THE USBORNE ILLUSTRATED
ATLAS OF THE
20th CENTURY

LISA MILES AND MANDY ROSS

DESIGNED BY RUTH RUSSELL

ILLUSTRATED BY KUO KANG CHEN, GUY SMITH,
KEVIN JONES ASSOCIATES AND JOHN LAWRENCE

COVER DESIGN BY RUSSELL PUNTER
COVER ILLUSTRATION BY MARK FRANKLIN

CONSULTANTS
ANNE MILLARD, GRAHAM ROBERTS
AND CHRISTOPHER SMITH

CONTENTS

THE TWENTIETH CENTURY

The twentieth century has been a time of great change and conflict. In its early years, the powerful empires of Britain and France were still expanding, while Germany and Italy had also begun to take control of territories abroad. European countries dominated the world. But conflicts within Europe were later to cause two world wars, more terrible than any other war before them.

THE POST-WAR WORLD

In the years after World War Two, the empires were broken up, creating independent nations in Asia and Africa. The new, post-war world was dominated by a period of tension between the great superpowers, the United States of America and the Soviet Union. In the late 1980s, this tension was eased and the mighty Soviet Union was broken up.

THE WORLD TODAY

There are around 180 nation states in the world today. The situation, though, is ever-changing, as national and international conflicts continually alter the political map of the world.

THE EARLY YEARS

In the first years of the twentieth century, European nations competed to establish colonies around the world. As the struggle for land continued, Europeans fought Europeans, and settlers fought native peoples for supremacy.

The Queen's South Africa medal, awarded to British soldiers who fought in the Boer War.

British drummer boy from the Boer War, writing a letter home.

THE BRITISH AND THE BOERS

In southern Africa in 1899, a war broke out between the British and the Boers. The Boers were descendants of Dutch farmers who had colonized southern Africa in the mid-seventeenth century. The Boer War was fiercely fought. Boer guerillas inflicted heavy casualties on British troops, while the British burned Boer farms and herded women and children into camps. The war ended in 1902, when the Boers asked for peace. A new state, the Union of South Africa, was set up in order to reconcile the two sides.

MOROCCAN CRISIS

At this time, France controlled Algeria and Tunisia, and was trying to extend its influence in Morocco too, where Germany also wanted to gain influence. To provoke France, in 1905 the German Kaiser referred in a speech to the Sultan of Morocco as an independent ruler. He was implying that France had no right to interfere in Morocco's affairs. To further provoke France, in 1911, Germany sent a gunboat to the port of Agadir to pressurize Morocco. This tense situation became known as the Agadir Incident.

HERERO REBELLION

By 1900, almost all of Africa had been colonized by European nations. Native peoples often lost their land and were forced to accept European rule. In German Southwest Africa, the Herero people became angry at the loss of their grazing lands and water sources to German settlers.

In 1904, their anger turned into violence and they massacred 123 German colonists. Despite the fact that the Herero had only spears and clubs, it took 14,000 German troops armed with guns to crush the rebellion. They drove 5,000 Herero people into the desert in reprisal. This act of cruelty caused an outcry in Germany.

AFRICA

Some areas of conflict in Africa – Morocco, German Southwest Africa and South Africa.

GERMAN SOUTHWEST AFRICA

HERERO TERRITORY

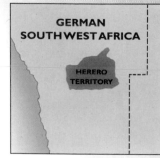

The Herero homeland in German Southwest Africa.

Mediterranean Sea

TUNISIA

Agadir

MOROCCO

ALGERIA

Sahara Desert

Niger

AFRICA

Nile

Atlantic Ocean

Congo

Lake Victoria

Lake Tanganyika

Lake Malawi

Zambezi

Kalahari Desert

GERMAN SOUTHWEST AFRICA

MADAGASCAR

N
W E
S

0   1000 km
0   625 miles

SOUTH AFRICA

THE RUSSO-JAPANESE WAR

In the early twentieth century, Japan was modernizing. It fought a war with Russia in 1904 because they both had plans to annex (take control of) Manchuria and Korea.

Russia suffered a series of defeats, including the Battle of Mukden and the loss of its fleet at Tsushima. This was a serious blow to the Russians who had sailed their fleet almost all the way around the world to fight Japan.

The Russian fleet sailed 29,000km (18,000 miles) from the Baltic Sea to fight Japan.

After the war, Japan gained more territory and also influence over Korea.

THE OTTOMAN EMPIRE

During the nineteenth century, the Turkish Ottoman Empire slowly lost its grip on its European provinces and became known as the "sick man of Europe". In the early years of the twentieth century, there was a surge of nationalism – a feeling of patriotism and a desire to bring the Turkish people together. In 1908, the nationalists, called the Young Turks, seized power. Immediately, however, the empire began to lose territory.

Enver Pasha, Young Turks' leader. He helped to forge closer links with Germany.

In 1908 Bulgaria declared full independence and the Austro-Hungarian Empire annexed Bosnia.

THE BALKAN WARS

More troubles followed with the outbreak of the Balkan Wars in 1912. Serbia, Bulgaria, Greece and Montenegro banded together to expel the Turks from Europe. Within a month they had pushed the Turks back to Constantinople. Albania, too, gained independence. Then in 1913, war broke out again. Serbia and Greece fought Bulgaria for control of territory in the area. Serbia won and became the major power in the Balkans.

Balkan countries at the outbreak of the first Balkan War in October 1912.

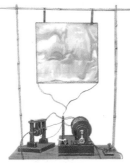
The Balkans in 1914. Serbia had enlarged its territory and now it was the major power.

TRAVEL AND COMMUNICATION

During this era, there were many developments in transportation and communication that were to have a huge effect on the twentieth century. In the USA in 1903, Orville Wright made the first flight in a plane. From then on the power, size and safety of planes developed rapidly. In 1908 the motor car became more popular when Ford began to mass-produce the Model-T. Then in 1914 the Panama Canal opened, cutting out the long route for ships around South America.

Communication improved with the development of the telegraph and the telephone. In 1901 Marconi sent the first radio signals across the Atlantic Ocean. In 1911, radio messages helped to bring the English murderer Dr. Crippen to justice. He was escaping on a ship to Canada, but the crew received a signal that he was on board.

The Marconiphone, patented in 1896, for sending radio messages.

Henry Ford's Model-T car. Mass production made the car much cheaper and more available to ordinary people. At first, the Model-T was manufactured in black only. In later years, other paintwork was used.

See above pages for more information.

By 1920, half the cars in the world were Model-T Fords.

WORLD WAR ONE

World War One, also known as the Great War, involved more nations and killed more soldiers than any other war that had been fought before. At first people believed that the war would be over quickly, but it dragged on for four destructive years.

A British wartime poster, encouraging men to enlist in the army or "join up".

Archduke Franz Ferdinand, the heir to the throne of the Austro-Hungarian Empire, who was shot dead.

THE FLASH POINT

The flash point which triggered the war happened in June 1914. Austria had annexed nearby Bosnia, but Serbia wanted to control Bosnia too. On June 28 the heir to the Austro-Hungarian throne and his wife were on a visit to Sarajevo, the Bosnian capital. While driving in an open car through the streets, they were shot dead by a Serbian nationalist. The Austrian government wrongly blamed the Serbian government for the killing. Diplomats tried to ease the tense situation but on July 28, Austria declared war on Serbia. Stability in Europe was now shattered beyond repair. Russia backed Serbia, while Germany supported Austria.

HOW DID IT HAPPEN?

The killing of the Archduke was the immediate cause of the war, but there were deeper causes that had been building up for some time. There were intense trade rivalries between the European nations. Germany was also jealous of Britain, France and others who had acquired colonies abroad. These tensions led to alliances being formed. Britain, France and Russia had drawn together on one side. Germany and Austria were on the other. It was now impossible to prevent all sides from declaring war.

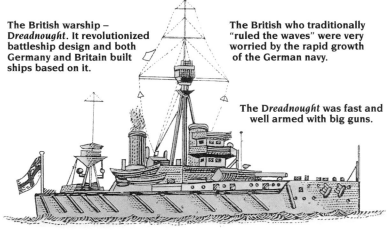

The British warship – *Dreadnought*. It revolutionized battleship design and both Germany and Britain built ships based on it.

The British who traditionally "ruled the waves" were very worried by the rapid growth of the German navy.

The *Dreadnought* was fast and well armed with big guns.

Bosnia and Herzegovina in 1914. It was in Sarajevo, the capital city, that Archduke Franz Ferdinand and his wife were shot.

Central Powers **Allies**

Europe was now split into two camps – the Central Powers (Austria and Germany), versus the Allies (Britain, France and Russia).

THE WESTERN FRONT

As soon as war was declared, the Germans attacked. The plan was to make a dash through neutral Belgium, and inflict a quick defeat on their old enemy France. Then, they planned to turn around and attack Russia. This idea very nearly succeeded, but the Battle of the Marne halted their advance 80km (50 miles) from Paris. Their advance to the north was also stopped by the Allies at the Battle of Ypres, which prevented them from reaching the ports on the coast of the English Channel.

After that, the war became a stalemate across Belgium and northeast France. This area, known as the Western Front, was crisscrossed by a network of trenches, protected by lines of barbed wire.

Frontline **Invasion**

The German route of attack. It was based on the Schlieffen Plan, which had been devised as early as 1905 in readiness for any war that might break out with France.

Battle **Frontline**

The Western Front. Trenches were dug across northern France to Switzerland. After autumn 1914, the frontline hardly moved until the end of the war.

NEW WEAPONS

To gain the upper hand, both sides used new weapons, such as poison gas and tanks. Another major development was the use of aircraft. Planes were first used to find out what was happening behind enemy lines (called reconnaissance). They were later used as fighters. During the war, the British Sopwith Camel shot down more planes than any other fighter.

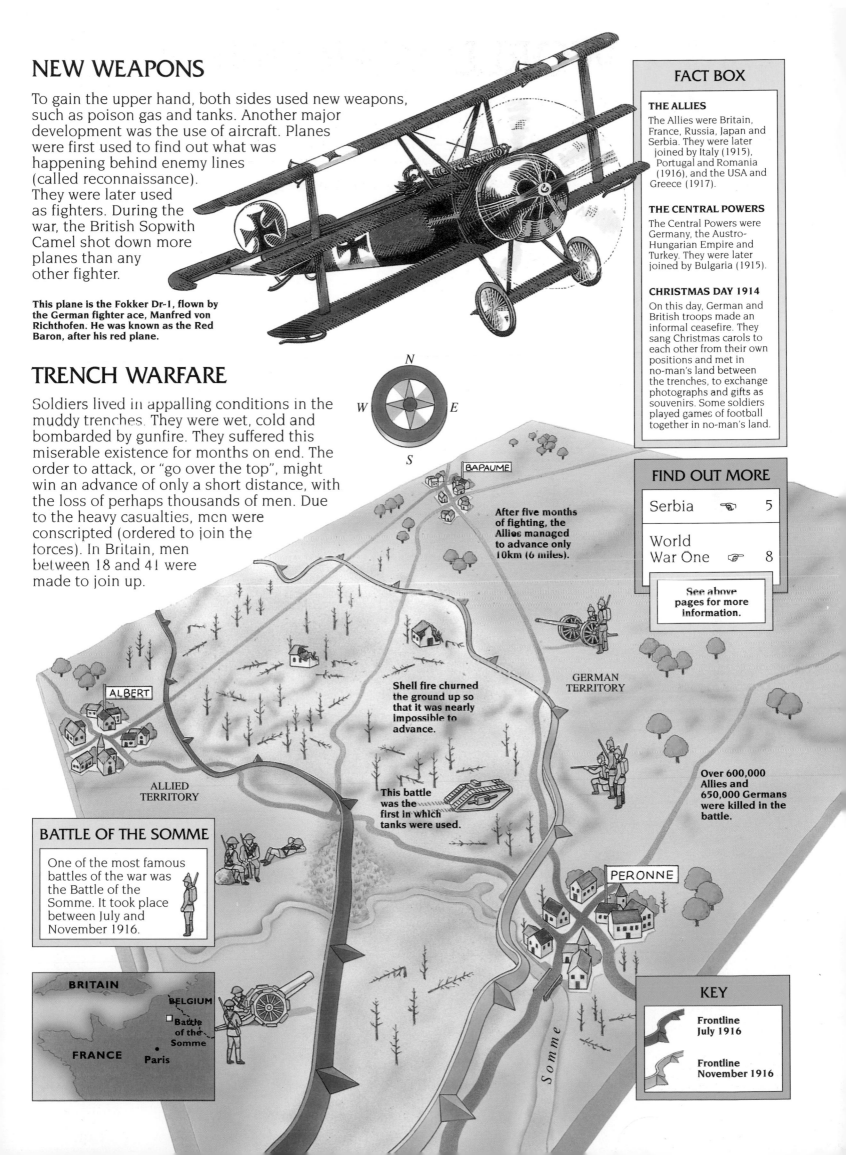

This plane is the Fokker Dr-1, flown by the German fighter ace, Manfred von Richthofen. He was known as the Red Baron, after his red plane.

TRENCH WARFARE

Soldiers lived in appalling conditions in the muddy trenches. They were wet, cold and bombarded by gunfire. They suffered this miserable existence for months on end. The order to attack, or "go over the top", might win an advance of only a short distance, with the loss of perhaps thousands of men. Due to the heavy casualties, men were conscripted (ordered to join the forces). In Britain, men between 18 and 41 were made to join up.

BATTLE OF THE SOMME

One of the most famous battles of the war was the Battle of the Somme. It took place between July and November 1916.

FACT BOX

THE ALLIES
The Allies were Britain, France, Russia, Japan and Serbia. They were later joined by Italy (1915), Portugal and Romania (1916), and the USA and Greece (1917).

THE CENTRAL POWERS
The Central Powers were Germany, the Austro-Hungarian Empire and Turkey. They were later joined by Bulgaria (1915).

CHRISTMAS DAY 1914
On this day, German and British troops made an informal ceasefire. They sang Christmas carols to each other from their own positions and met in no-man's land between the trenches, to exchange photographs and gifts as souvenirs. Some soldiers played games of football together in no-man's land.

After five months of fighting, the Allies managed to advance only 10km (6 miles).

BAPAUME

GERMAN TERRITORY

Shell fire churned the ground up so that it was nearly impossible to advance.

This battle was the first in which tanks were used.

Over 600,000 Allies and 650,000 Germans were killed in the battle.

ALBERT

ALLIED TERRITORY

PERONNE

BRITAIN

BELGIUM

Battle of the Somme

FRANCE

Paris

Somme

KEY

Frontline July 1916

Frontline November 1916

THE WIDER WAR

T. E. Lawrence, known as Lawrence of Arabia.

As World War One settled into a stalemate on the Western Front, fighting broke out in other regions. In the west, the Germans had failed to defeat France as planned, and were faced with the task of fighting Russia in the east at the same time.

A soldier from the Australia and New Zealand Army Corps (ANZAC), which fought at Gallipoli.

THE EASTERN FRONT

The Russians, though brave fighters, were ill-prepared for war. They were badly equipped and they suffered several defeats with heavy casualties. Poverty plagued the Russian people and by 1917 they were deeply unhappy with their leader, Czar Nicholas II. A revolution broke out, forcing the Czar to abdicate. A new Russian government eventually made peace with Germany.

The Eastern Front in 1915. The Russians and the Poles had attacked first, but the Germans drove them back.

THE ARAB REVOLT

Arabia had been dominated by the Ottoman Empire for many years. The Sharif of Mecca, Hussein ibn Ali, now took his chance and rose in revolt. His son, the Emir Feisal, worked with the British officer T. E. Lawrence to combine their forces against the Turks. From 1916, the Arabs kept in close contact with the British army. In 1918, they entered Damascus together – victorious.

Arabia and the Ottoman Empire in 1914. The empire had been weakening for many years and the Arabs wanted independence.

GALLIPOLI

For the Allies, the defeat of the Turkish Ottoman Empire would open routes through the Black Sea to Russia, India, and the oil wells in Persia. In 1915, they invaded the Gallipoli peninsula on the Turkish coast.

The attack was badly planned and the Turks held strong positions above the beaches. Allied troops, many from the Australia and New Zealand Army Corps (ANZAC), endured eight months of fighting, gaining nothing. Many lives were lost and Allied forces were eventually evacuated.

THE INVASION

This map shows the Gallipoli peninsula. The Allies tried to force their way through the Dardanelles by ship, but when that failed, troops were landed on the beaches. The invasion was a terrible failure.

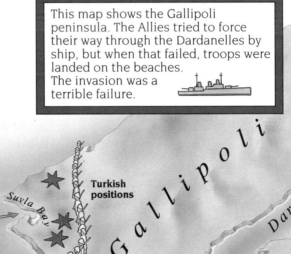

Turkish positions

Suvla Bay

Aegean Sea

Anzac Cove

The tiny beach assaulted by the ANZAC forces was nicknamed Anzac Cove.

Turkish positions

Gallipoli

Dardanelles

GALLIPOLI

ÇANAKKALE

TURKEY

The Dardanelles channel leads from the Aegean Sea to the Black Sea, and so to Russia.

Imbroz

Cape Helles

KEY

→ Allied invasion

★ Battle

• Turkish mines

WAR AT SEA

The main sea battle took place at Jutland in 1916. There was no winner.

The battleships of Britain and Germany did not play such a big role in the war as expected. Instead, Germany used submarines to attack supply ships, and very nearly starved Britain. In 1915, the Germans sank two passenger ships, the *Lusitania* and the *Arabia*, with great loss of life. This later helped to persuade the USA to enter the war against Germany.

German submarines (U-boats) attacked Allied shipping around Europe.

WOMEN'S ROLES

Edith Cavell, a British nurse, was executed by the Germans for helping Allied prisoners to escape.

While their menfolk were away fighting on the frontline, many women occupied roles traditionally filled by men. At home they took on jobs such as working in arms factories and driving buses.

Some became involved in the actual war, serving as ambulance drivers and nurses. A few took on more daring roles. They became spies and resistance fighters, working behind enemy lines.

The Dutch dancer, known as Mata Hari. She was executed by the British for being a German spy.

PACIFISTS

Few countries managed to stay neutral in the war. Within some countries, however, were groups of pacifists who refused to fight on principle. They did this because they disagreed so strongly with the whole idea of warfare, for whatever cause. Some pacifists were prepared to act on the frontline as stretcher-bearers for the injured.

Pacifist societies used emblems such as this one. The dove represents peace.

THE USA ENTERS THE WAR

In April 1917, the USA declared war on Germany. Submarine warfare had killed many of its citizens and Americans rallied behind the Allies. By now Allied forces were weak, so fresh troops and equipment were valuable. With so many men and resources against them, defeat for Germany was certain.

THE END AT LAST

The Allies gained control of the sea and Germany grew short of food and raw materials. One by one, the Central Powers surrendered. The guns finally fell silent on November 11, 1918. At least ten million people died in World War One. It is possible that this figure may be much higher as some records are inadequate. Peace treaties were made separately with each of the Central Powers. There were enormous problems to solve and the suffering left many feeling very bitter.

For the people of the Allied nations, the end of the war was a joyous celebration. These people took to the streets on Armistice Day – November 11, 1918.

FACT BOX

CASUALTY FIGURES
Gallipoli, 1915

25,000 Allied troops dead
76,000 wounded
13,000 missing.

Total deaths 1914-1918
British Empire 947,000
France 1,375,000
Italy 460,000
USA 115,600
Russia* 1,700,000
Germany 1,808,500
Ottoman Empire* 325,000
Austro-Hungarian
  Empire* 1,200,000

*These figures may be inaccurate and are likely to be much higher.

T. E. LAWRENCE (1888-1935)

Lawrence of Arabia, as he was known, studied the Middle East at Oxford University. In 1916, he went to Arabia to help the Emir in his revolt against the Turks, Germany's allies.

After the war, he became a special adviser on Arab affairs to the British government. He felt that the Arab cause was betrayed when control over the area was given to Britain and France.

FIND OUT MORE

| Russian Revolution | ☞ 10 |
| Peace treaties | ☞ 12 |

See above pages for more information.

RUSSIAN REVOLUTION

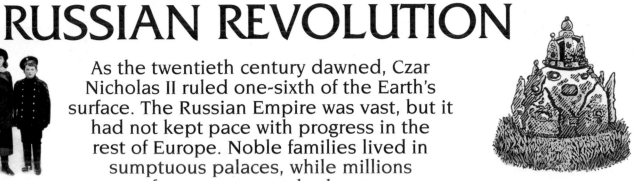

Czar Nicholas II, with his family. They were murdered in 1918, in the aftermath of the revolution.

As the twentieth century dawned, Czar Nicholas II ruled one-sixth of the Earth's surface. The Russian Empire was vast, but it had not kept pace with progress in the rest of Europe. Noble families lived in sumptuous palaces, while millions of peasants scratched out a miserable life of hardship.

The Czar's jewel-encrusted crown was a symbol of his immense wealth and power.

CZARIST RUSSIA

The Russian Empire was trying to catch up with European industrial progress. But factory workers and peasants, poor and hungry, were growing restless. A disastrous war against Japan in 1904-5 caused mutiny in the army, and riots at home. In 1905 troops fired at demonstrators at the Czar's Winter Palace. This event sparked a rebellion. In a panic, the Czar set up a new parliament, the Duma. But it had little real power. Whenever it criticized the Czar, he simply closed it down.

WORLD WAR ONE

In 1914 Russia entered World War One. The Czar hoped that war might quieten unrest at home. But the troops were hopelessly ill-prepared. By the end of 1914, a quarter of the army was lost. Although he was no soldier, the Czar himself went off to take charge at the front. Back in Russia, the war caused terrible food and fuel shortages. Women lay on the rails to stop troop trains from leaving. Left in charge, the Czarina and her adviser, Rasputin, grew unpopular. "Revolution!" was whispered everywhere.

FEBRUARY 1917

Tired of waiting in frozen streets for rationed bread, in 1917 the women of Petrograd (now St. Petersburg) sparked off the February Revolution. Millions of factory workers went on strike. Instead of firing on them, troops joined the demonstrators. Czar Nicholas tried to get home, but railway workers stopped his train outside Petrograd. There, in a train siding, he abdicated. The Duma took over, but could neither win the war nor end it. The Czar's fall seemed to change nothing.

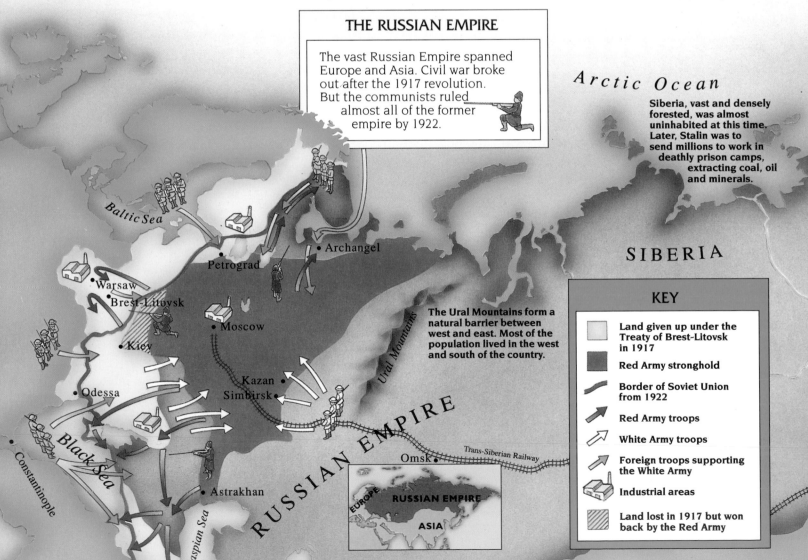

THE RUSSIAN EMPIRE

The vast Russian Empire spanned Europe and Asia. Civil war broke out after the 1917 revolution. But the communists ruled almost all of the former empire by 1922.

Arctic Ocean

Siberia, vast and densely forested, was almost uninhabited at this time. Later, Stalin was to send millions to work in deathly prison camps, extracting coal, oil and minerals.

SIBERIA

The Ural Mountains form a natural barrier between west and east. Most of the population lived in the west and south of the country.

Baltic Sea
Archangel
Petrograd
Warsaw
Brest-Litovsk
Moscow
Kiev
Ural Mountains
Odessa
Kazan
Simbirsk
Black Sea
Constantinople
Astrakhan
Caspian Sea
Baku
Omsk
Trans-Siberian Railway

RUSSIAN EMPIRE

EUROPE
RUSSIAN EMPIRE
ASIA

KEY

Land given up under the Treaty of Brest-Litovsk in 1917

Red Army stronghold

Border of Soviet Union from 1922

Red Army troops

White Army troops

Foreign troops supporting the White Army

Industrial areas

Land lost in 1917 but won back by the Red Army

PEACE! BREAD! LAND!

The Bolsheviks, followers of Karl Marx's communist teachings, wanted to create a socialist society. All men and women would be equal. Wealth was to be shared, putting an end to poverty and injustice. With their slogan "Peace! Bread! Land!", the Bolsheviks won support among the war-weary, hungry people. In April 1917 the Bolshevik leader, Vladimir Il'yich Ulianov, known as Lenin, returned from exile. Under his leadership, the Bolsheviks' power grew rapidly.

Communism offered real change to peasants, like these women hauling a barge.

BOLSHEVIK REVOLUTION

In the small hours of October 25, 1917, groups of Bolsheviks quietly occupied Petrograd's railway stations, telephone exchanges and post office. At 2am they stormed the Winter Palace, arrested the Duma, and declared a new revolutionary government. Hardly a drop of blood was shed.

Lenin's first act, as he had promised, was to bring Russia out of the war. Then – because he needed the peasants' support – he ordered the nobles' land to be shared among the people. This won the Bolsheviks huge popularity.

Petrograd's landmarks, seized by the Bolsheviks.

FACT BOX

KARL MARX 1818-83
Karl Marx was the founder of communism. Born in Germany, in 1848 he wrote the Communist Manifesto with Friedrich Engels. This work described the class struggle which he believed would lead to revolution.

RASPUTIN 1873-1916
Grigory Rasputin was a Russian holy man. He won immense power at the Czar's court because he seemed to be able to heal Alexis, the sickly heir to the throne. But the drunken "mad monk", as he was known, was believed to be a German spy, and he was murdered in 1916.

THE PRICE OF PEACE
The Germans demanded a heavy price for Russia's exit from World War One. By the Treaty of Brest-Litovsk in 1917, Russia lost a third of her population and farmland, and more than half her industry, which was concentrated in this area.

CIVIL WAR

There was an immediate backlash from the Czar's supporters, nobles and liberals, who formed the White Army. Foreign countries sent massive support to try to stop communism from spreading. By the summer of 1918, a murderous civil war raged throughout the old Czarist Empire.

By the spring of 1919, the Bolsheviks' newly-formed Red Army had begun to turn the tide. But the fighting dragged on, followed in 1921 by a catastrophic drought and famine. Millions died of hunger and thirst. There were even reports of cannibalism.

This Bolshevik propaganda poster asks "Have you joined the Red Army?"

FIND OUT MORE

Russo-Japanese War ☞	5
World War One ☞	6
Stalin's Soviet Union ☞	20

See above pages for more information.

Sea of Okhotsk

During the civil war, foreign troops came from the east to support the White Army. They came on the Trans-Siberian railway.

JAPAN

Vladivostock

BIRTH OF THE SOVIET UNION

By 1922, the Communists (the Bolsheviks' new name) had won the civil war. But the economy was in ruins. Lenin encouraged people to buy and sell freely. Soon the markets were full of food and goods.

The mid-1920s was a hopeful, exciting time in the Soviet Union (as the nation was renamed). Education was free to all. The revolution was celebrated with art, music and film. Women welcomed their new rights, such as education and divorce.

But the Communists' state police force, the Cheka, dealt ruthlessly with anyone who disagreed with the government. The seeds were sown for the reign of terror under the next Soviet leader, Stalin.

The Communist Party symbol, the hammer and sickle, decorated all kinds of objects, like this hand-painted plate.

PEACE AFTER WAR

After the war German weapons, such as tanks, were broken up.

At the end of World War One, international conferences were held to decide the peace settlements. The settlements were to state what should happen to the countries involved in the war – especially the losers.

War memorials were built after the war to commemorate those who died.

THE TREATY OF VERSAILLES

In 1919 at the Palace of Versailles near Paris, a conference was held to make a settlement between Germany and the Allies. A treaty was signed by 27 nations, of which 17 were non-European. Also at the conference, an organization called the League of Nations was set up to try to prevent war in future. The failure of the USA and the Soviet Union to join the League, however, made it weak. Separate treaties followed with Germany's allies.

British children celebrating the Versailles Peace Treaty with a tea party.

GERMANY'S FATE

A German stamp valued at 5,000 million marks.

The main outcome of the Treaty of Versailles was that Germany was made to admit its guilt and to take full responsiblity for causing World War One. It was made to agree to enormous sums as reparations – financial payments to the Allies. Germany also had to reduce its army and navy drastically, and was not allowed tanks or submarines.

It also had to give up land to its former enemies. The colonies were handed to the Allies as mandates – regions that the Allies should rule for the time being until they could be given independence. Germany found it impossible to pay the reparations and the value of its currency fell. Before long, the value of the German mark sank to 10,000 million for £1 and 48,000 million for $1.

NEW COUNTRIES

Separate treaties were made with the old Austro-Hungarian Empire and the Ottoman Empire, which were both broken up. A separate treaty was also made with their ally Bulgaria. The map of Europe was now redrawn in order to give independence to nations that had previously been part of the old empires. Several of these new countries, however, contained two or more different nationalities and also different religious groups.

For instance, a third of Poland's population did not speak Polish. Among its new inhabitants were Russian and German speakers. This problem made many of the new countries unstable, as the different cultural groups vied with each other for dominance within the new nations.

The flag of Poland – one of the new countries in 1919.

After the treaty, Germany had to give up territory. The Rhineland was to be occupied by Allied troops for 15 years and no German troops were ever to be stationed there.

German Southwest Africa became a South African mandate and German East Africa became a British one. The Cameroons and Togoland were divided between Britain and France.

Europe after the peace treaties. Germany and the Austro-Hungarian and Ottoman Empires were broken up and new countries in central Europe came into being. In addition, although not part of the treaties, Finland became independent from Russia in 1917 and the Irish Free State (formally part of Britain) was created in 1921.

THE MIDDLE EAST

The former Middle East territories of the Ottoman Empire either became mandates or gained independence. During the 1920s and 30s, there was an increasing worldwide demand for oil as motor transportation took over and the use of oil in industry increased. The huge amounts of oil that were being discovered in the Middle East made it very valuable territory.

NEW ARAB NATIONS

This map shows the Middle East during the 1920s. Britain and France held mandates over some areas. Other areas gained independence.

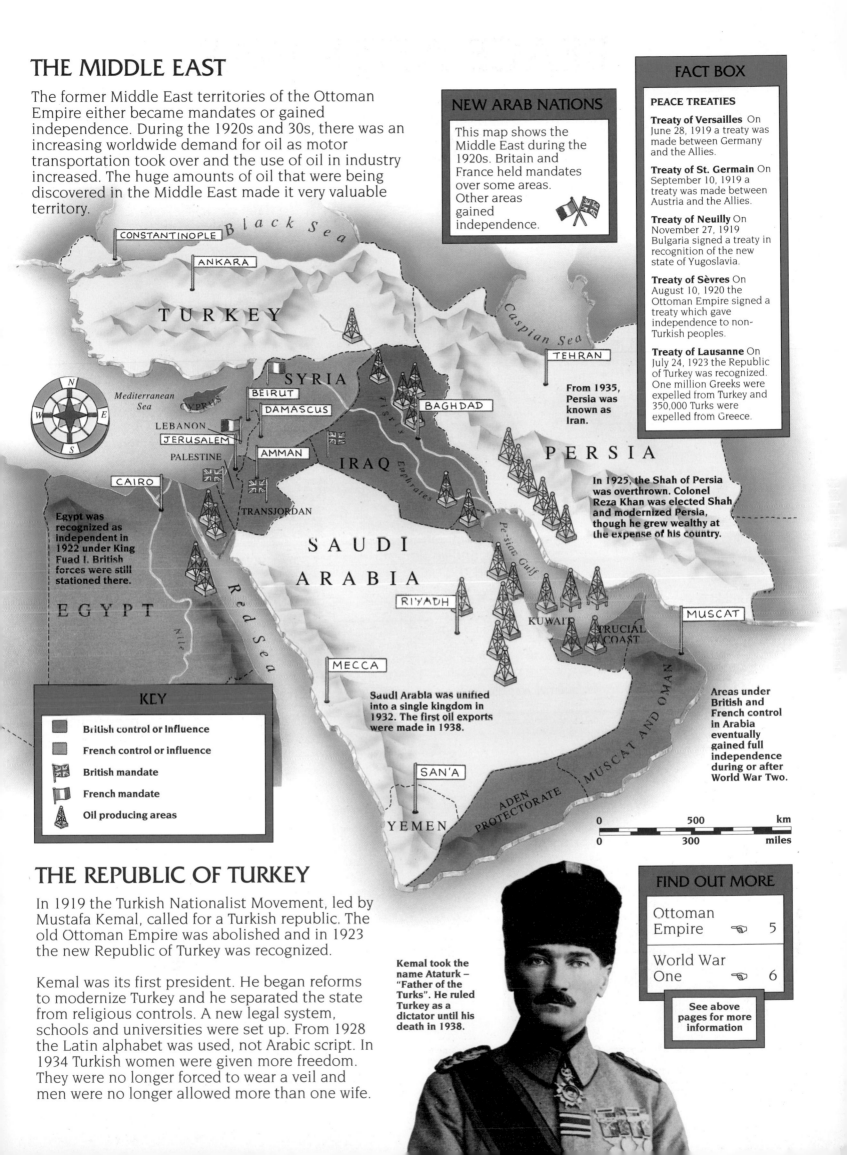

Black Sea

CONSTANTINOPLE
ANKARA

TURKEY

Caspian Sea

TEHRAN

From 1935, Persia was known as Iran.

Mediterranean Sea

CYPRUS

SYRIA

BEIRUT
DAMASCUS
LEBANON
JERUSALEM
PALESTINE
AMMAN
Tigris
Euphrates
BAGHDAD

IRAQ

PERSIA

TRANSJORDAN

CAIRO

In 1925, the Shah of Persia was overthrown. Colonel Reza Khan was elected Shah and modernized Persia, though he grew wealthy at the expense of his country.

Egypt was recognized as independent in 1922 under King Fuad I. British forces were still stationed there.

EGYPT

SAUDI ARABIA

Nile
Red Sea

RIYADH

Persian Gulf

MUSCAT

KUWAIT
TRUCIAL COAST

MECCA

Saudi Arabia was unified into a single kingdom in 1932. The first oil exports were made in 1938.

MUSCAT AND OMAN

Areas under British and French control in Arabia eventually gained full independence during or after World War Two.

SAN'A
ADEN PROTECTORATE
YEMEN

KEY

- British control or influence
- French control or influence
- British mandate
- French mandate
- Oil producing areas

```
0        500    km
0      300      miles
```

THE REPUBLIC OF TURKEY

In 1919 the Turkish Nationalist Movement, led by Mustafa Kemal, called for a Turkish republic. The old Ottoman Empire was abolished and in 1923 the new Republic of Turkey was recognized.

Kemal was its first president. He began reforms to modernize Turkey and he separated the state from religious controls. A new legal system, schools and universities were set up. From 1928 the Latin alphabet was used, not Arabic script. In 1934 Turkish women were given more freedom. They were no longer forced to wear a veil and men were no longer allowed more than one wife.

Kemal took the name Ataturk – "Father of the Turks". He ruled Turkey as a dictator until his death in 1938.

FIND OUT MORE

Ottoman Empire	☞	5
World War One	☞	6

See above pages for more information

THE GREAT DEPRESSION

In the USA, the period after World War One was called the "Era of Big Business". The capitalist economy brought new wealth, as mass production improved and new consumer goods became available. But within ten years, this prosperity vanished. The USA entered a period of poverty that deeply affected the rest of the industrialized world.

The Ku Klux Klan wore white robes and hats and usually masked their faces.

This car was used as a home by a farmer and his family, who left the Midwest to find work in California.

THE KU KLUX KLAN

One of the more sinister aspects of the postwar period was the rise in popularity of a group called the Ku Klux Klan. Founded in 1915, the Klan attacked nonwhites, Jews and Catholics – in fact anyone whose ideas and values they disagreed with.

They terrorized their victims with violence and were particularly active in the 1920s in the south of the United States and also the Midwest.

THE USA

The United States of America in the 1920s and 30s. Dust storms from drought-hit areas blew as far as New York on the east coast.

THE DUSTBOWLS

The 1920s and 30s were troubled times for people in America's farming regions. Farmers felt that their interests were being neglected. They made little money from their produce. Severe droughts caused the land to become very dry. Bad farming practices made the problem worse. In some areas, soil erosion was so bad that farms became giant dustbowls. Many small farmers were ruined and could not support their families.

GANGSTERS

In 1920, the 18th Amendment to the Constitution banned the production and sale of alcohol in the USA. The period during which alcohol was illegal is called the Prohibition. It lasted until 1933. The law was an attempt to stop people from drinking alcohol, but it soon became unpopular. Organized crime flourished as groups of gangsters, such as the Mafia, controlled businesses and alcohol smuggling.

A 1920s gangster and his female accomplice.

CANADA

Rocky Mountains

UNITED STATES OF AMERICA

Great Lakes

Midwest

Milwaukee • Detroit • Boston
Omaha • • Chicago Pittsburgh • New York
Kansas City • Cleveland Baltimore • Philadelphia
St. Louis
Mississippi Tennessee
• Oklahoma City
Atlanta •

• San Francisco

Los Angeles •

Rio Grande

Gulf of Mexico

• New Orleans

Atlantic Ocean

Pacific Ocean

MEXICO

CUBA
Caribbean Sea

KEY

- Industrial city

Dustbowl

Migrant workers leaving the dustbowl

THE WALL STREET CRASH

October 24, 1929 is known as Black Thursday – the day that the New York Stock Exchange crashed, making stocks and shares virtually worthless. The crash was caused by weaknesses in basic industries, such as agriculture, mining and textiles. Many people were investing money on the stock exchange. Share prices fell suddenly and panic set in. This disaster is called the Wall Street Crash after Wall Street, the home of the New York Stock Exchange.

After the crash, industrial production in the USA fell by over a half. Banks called in their loans and businesses everywhere were ruined. These problems spread worldwide. Around 15 million people in the USA, 6 million in Germany and 3 million in Britain became unemployed. This period of severe poverty is known as the Great Depression. The hardship lasted until 1934, when the economy began to recover at last.

These unemployed men are waiting for free soup, which was handed out to the poor during the Great Depression.

LINE FOR
1¢ RESTAURANT

20 MEALS FOR 1¢

DONATIONS WANTED
HELP FEED THE HUNGRY
I WILL FEED 20

1¢ RESTAURANT
107 W 43ᴿᴰ ST

FACT BOX

CAPITALISM

Capitalism is the economic system in which businesses and industry are run for profit and owned by a minority, for which the majority work. This is the economic system traditionally followed by the USA and other countries in Western Europe (known together as the West).

UNEMPLOYMENT

In 1932, industrial production in the United States and Germany was only just above half of that in 1929. In all, around 30,000,000 people may have been unemployed in the industrial world.

F. D. ROOSEVELT (1882-1945)

Roosevelt was US President from 1932 to 1945. About the Depression, he said, "I see one third of a nation ill-housed, ill-clad, ill-nourished." He oversaw the entry of the USA into World War Two in 1941.

THE NEW DEAL

In 1932, Franklin D. Roosevelt was elected President and he announced a series of emergency measures, known as the New Deal, to end the Great Depression. There were plans to help both industry and farming, while public building projects were started to create jobs.

One of these projects was the setting up of the Tennessee Valley Authority. This organization worked on the Tennessee River to improve the irrigation (watering) of the land. It also built power stations to supply energy to new industries, and planted trees to prevent soil erosion.

Symbols against depression – a badge from Roosevelt's Democratic Party (left) and the logo of the Tennessee Valley Authority (right).

FIND OUT MORE

| World War One | ☞ | 6 |
| World War Two | ☞ | 22 |

For more information see above pages.

ISOLATIONISM

After World War One, many Americans wanted to keep out of European affairs. This idea, which had often been part of American policy, was known as "isolationism". Despite strong opposition, however, President Roosevelt started to establish closer relations with foreign countries. When Europe went to war in 1939, opinions in the USA were split over whether or not to get involved.

A cartoon dated September 1939, showing the indecision of the American people over whether or not to get involved in World War Two.

HELP THEM!

DO NOTHING!

ISOLATION

LAOCOON 1938

15

CHINA AND JAPAN

In the nineteenth century, Japan had begun to modernize. Services, such as schools and the police, were organized along European lines. A parliament was introduced and in 1925 adult men got the vote. China, in contrast, avoided Westernization as much as possible.

Pu-Yi, the last Emperor of China, was deposed in 1912.

Emperor Hirohito of Japan ruled from 1926-1989.

THE FALL OF THE EMPEROR

In China, the government of the six-year-old Emperor, Pu-Yi, was becoming increasingly weak and unpopular. In 1911, a revolution broke out. One of the most important revolutionaries was Dr. Sun Yat-sen, founder of the Kuomintang – the National People's Party. His ideas were based on no interference by foreign powers, democracy and a guaranteed income for all. For a short while after the revolution, he became President of the new republic.

THE WARLORDS

After the revolution, the Nationalist government found it hard to bring its huge country under control. Local military leaders, called the Warlords, set themselves up as rulers in their own districts. They recruited private armies which they used to terrorize peasants and increase their own power and wealth. Civil war followed.

Chiang Kai-shek (1887-1975).

Between 1926 and 1928 the head of the Nationalists, Chiang Kai-shek, led a victorious campaign against the Warlords. He also achieved other improvements, such as the building of roads, railways and some hospitals and factories.

JAPAN BETWEEN THE WARS

While China struggled, the 1920s were troubled times for Japan too. As one of the victors in World War One, it was given German territory in the Pacific Ocean, but there were financial scandals and in 1923 an earthquake devastated Tokyo and Yokohama. Like other industrialized nations, it also suffered during the Great Depression. When Hirohito became Emperor of Japan in 1926, the country was unstable and a spate of political murders in the 1930s made matters worse.

Japan had been trying to influence China for some years. In a bid for colonial power, in 1931 Japan occupied Manchuria (part of China) and renamed it Manchukuo. Pu-Yi, the former Emperor of China, was set up as its head of state under Japanese control.

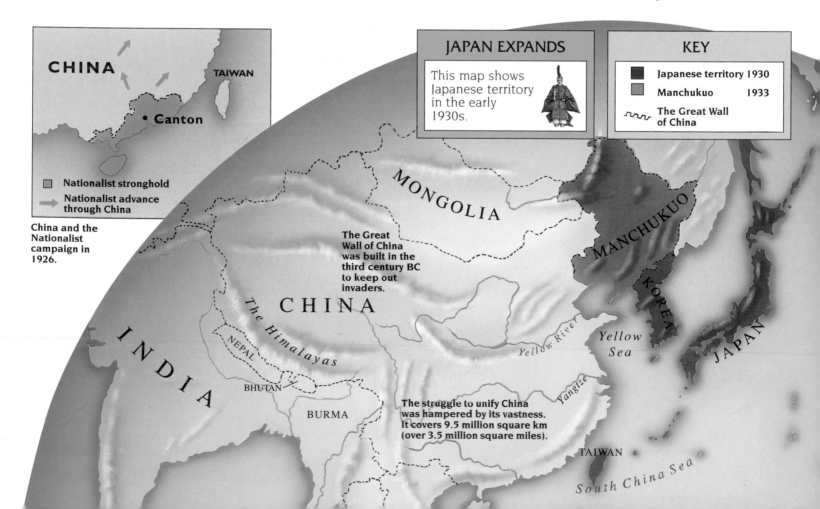

CHINA

TAIWAN

• Canton

☐ Nationalist stronghold
→ Nationalist advance through China

China and the Nationalist campaign in 1926.

JAPAN EXPANDS

This map shows Japanese territory in the early 1930s.

KEY

■ Japanese territory 1930
■ Manchukuo 1933
〰 The Great Wall of China

MONGOLIA

MANCHUKUO

KOREA

JAPAN

The Great Wall of China was built in the third century BC to keep out invaders.

CHINA

Yellow River

Yellow Sea

INDIA

NEPAL

The Himalayas

BHUTAN

BURMA

Yangtze

The struggle to unify China was hampered by its vastness. It covers 9.5 million square km (over 3.5 million square miles).

TAIWAN

South China Sea

THE LONG MARCH

Meanwhile the Chinese Communist Party was growing powerful. Originally, it had worked with the Nationalists, but in 1927 it broke away and set up its own government in Kiangsi. In 1934, the Nationalist army encircled the Communists. During this siege up to one million people may have been starved or killed. The communist Red Army escaped by trudging 8,000km (5,000 miles) to Yenan in the north. Out of 100,000 people, only 30,000 survived this journey, called the Long March.

Japan was suspicious of the both the Chinese and the Soviet communists. So, it joined the Anti-Comintern Pact with Germany and Italy in 1936, in order to work against communism.

The Long March, which began in October 1934, took a whole year to complete. The marchers crossed 18 mountain ranges and 24 rivers, fighting skirmishes almost every day. For years after this, the Chinese Communist Party was dominated by its survivors, including Mao Zedong.

THE SINO-JAPANESE WAR

In 1937 there was a clash between Chinese troops and the staff of the Japanese Embassy in Beijing. This incident sparked off a full-scale war. Japan invaded China, bombing Chinese cities and occupying important industrial regions near the coast. Troops behaved with appalling cruelty to civilians, looting and killing. The Chinese Nationalist government enlisted the help of the Communists to help fight the invaders, but the Japanese army was too strong. Although the Japanese were unable to occupy the whole country, it was impossible for the Chinese to expel them.

The invasion was condemned by the League of Nations but Japan took no notice. It had been disappointed in the League right from the start because it had failed to include a clause of racial equality in its covenant (agreement). Japan now responded to the League's protests by just resigning from it.

Only the Soviet Union, determined not to lose any of its own territory, stood up to Japan, defeating it at Nomonchau in 1939. In the same year, World War Two broke out, leaving China and Japan to struggle on until 1945.

Japan's invasion route into China in 1937. Troops swept swiftly down from Manchukuo and captured Beijing. A second force, brought by the Japanese navy, took Shanghai.

Japanese territory in 1938. By this time, Japan had conquered large areas of northern China, including the important industrial areas, such as Canton.

Pacific Ocean

Japanese troops entering Beijing in 1937.

FACT BOX

SUN YAT-SEN (1867-1925)

Born as the son of a Chinese peasant, Sun Yat-Sen was an American citizen for some years and trained as a doctor in Hong Kong. After the Chinese Revolution in 1911, he became President in 1913.

He soon resigned, however, in the interests of unity. He remained a great influence on the government but died of cancer before China could be unified.

HENRY PU-YI (1906-67)

Pu-Yi became the last Manchu Emperor of China in 1908 when he was two years old. After the Chinese Revolution in 1911, he was allowed to live in a palace in Beijing.

Disorder in China caused him to seek safety in Japanese-held territory. The Japanese made him Emperor of Manchukuo in 1934, but he was just a figurehead. In 1945 he was captured by the Soviets and was imprisoned in Siberia. In 1950 he was handed back to China and lived as a private citizen.

THE 21 DEMANDS

As far back as 1915, Japan had been trying to influence China. It demanded a list of concessions from China known as the 21 Demands. They included: Japanese advisors to be employed by the Chinese government; major industries to be put under joint control; police in trade areas to be under joint control; and no bay or island to be leased to any country except Japan.

THE RISE OF FASCISM

The horrors of World War One shattered many of the old certainties in Europe. Empires had fallen, and governments seemed unsure. In many countries, people turned to a new movement, called fascism. Its leaders offered simple answers to problems caused by the war.

Mussolini, like other fascist dictators, stirred crowds into a frenzy of rage and hatred with his passionate speeches.

Nazi Germany used the eagle as a symbol of strength and nationalism.

Fascism took its name from the bundle of rods, or *fasces*, which symbolized authority in Ancient Rome.

WHAT IS FASCISM?

Fascism, which first emerged in Italy, was a new and violent political movement. It appealed to traditional virtues, such as unity, nationalism and love of the motherland. Its leaders – mainly military men – offered strong discipline and demanded absolute obedience to their orders. Fascism quickly gathered strength, spreading across Europe and South America.

The fascists hated communism, but they also wanted to destroy the old aristocracy. Just like classroom bullies, they built up a feeling of fearful unity by picking scapegoats, and encouraging people to attack them. This combination of ideas appealed to the poor, and also to the middle classes whose comfort and savings were threatened by the chaos of inflation (steep price rises), falling wages and unemployment.

ITALY

Following World War One, Italy faced unemployment and soaring prices, despite being on the winning side. People lost faith in the faltering government. Many, especially powerful factory owners and Church leaders, feared a communist takeover.

The time was ripe for Benito Mussolini, a journalist and ex-soldier, to launch the first fascist movement, *fascio di combattimento*, or "fascists for the battle". He promised to smash the threat of communism and make Italy a powerful nation. Many people welcomed his strong leadership.

Mussolini's supporters, black-shirted young thugs, fought on the streets and terrorized politicians. The government was unable to tame them. King Victor Emmanuel III was afraid of a communist revolution, so in 1922 he agreed to make Mussolini prime minister. Gradually Mussolini removed all his enemies and became a dictator.

GERMANY

The German economy was shattered by World War One. After the New York Stock Exchange crash in 1929, German money became almost worthless. Inflation meant that people needed a suitcase full of cash to buy a loaf of bread. In this climate, a new form of fascism quickly took hold. It was called Nazism, and was built on violent race hatred. The Nazis encouraged anti-Semitism, or hatred of Jews, whom they blamed for all Germany's economic problems.

Hitler adopted the swastika as the Nazi emblem.

ADOLF HITLER AND THE NAZIS

Adolf Hitler, a fanatical anti-Semite, had set up the Nazi party in 1920. It grew rapidly. His rabble-rousing speeches offered a vision of a glorious German master race, superior to Jews and dark-skinned peoples. Led by a powerful leader, or *Führer*, they would build a thousand-year empire. Hungry, desperate and still resentful of the terms of the Treaty of Versailles, millions of Germans rallied to Hitler's call.

Elected as chancellor, or head of government, in 1933, Hitler soon removed all other parties from power. He set up vicious prison camps such as Dachau, and on the "Night of the Long Knives", in June 1934, his henchmen murdered over a hundred of his rivals. Nazi thugs attacked German Jews and their homes and shops. Jewish children were expelled from schools. On *Kristallnacht* (Crystal Night) in 1938, hundreds of synagogues were burned down and thousands of Jews were arrested – a grim sign of things to come.

THE SPANISH CIVIL WAR

Isolated and backward, Spain kept out of World War One. In 1931, a new Republican government set out to improve the lives of the poor. But in doing so, they made many powerful enemies.

SPAIN

■ Franco's conquests
□ Republican areas

Republicans in northern and eastern Spain held out against Franco until 1939.

By 1936, General Franco had united the government's enemies under a fascist banner. Civil war broke out. To support Franco, German planes carried out devastating air raids on Spanish cities. Over 30,000 men from 54 countries joined the Republicans' fight against fascism. But they were no match for Franco's professional army. In 1939 the fascists won. Franco became Spain's dictator until his death in 1975.

In the Spanish Civil War, both sides used propaganda to get their message across. Some was even aimed at children. This doll, with its cut-out uniforms, is making a fascist salute.

DICTATORS IN EUROPE

This map shows how the nations of Europe were governed in 1938. Many countries were in the grip of fascist rulers or other harsh, unelected dictators.

FASCIST AGGRESSION

Having promised their people glory, fascist leaders needed to produce victories to satisfy them.

By the mid-1930s, Mussolini's economic plans were in ruins and the people were growing restless. To distract them, in 1935 he launched an attack on Ethiopia. The Ethiopian Emperor, Haile Selassie, asked for support from the League of Nations. But it failed to stop Mussolini.

Emperor Haile Selassie, ruler of Ethiopia, which was also then known as Abyssinia.

Watching in Germany, Hitler seized the moment. He ordered troops into the Rhineland, although this was forbidden by the Treaty of Versailles. The League of Nations made no response at all.

The Rhineland acted as a buffer between Germany and France.

Morocco was still under French and Spanish control. Franco's troops included many Moroccan divisions.

Ethiopia was the last part of Africa to be colonized by a European power.

Liberia was the only other African nation which was not a European colony.

Mussolini used planes and poison gas against the poorly armed Ethiopian fighters.

KEY

■ Fascist dictatorships
■ Other dictatorships
■ Democracies
■ Communist states
↘ Italy's invasion route to Ethiopia

| 0 | 500 | 1000 km |
| 0 | 300 | 600 miles |

FIND OUT MORE

After World War One	☞	12
League of Nations	☞	12
Treaty of Versailles	☞	12

See above pages for more information.

Indian Ocean

Atlantic Ocean

STALIN'S SOVIET UNION

This propaganda poster shows agricultural workers as heroes.

Joseph Stalin chose his own name, meaning "man of steel".

By 1924, the civil war and famine that followed the Russian Revolution were over. Communism was starting to succeed. Joseph Stalin emerged as the new leader when Lenin died. He modernized the Soviet Union, transforming it from a backward agricultural nation to an industrial giant and an atomic superpower. But these changes cost immeasurable human suffering.

RISE TO POWER

After Lenin's death, Stalin worked his way to power by encouraging quarrels between his rivals, including Leon Trotsky, Lenin's second in command. By 1929 he was every bit as powerful as the Czar had once been. Stalin was seen as a trusted father figure who would lead the country to peace and plenty. But he was ruthless. He silenced his critics at home and exiled Trotsky, whom he later had assassinated.

THE FIVE YEAR PLANS

"We are fifty or a hundred years behind the advanced countries," said Stalin. "We must catch up in ten years, or we shall be crushed." In 1928, he announced the first Five Year Plan. It set gigantic targets for every kind of heavy industry.

The people responded to Stalin's call. They set to work with energy and enthusiasm. Across the Soviet Union, armies of volunteer workers lived in tents, sharing beds in shifts, as they built vast new coal, iron and steel works, massive factories and Europe's largest dam on the River Dnieper.

AGRICULTURE

Stalin tightened his grip over the peasants. He wanted them to increase production by giving up their own farms and working under communist orders on vast collective farms, called *kolkhoz*.

When the peasants resisted, their villages were surrounded by machine gunners. In a great wave of anger, millions of Russian peasants burned their crops and slaughtered their cows and pigs, rather than hand them over to the new collective farms.

STALIN'S PRISON CAMPS

Stalin built up a vast system of prison camps, called Gulags. They became a vital part of the Soviet economy. During Stalin's rule, on average eight million prisoners slaved in the Gulags' deadly conditions, opening up frozen and remote areas of the country.

KEY

Prison camps		Railways built by prisoners
Tundra (frozen land)		Canal built by prisoners
Dense forest		
Areas set aside for prison camps alone		

CHAOS AND FAMINE

Millions of peasants were denounced as enemies of the people, and sent to prison camps in remote areas. In the chaos, few crops were sown. In 1932-33 up to three million people died in a man-made famine which swept through the Ukraine. People ate mice, ants or bark to survive. But factory workers received just enough food to keep up production.

THE GREAT TERROR

By 1934, Stalin was determined to get rid of anyone who opposed him. No one was safe. For little or no reason, millions of men and women were imprisoned, tortured or shot in the purges of the "Great Terror". Survivors were sent to join the peasants in the prison camps, where few lived longer than a couple of years.

THE AFTERMATH

By 1938 the Cheka, or State Police, had files on more than half the population of the cities. One in twenty of all the people in the Soviet Union had been arrested, and millions had died. The Terror had finally run its course. But now the Soviet people faced another deadly onslaught. In Germany, Adolf Hitler was preparing for war.

These prisoners, who were known as *zeks*, are dragging a massive cable. Others mined gold, felled trees and laid railways.

A Gulag watchtower. Prisoners were kept cold and hungry, and were treated brutally.

During World War Two, Hitler's forces were to invade the western part of the Soviet Union. Supplies from the industries in the Gulags helped the Soviet Union to survive Germany's attack.

N O R Y L L A G
It is said that several hundred camps of complete isolation were built within this region, in places impossible to escape from.

Dalstroi region, over 1,000 miles (1,600km) long, was uninhabited except for prison camps.

DALSTROI

Arctic Circle

Sea of Okhotsk

U N I O N

C H I N A

FIND OUT MORE

| Russian Revolution | ☞ 10 |
| Stalin and Hitler | ☞ 22 |

For more information see above pages.

These women are learning to read and write. A massive literacy campaign, which reached millions of people in the first ten years of Soviet rule, was one of communism's great early achievements.

WORLD WAR TWO

In the 1930s, the German leader, Adolf Hitler, started to break the terms of the Versailles Treaty. He began by rearming Germany and by sending soldiers into the Rhineland on France's border. He also formed an alliance with Italy's leader, Benito Mussolini.

A British wartime identity card. Every citizen had one.

The war separated families. This baby girl was born in 1939. Her photo was taken to send to her father, on the frontline in 1940.

THE ANSCHLUSS

One of Hitler's aims was to gain control of countries where German-speakers lived. His first target was Austria, which was put under pressure to unite with Germany. Austria's Chancellor asked the people to take part in a referendum (vote) to decide if that was what they wanted. Before the vote took place, in March 1938 German troops entered Austria. This joining of Austria and Germany is called the Anschluss ("union"). It was forbidden by the Treaty of Versailles.

Here Austrians greet German soldiers. Many Austrians agreed with the Anschluss.

GERMAN EXPANSION

This map shows how Germany acquired more and more territory between 1937 and 1939.

0 — 500km
0 — 100 — 200 — miles

NETHERLANDS
BELGIUM
RHINELAND
GERMANY
Berlin
SUDETENLAND
Prague
CZECHOSLOVAKIA
Vienna
AUSTRIA
LITHUANIA
MEMEL
Danzig
EAST PRUSSIA
POLAND
Warsaw

KEY

- Germany in 1937
- Occupied by Germany 1938
- Occupied by Germany 1939
- Occupied by the Soviet Union 1939

"The scum of the Earth, I believe?"

"The bloody assassin of the workers, I presume?"

A 1939 cartoon, depicting Stalin and Hitler gleefully greeting each other over the body of the dead Poland.

HITLER ADVANCES

France and Britain protested, but did nothing to stop the Anschluss. In September 1938, German troops occupied the Sudetenland in Czechoslovakia. The British Prime Minister tried to appease (pacify) Hitler, signing an agreement allowing him to keep the territory. Hitler now went in search of more *Lebensraum*, or "living space" for Germans.

British Prime Minister Chamberlain declares that his agreement with Hitler is "peace for our time".

ATTACK ON POLAND

Within six months, Germany occupied the rest of Czechoslovakia and also Memel in Lithuania. Stirred to action, Britain and France promised to help Poland, Romania and Greece if they were attacked. In August 1939, the Soviet Union and Germany signed a non-aggression pact. Secretly, they agreed to divide Poland up between them.

On September 1, Hitler invaded Poland. Britain and France had no choice but to declare war. The Poles fought bravely, but by the end of September the Germans had occupied the western half of their country, while the Soviets had occupied the east.

BLITZKRIEG

The first six months of the war were surprisingly uneventful. A small British Expeditionary Force crossed to France and all sides prepared for war. American journalists called it a "phony war". Then in April 1940, the Germans swept into neutral Denmark and Norway. They attacked Belgium, the Netherlands and Luxembourg, and pushed on into France. The Germans used the speed of tanks and planes in a tactic known as Blitzkrieg, or "lightning war".

As well as planes and tanks, German soldiers used motorcycles to speed their way across Europe.

The advance across Europe. German forces moved across Belgium, the Netherlands, Luxembourg and into France with frightening speed. They reached the English Channel within a week.

THE DUNKIRK EVACUATION

In May 1940, British and French troops were pushed back to a strip of land around Dunkirk. To save them from capture, a rescue operation was mounted. The Royal Navy, with the help of hundreds of private boats, ferried troops back to England. Northern France was occupied by Germany and the south, known as Vichy-France, was ruled by a German-controlled government at Vichy.

This 1939 Christmas card was printed for soldiers of the British Expeditionary Force to send back to their families.

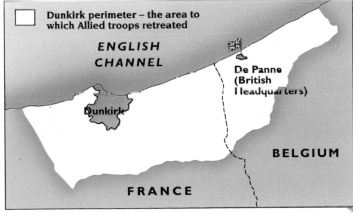

Dunkirk perimeter – the area to which Allied troops retreated

ENGLISH CHANNEL

De Panne (British Headquarters)

Dunkirk

BELGIUM

FRANCE

The area around Dunkirk, from which the British Expeditionary Force and some French troops were evacuated.

Paris
OCCUPIED FRANCE

Vichy

VICHY-FRANCE

Occupied France and Vichy-France.

FIND OUT MORE

Treaty of Versailles	☞	12
Germany	☞	18
War continues	☞	24

See above pages for more information

A British Vickers Supermarine Spitfire, flown in the Battle of Britain. It was one of the most successful fighters in the war.

German Messerschmidt 109E

THE BATTLE OF BRITAIN

With the support of the British Empire, Britain kept fighting. To subdue her, Hitler planned to invade. But to do this he realized that first he would have to wipe out the Royal Air Force. In August and September 1940, the Battle of Britain raged in the skies. Despite heavy losses, the RAF kept the German airforce, the Luftwaffe, at bay.

The Luftwaffe then changed tactics. It began to bomb British cities at night to crush morale. Bombers raided night after night, from September 1940 to May 1941 in a prolonged attack known as the Blitz. British bombers, in turn, pounded German cities. Civilians were now in the frontline. Many were killed or lost their homes and possessions.

There were eight machine guns in the wings.

THE WAR SPREADS

A British child's food rationing book. Ration books were issued to all.

By the end of 1940, much of Europe was under German occupation. Italy had also entered the war on Germany's side. Together they were known as the Axis Powers. With much of Europe occupied, Britain and its allies were now alone in resisting the Nazi threat.

Erwin Rommel, who commanded the Axis forces in North Africa.

BATTLE OF THE ATLANTIC

In order to continue the war, Britain relied on supply by ship. Battles took place at sea and German aircraft and U-boats (submarines), sank many supply ships. This was a serious threat to the Allies. In response, ships sailed in groups, called convoys, protected by warships. They also used a new tracking device called sonar to find and destroy the U-boats. This struggle, called the Battle of the Atlantic, continued to the end of the war.

HELP FROM THE USA

Although the USA did not enter the war straight away, President Roosevelt persuaded his government to support the Allies against Nazi Germany. Help was given through the Lend-Lease Act of 1941. The act enabled the USA to send supplies to any country if this action might help defend the USA itself. This meant that essential supplies of food, arms and materials could be sent to Britain to help them in the war effort.

The men, women and children left at home in Britain also threw themselves into the war effort. Food and clothes were rationed and everyone made an effort to save materials. A famous slogan, "Dig for Victory", encouraged people to grow their own food.

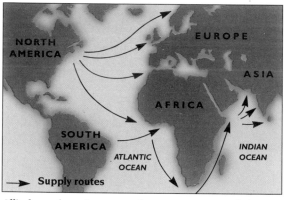

Allied supply routes across the oceans. To try to foil German attacks in the Atlantic, merchant ships sailed in convoys, guarded by warships.

British women working on a farm during the war. Known as the "Land Army", they took the place of male farmworkers who were away fighting. Women also did other jobs, such as working in arms factories and on buses and trains.

WAR IN NORTH AFRICA

From its colonies of Libya and Ethiopia, Italy attacked the Allies in North Africa. Successful at first, they were soon pushed back. To support them, Hitler sent in his Afrika Korps troops under Field Marshall Rommel. In 1941, the Germans advanced and by mid-1942, Rommel was just 100km (60 miles) away from Egypt – the British stronghold in North Africa. After losing a fierce battle at El Alamein, the Axis forces retreated, finally evacuating to Sicily.

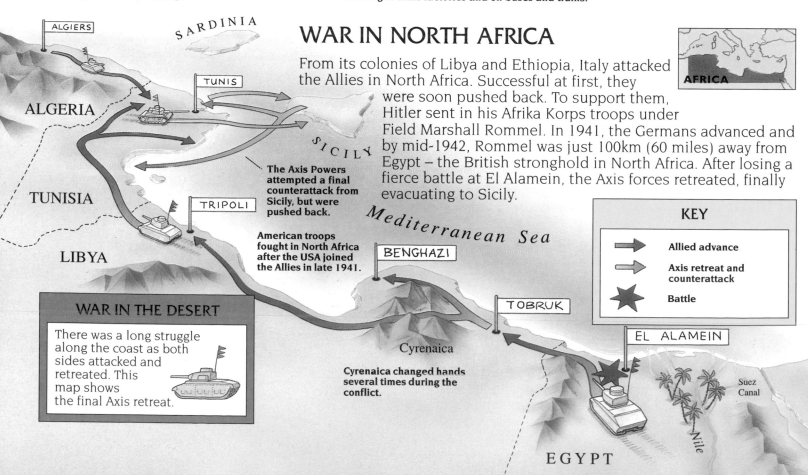

ALGIERS

SARDINIA

TUNIS

ALGERIA

SICILY

TUNISIA

The Axis Powers attempted a final counterattack from Sicily, but were pushed back.

American troops fought in North Africa after the USA joined the Allies in late 1941.

TRIPOLI

Mediterranean Sea

BENGHAZI

LIBYA

TOBRUK

WAR IN THE DESERT

There was a long struggle along the coast as both sides attacked and retreated. This map shows the final Axis retreat.

Cyrenaica

Cyrenaica changed hands several times during the conflict.

EL ALAMEIN

KEY

→ Allied advance

→ Axis retreat and counterattack

★ Battle

AFRICA

Suez Canal

Nile

EGYPT

WAR AGAINST THE SOVIETS

In June 1941, Hitler went back on his pact with Stalin and ordered the invasion of the Soviet Union. Forgetting past tensions, the Soviets entered into an alliance with Britain. The Germans had expected the campaign to last only a few weeks, but fanatical Soviet resistance and the sheer size of the Soviet army held them back. The Russian winter arrived, and the Germans lacked equipment and suffered in the bitter cold. Far from victory, they were now fighting on two fronts.

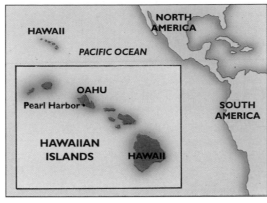

German forces blasted their way into the Soviet Union. The invasion was codenamed Operation Barbarossa.

PEARL HARBOR

The Japanese, who were at war with China, had made a pact with Nazi Germany in 1936. With Europe at war, Japan saw an opportunity to expand into mainland Asia and also across the Pacific. Only the American Pacific fleet stood in their way. Without warning, on December 7, 1941, Japan invaded Malaya and Thailand and attacked the American fleet in Pearl Harbor, Hawaii, killing nearly 2,500 people. The USA immediately declared war on Japan, bringing both nations into World War Two.

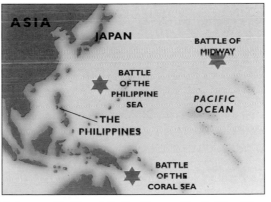

Pearl Harbor. 19 warships were sank or damaged, but the US aircraft carriers escaped – they were not there.

IN THE FAR EAST

At first the British forces were unable to stop the Japanese advance. Thousands of prisoners were taken by the Japanese and treated with such terrible cruelty that many died. The Japanese also conquered much territory in the Pacific, but their advance was finally halted in 1942. The British advanced overland and the Battles of the Coral Sea, Philippine Sea and Midway were victories for the US navy, although casualties were heavy. The Americans began to capture territory in the Pacific, island by island.

Major naval battles of the Pacific war. The Battle of the Philippine Sea was a particularly harsh defeat for Japan.

For more information see above pages.

THE FINAL SOLUTION

In 1941, the German leadership devised the "Final Solution" – all Jews were to be rounded up, sent to concentration camps and exterminated. The camps were heavily guarded and it was impossible to escape. While the war went on, Jews and other enemies of the Nazis suffered terribly as the Final Solution was carried out unmercifully.

Persecution of Jews had been going on for many years. Jews in German-occupied territory had to wear the yellow Star of David to identify them.

THE TURNING TIDE

In November 1942, General Montgomery defeated the Axis Powers in Egypt at the Battle of El Alamein. General Eisenhower led an Anglo-American landing in Morocco and Algeria, joined by the Vichy-French forces there. German forces were trapped in Tunisia and surrendered in May 1943. The German attack on the Soviet Union had failed and the U-boats were being driven out of the Atlantic. The Axis Powers were now halted and under pressure from all sides.

Anne Frank, a victim of the Nazis, whose diary became world famous. The writing says, "This is a photo of me as I wish I looked all the time. Then I might still have a chance of getting to Hollywood."

VICTORY FOR THE ALLIES

General de Gaulle, leader of the Free French army, inspects troops.

By July 1943, the Allies were in a stronger position than they had ever been. Allied troops gathered in Britain and North Africa, preparing for an invasion of mainland Europe. The liberation of Nazi-occupied territory was about to begin.

ITALY INVADED

After their victory in North Africa, Allied troops landed in Italy on the Sicilian beaches. At first the Germans resisted, but were pushed back to the mainland. Welcomed by the people, the invading forces followed the retreating Germans north.

The Italian people were unhappy with their continued involvement in the war. Mussolini was ousted and imprisoned. The new Italian government made peace with the Allies and joined in against the Nazis. But the Allied campaign was hard-going and the push through Italy was slow.

A landing craft – a troop carrying ship used in the invasion of the Italian mainland and other seaborne invasions.

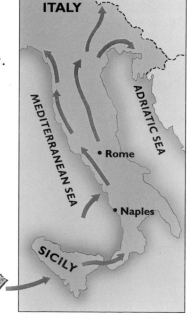

The route of the invasion of Italy, in which nearly half a million Allied troops took part.

D-DAY

As the Allied troops were battling through Italy, Allied commanders were planning to launch an invasion of northern France. Troops and arms were collected together in southern England, waiting for the word to attack. The first day of the great invasion was to be codenamed "D-Day".

On June 6, 1944, landing craft in the English Channel made their way to the Normandy coast. Five strips of beaches had been identified as landing places for American, Canadian and British troops. Soldiers now poured ashore under German fire. Bombing raids had destroyed many German lines of communication, but heavy fighting still followed. The Allies did not break away from the Normandy coast until the end of July 1944.

FRANCE IS LIBERATED

The Allies began to fight their way through France, despite strong counterattacks. A second Allied army, containing units of General de Gaulle's Free French army, landed in southern France. On August 25, 1944, Paris itself was liberated due to the joint efforts of the Allies and the French Resistance – civilians who worked to undermine their German occupiers. Although it was not necessary to do this for military reasons, the Allies decided to enter Paris to boost the Allies' morale.

The next day de Gaulle led a triumphant march through the streets cheered by jubilant crowds. Belgium and the Netherlands were also liberated from German occupation. But German counterattacks still threatened the Allies' progress across Europe.

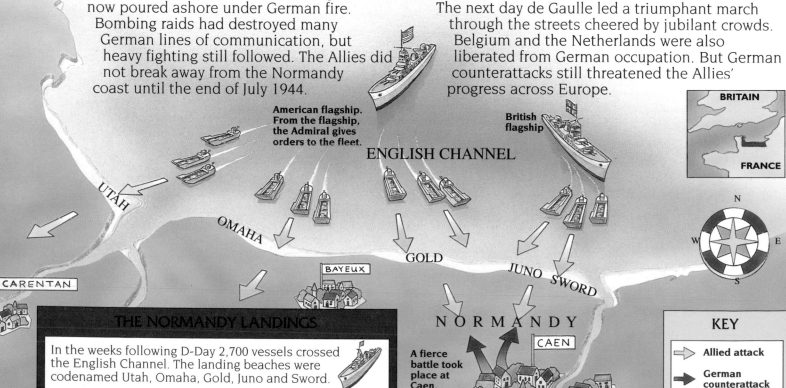

American flagship. From the flagship, the Admiral gives orders to the fleet.

British flagship

ENGLISH CHANNEL

UTAH

OMAHA

GOLD

JUNO

SWORD

CARENTAN

BAYEUX

NORMANDY

CAEN

A fierce battle took place at Caen.

THE NORMANDY LANDINGS

In the weeks following D-Day 2,700 vessels crossed the English Channel. The landing beaches were codenamed Utah, Omaha, Gold, Juno and Sword.

FRANCE

BRITAIN

FRANCE

KEY

⇨ Allied attack

➤ German counterattack

INTO GERMANY

In September 1944, Allied troops were crossing the western German frontier, but a struggle lay ahead of them. At Arnhem in the Netherlands, British paratroops tried to secure a bridge over the Rhine and were defeated with heavy losses, but this was only a temporary setback. Meanwhile, Soviet troops were advancing from the east.

A British paratrooper. Over 20,000 Allied troops were dropped into the Netherlands. 8,000 British paratroopers landed at Arnhem, of which only 2,000 escaped.

HITLER'S LAST WEAPON

Hitler refused to acknowledge this dire situation. In June 1944, he ordered his new secret weapon to be put into action. This was the rocket-propelled flying bomb, called the V-1 ("V" stood for *Vergeltung*, meaning "Revenge"). Known as "doodlebugs", they were capable of reaching London from France.

Shortly after the V-1, an even greater threat was developed – the V-2. But Hitler's flying bombs could not save him. By spring 1945 the Allies were advancing from both sides. Unable to face defeat, Hitler killed himself on April 30. On May 8, the German government surrendered.

In April 1945, the Allies were closing in on Berlin from both east and west.

DEATH CAMPS DISCOVERED

As Allied armies moved across Europe, they made a terrible discovery. In the some of the areas they liberated were concentration camps where Jews, Slavs, gypsies, the mentally ill and enemies of the Nazis had been sent to work as slaves or simply to be exterminated under the Nazi's Final Solution.

The Allies liberated the surviving prisoners in the death camps, but it was too late for most of them. Most had died of disease or overwork, or had been murdered. About 15 million people in all were killed in this way. Six million of these people were Jews. This event is known as the Holocaust.

△ Concentration camps

Europe's concentration camps. Those in Poland were set up specifically as extermination camps.

JAPAN SURRENDERS

Meanwhile, the Allies were still fighting Japan. American troops were advancing in the Pacific, Allied armies were moving into Burma, and the Soviets invaded Manchuria. Japan was already being heavily bombed, when a devastating weapon was used against it. On August 6, 1945 the US Air Force dropped an atom bomb on Hiroshima. Two days later a second bomb was dropped on Nagasaki. Both cities were completely destroyed and Japan surrendered on August 14, 1945.

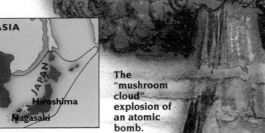

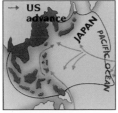

Japanese territory in mid-1943. US marines advanced across it.

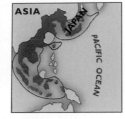

Japanese territory in August 1945. Japan itself was not invaded.

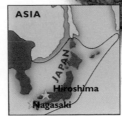

Hiroshima and Nagasaki – the cities destroyed by atomic bombs.

The "mushroom cloud" explosion of an atomic bomb.

FACT BOX

FRENCH RESISTANCE

In occupied France, some anti-Nazis took up arms and worked under cover to help the Allies. Known as the French Resistance, or the Maquis, they sabotaged German equipment and helped Allied prisoners to escape back to Britain. Resistance groups flourished in all occupied countries.

THE JULY PLOT

Hitler had always had enemies, but by mid-1944, they were becoming bold. In July, senior members of his staff attempted to kill him with a bomb, in the so-called July Plot. They failed and the leaders were executed. Some opted for suicide.

WINSTON CHURCHILL

Churchill was one of the great Allied leaders of the war. He had served in the army before becoming a war correspondent during the Boer War. He became Prime Minister of Britain in May 1940. His stirring speeches helped to keep morale high and keep the Allies together.

MUSSOLINI'S FATE

A daring German raid rescued Mussolini from his prison in the Apennine Mountains. His rescuers flew him to northern Italy where he was set up as leader of a puppet Italian government by Hitler. In April 1945, as the war drew to a close, Mussolini was captured by Italian partisans and executed.

HIROSHIMA

Hiroshima was flattened by the atomic bomb. An 8km (5 mile) high cloud covered the city and the explosion was said to be as bright as the sun. 80,000 were killed and within a year 60,000 more died of injuries and disease caused by the bomb's radiation.

EUROPE DIVIDES

By the end of World War Two, much of Europe was in ruins. While the people started to rebuild their lives, their leaders set about making a lasting peace. But without a common enemy to unite them, the bonds between the Allies were soon to unravel.

British Prime Minister Churchill, US President Roosevelt and Stalin, the Soviet leader, at Yalta.

THE AFTERMATH

The war created millions of orphans and widows. Throughout Europe, air raids and street fighting had turned cities into rubble. Homes, factories and farms were devastated. Shelter and food were in desperately short supply. Many went hungry.

Millions had been forced away from their homelands by the war. Great trudging masses of people were trying to get back home, or to build a new life elsewhere. Refugees, ex-slave workers, freed prisoners of war, and survivors of the concentration camps – all were on the move. As the new borders were drawn in areas such as Poland and the Baltic coast, people who for generations had been settled were now forced to uproot and return to their original homelands. Many fled west because they did not want to live under a communist regime.

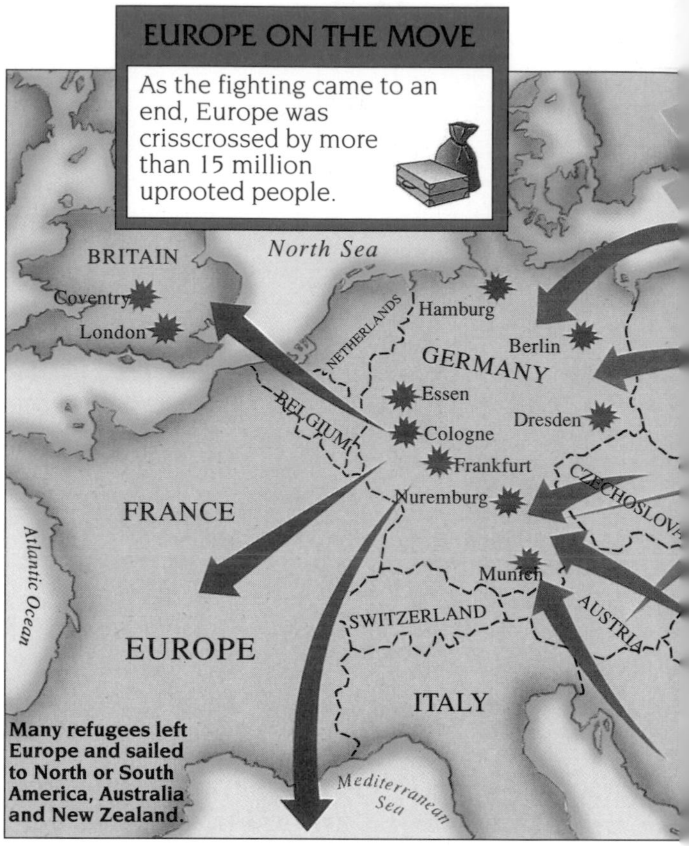

EUROPE ON THE MOVE

As the fighting came to an end, Europe was crisscrossed by more than 15 million uprooted people.

Many refugees left Europe and sailed to North or South America, Australia and New Zealand.

(Map labels: North Sea, BRITAIN, Coventry, London, NETHERLANDS, Hamburg, Berlin, GERMANY, Essen, Dresden, BELGIUM, Cologne, CZECHOSLOVA..., Frankfurt, FRANCE, Nuremburg, Atlantic Ocean, Munich, AUSTRIA, SWITZERLAND, EUROPE, ITALY, Mediterranean Sea)

UNITED NATIONS

The old League of Nations, set up after World War One, had failed to prevent another global war. In 1945, world leaders decided to set up a new organization. The United Nations (or UN), as it was called, had more power than the old League of Nations because now both the superpowers, the USA and Soviet Union, were members. The UN set out its aim: "to save succeeding generations from the scourge of war".

The symbol of the United Nations. The olive branches represent peace.

Much of Europe was bombed to ruins. Here in Dresden and elsewhere, the *Trümmerfrauen*, "women of the rubble", rebuilt their cities brick by brick.

GERMANY'S FUTURE

In February 1945, now certain of victory, the Allied leaders had held a conference at Yalta by the Black Sea to discuss Germany's future. The Soviet Union, which had lost 20 million people, wanted to punish Germany for the war. But the other leaders wanted to avoid the problems that had brought Hitler to power. Germany (and her capital city, Berlin) was to be divided and occupied by foreign powers. She was forbidden to make weapons or to have an army capable of military action.

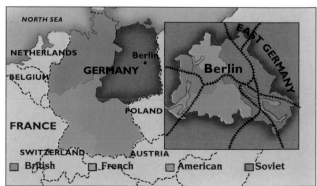

(Map labels: NORTH SEA, NETHERLANDS, Berlin, GERMANY, EAST GERMANY, Berlin, BELGIUM, FRANCE, POLAND, SWITZERLAND, AUSTRIA)

| ■ British | ■ French | ■ American | ■ Soviet |

Germany and Berlin were divided into four zones. Berlin, inside the Soviet zone, had special access routes to the West.

GROWING SUSPICIONS

As the war drew to a close, the superpowers grew suspicious of each other. Stalin was alarmed to discover that the USA had built the atom bomb – and furious that it had dropped two of them on Japan without consulting him. The Soviets urgently started work on their own bomb. For their part, American leaders suspected that the Soviet Union wanted to build a communist empire across Europe and beyond.

Thousands of anti-communist Russians were forced back to the Soviet Union against their will. Many were executed or sent to prison camps in Siberia.

SOVIET UNION

POLAND

Warsaw

NGARY

ROMANIA

GOSLAVIA

Baltic Sea

KEY

→	1 million concentration camp survivors and refugees
→	5 million Russians
→	11 million Germans
→	Russians leaving for the Baltic States
→	Baltic peoples
→	Poles
✹	Some bombed cities

US TROOPS AND AID

America watched with alarm as Eastern European nations fell under Soviet influence. Would Western Europe, hungry and demoralized after the war, turn to communism? In 1947, both Greece and Turkey teetered on the brink of communist revolution. US President Truman sent American aid and weapons to support the "free peoples" there against what he saw as a communist threat.

The US offered European governments massive amounts of aid, in the form of food, goods and cash to rebuild factories, roads and transportation. Eagerly, the nations of Western Europe accepted. But the Soviet Union and other communist countries refused the offer. The Marshall Plan, as it was called, pumped $14,000,000,000 into Western Europe between 1948-52. As a result, the West recovered quickly from the war.

This poster promoted the new Common Market, set up in 1955 to strengthen trade in Western Europe. It later became known as the European Community. The region's industry flourished with Marshall Plan money received from the US.

FACT BOX

NUREMBERG TRIALS

In 1945-47 at Nuremberg in Germany, 177 Germans and Austrians were tried for war crimes. Survivors of the concentration camps gave harrowing evidence against them. In total, 25 Nazi leaders were sentenced to death for crimes against humanity, and 117 were sent to prison.

KATYN FOREST MASSACRE

Tensions arose at the Nuremberg Trials over the mass graves discovered in Katyn Forest in Poland. Thousands of Polish officers had been massacred there in 1940. Soviet and Nazi generals accused each other's troops. To this day, neither side has admitted that they carried out the mass killings.

EASTERN EUROPE

In 1945, Soviet troops raced across Eastern Europe, freeing it from Nazi control. They stayed on to create a communist zone right along the Soviet border. Despite agreeing at Yalta to a "free and independent Poland", Stalin now insisted on communist leaders there. He had the old rulers of Bulgaria and Romania arrested as Nazi sympathizers, and replaced them with his own supporters. Even Czechoslovakia, with its stronger democratic traditions, soon fell to Stalin's pressure.

NETHERLANDS
Berlin POLAND
EAST
WEST GERMANY
CZECHOSLOVAKIA
FRANCE
AUSTRIA HUNGARY
ROMANIA
SWITZERLAND
YUGOSLAVIA
BULGARIA
ITALY
BLACK SEA
MEDITERRANEAN SEA
GREECE
SOVIET UNION
☐ Communist countries

Europe divides. In 1946, Churchill spoke of an "iron curtain" separating the communist East from the capitalist West.

BERLIN AIRLIFT

Berlin, where East and West were face to face, became a focus for tension. In 1948, frustrated by this island of capitalism inside communist territory, Stalin blockaded all road and rail routes into West Berlin.

Planes brought basic rations into West Berlin – including food for the city's zoo animals.

Defiantly, the Western powers started a massive, regular airlift of food, fuel and mail. The Soviets knew that to shoot down the planes would lead to war. For nearly a year, West Berliners survived on airlifted rations. Eventually, in 1949, the Soviet Union backed down. East and West Germany became two countries.

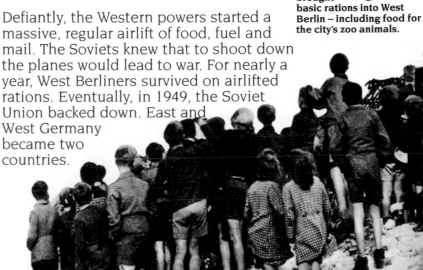

THE BIRTH OF ISRAEL

The Jewish people had been stateless since the Romans forced them out of Palestine in AD98. Since the end of the nineteenth century, Jews had campaigned for a nation. As news of the Holocaust emerged after World War Two, support grew for the idea. Palestine, the Jews' ancient homeland, seemed the obvious place.

Jewish children who came from Yemen to settle in the new state of Israel.

Many Arabs fled from Palestine in 1948. They hoped to return later.

ZIONISM

Zionism is the belief that Jewish people should have their own independent homeland. The Zionist movement, founded in the late nineteenth century, flourished among European Jews in a climate of widespread anti-Semitism (hatred of Jewish people). Some rulers encouraged violent attacks against Jews, as a distraction from other problems. Zionists dreamed of a mass return to the Jewish homeland, Palestine.

BRITISH PROMISES

During World War One, the British promised to press for a Jewish state in Palestine. They hoped to win Jewish support in the United States, which had just entered the war. But the British had also promised an independent state to the Arabs who lived in Palestine, who were mainly Muslims. They did this to undermine their Turkish rulers, who were Germany's allies in the war. After the war, Britain was given a mandate to rule Palestine when the Ottoman Empire was broken up.

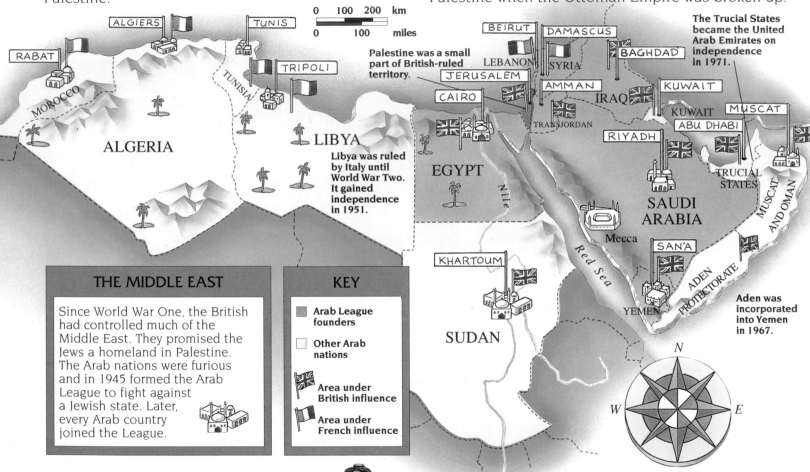

Palestine was a small part of British-ruled territory.

The Trucial States became the United Arab Emirates on independence in 1971.

Libya was ruled by Italy until World War Two. It gained independence in 1951.

Aden was incorporated into Yemen in 1967.

THE MIDDLE EAST

Since World War One, the British had controlled much of the Middle East. They promised the Jews a homeland in Palestine. The Arab nations were furious and in 1945 formed the Arab League to fight against a Jewish state. Later, every Arab country joined the League.

KEY

- Arab League founders
- Other Arab nations
- Area under British influence
- Area under French influence

JEWS IN PALESTINE

Fleeing anti-Semitic attacks in Europe, Jews had been settling in Palestine since the turn of the century. They bought land from Arab landlords. The settlers endured harsh conditions at first. Much of their land was stony or marshy. Many died of malaria. But full of hope, energy and idealism, they built new cities and set up communal farms, called *kibbutzim*.

An early Jewish settler working on the land in Palestine.

ARAB RESENTMENT

In the late 1920s, Arab resentment was growing in Palestine. In 1929 thousands of Arabs rioted in protest at Jewish immigration. Unrest spread quickly. To protect themselves, Jewish settlers later formed an armed security force called the Hagannah.

The British, now responsible for ruling Palestine, were getting desperate. To try to calm the Arabs, after 1933 they limited the number of Jews allowed to enter and settle in Palestine each month to just 1,500. They ignored the growing threat to European Jews from Nazi Germany.

JEWS FLEE HITLER

In 1933 the Nazis, fanatical anti-Semites, took power in Germany. Thousands of Jews fled for Palestine. But the British turned most away. Many drowned, and some were even returned to Europe where they were rounded up by the Nazis.

A refugee ship bound for Palestine. Even after World War Two, the British still turned away most Jewish refugees and survivors of the Nazi death camps.

TERRORISM

After World War Two, terrorism escalated in Palestine. Jerusalem was besieged by Arab guerilla fighters. Jewish terrorists killed 250 people at the Arab village of Deir Yassin. Although this was condemned by the Zionist leadership, the Arabs struck back, ambushing a medical convoy, killing many doctors and nurses. A world exhausted by war wanted a simple solution to the problems in Palestine. The United Nations suggested dividing the area into two halves, one Jewish and one Arab.

LEBANON
SYRIA
MEDITERRANEAN SEA
Jerusalem International Zone
PALESTINE
JORDAN
EGYPT
☐ Jewish areas
■ Arab areas

Palestine in 1947, as the UN planned to divide it. Jews and Arabs were to have an equal share.

LEBANON
SYRIA
MEDITERRANEAN SEA
JORDAN
Jerusalem
EGYPT
☐ Israel in 1948
— Israel's border in 1949
➤ Arab attacks

Israel in 1949. At first, Arab attacks forced Israeli troops back, but in the end Israel won some extra land.

A NEW STATE

The state of Israel was declared on 14 May 1948. The very next day the armies of five Arab nations attacked Israel. In Israel's War of Independence, as it became known, Arab troops outnumbered Israeli forces three to one. But united and fighting for survival, the Israelis won. They took some land which the UN had allocated to the Arabs. The rest became part of the new kingdom of Jordan.

The Zionists' dream had come true. The new state of Israel started to build schools, universities, hospitals and industries. But the war had brought a cease-fire without peace. Arab leaders called for the destruction of the Zionist state.

JORDAN
Walls of the Old City
Dome of the Rock
Church of the Holy Sepulchre
Western Wall
El Aksa Mosque
ISRAEL
Jerusalem

Part of the city of Jerusalem. Sacred to Jews, Muslims and Christians, in 1948 Jerusalem was divided after Israel's war of independence. Jews could not go to pray at holy sites in Arab territory, such as the Western Wall.

THE PALESTINIANS

Around 300,000 Arabs had fled from Palestine on the eve of war. Now homeless and stateless, they became known as the Palestinians. Many lived in refugee camps in the countries on Israel's borders. During the 1950s and 60s, they believed that the Arab states would help them to return to Israel. But despite strong words, Arab leaders did little. Instead, they used the plight of the Palestinians to keep up hatred of Israel. Around 200,000 Arabs remained in Israel in 1948. They had the right to vote, but were second class citizens, with poorer education, health care and housing than Jewish citizens.

A Palestinian refugee camp in Jordan. At first, many camps had no running water or electricity.

FACT BOX

THE MUFTI OF JERUSALEM

In 1921, the British appointed a vicious anti-Semite, Mohammed Amin al-Husseini, as senior judge, or *Mufti*, of Jerusalem. He organized the murder of many moderate Arabs who were prepared to live side by side with Jewish settlers.

HEBREW, THE NATIONAL LANGUAGE

Hebrew had always been the Jews' language of prayer. It was not used for everyday talk or writing. But early settlers in Palestine decided to use Hebrew, as part of their national identity. As Jewish immigrants arrived from all over the world, they learned Hebrew, a single language which bound them all together.

"OPERATION MAGIC CARPET"

Large Jewish communities in Arab countries had been allowed to live more or less peacefully until Israel was formed. But hostility to the new state meant that Jews in Arab countries became the target of attacks. Many came to settle in Israel. In "Operation Magic Carpet", between 1949-50, 49,000 Jews were airlifted from Yemen to safety in Israel.

INDEPENDENCE FOR ASIA

As the century progressed, demands for independence from European colonial powers grew steadily in Asia. Some nations achieved this peacefully, but for others it was a violent and bitter struggle.

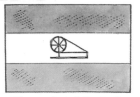

The symbol of the Indian National Congress Party.

THE INDIAN NATIONAL CONGRESS

In 1885, the Indian National Congress Party was founded by a group of middle-class Indians. They wanted a share in government, but Britain was reluctant to relax its control over its prize colony. The Indian Acts of 1909, 1919 and 1935 gave Indians a say in government, but not as much as they wanted.

In 1915, a young lawyer called Mohandas Karamchand Gandhi joined the Indian National Congress. He had already campaigned for Indian rights in South Africa (where many Indians lived). Gradually he emerged as the leader, encouraging non-violent protest, such as marches. He was imprisoned several times, but went on hunger strike to continue his protest.

Gandhi was assassinated by a Hindu fanatic in 1948. He became known to the Hindu people as the *Mahatma* or "Great Soul".

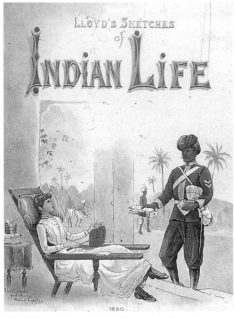

This illustration of 1890 shows the luxurious life of the British in India.

INDIA AND PAKISTAN

In India there were two main religious groups – Hindus and Muslims. The Indian National Congress was supported by Hindus, while the Muslims had their own party called the Muslim League. At first, the two parties worked together for independence, but Muslims were worried that they would have less say in an independent India. The Muslim League insisted on a separate state. Gandhi agreed, although he had hoped to keep India together.

After World War Two, Britain was struggling to rebuild itself and had to let its colonies go. In 1947, the Indian Empire became independent and two states were created – India for Hindus and Pakistan for Muslims.

Muslims from Hindu areas migrating to Pakistan. Thousands of refugees left their homes amid much violence.

NEW BEGINNINGS

Other parts of Asia had also been colonized in the nineteenth century. In World War Two, Japan had attacked the colonies, including Malaya (now Malaysia), Dutch East Indies (Indonesia), Burma (Myanmar) and the Philippines. It also occupied parts of Vietnam, where the Japanese became targets for Vietnamese nationalists, led by Ho Chi Minh. Calls for independence in Asia gathered strength, especially after Japan's defeat. The people no longer wanted to be dominated by foreign powers.

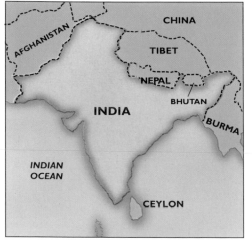

The Indian sub-continent in 1945. It had been ruled by Britain since the eighteenth century.

The separate states of India and Pakistan in 1947. East Pakistan became Bangladesh in 1971.

Japanese territory during World War Two. The Japanese wanted an empire in Asia.

FRENCH INDOCHINA

After World War Two, France tried to regain control over its colonies in French Indochina. Vietnamese nationalists were opposed to this and war broke out in 1946. French forces made a huge effort to win back their colony, but were no match for the Vietnamese guerillas in the jungles. The nationalists set up a republic in the north, which came under communist control.

After crushing the French at Dien Bien Phu, Vietnam declared itself independent in 1954. But it was a divided country – the communists still controlled the north, while the south was supported by the democratic powers in the West. Cambodia and Laos became independent in 1953.

Vietnamese villagers

The Thakin Party led the call for independence in Burma in the 1930s. Independence was granted in 1948. Renamed Myanmar, it is now under a military dictatorship.

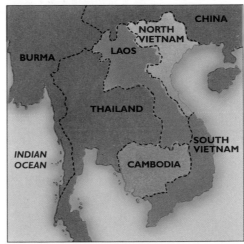

Three independent countries emerged from the former French Indochina – Laos, Vietnam and Cambodia.

FACT BOX

DIEN BIEN PHU

This was the decisive battle in the war for independence in Vietnam. French airborne troops seized the village of Dien Bien Phu in November 1953 and a battle followed. The French were besieged and defeated in May 1954. Two months later, France signed an armistice and withdrew its troops from Vietnam.

THE DUTCH EMPIRE

After the British and the French, the Dutch empire was the third biggest. Most of it was in Indonesia (then called the Dutch East Indies).

A NEW ASIA

This map shows the modern borders of the Asian countries. It also shows which areas were colonized by which European powers. China was not colonized by any European nation, although at times European influence there was strong.

Thailand (called Siam until 1939) was ruled by a king who had absolute power. In 1932, the people were granted a say in government. Since 1939, there have been several periods of military rule.

The Philippines were occupied by the USA in 1902. In 1946, independence was granted, but the USA kept military bases.

Britain gave Ceylon limited self-rule in 1931. It became independent in 1947 and was renamed Sri Lanka in 1972.

In Malaya, the Communist Party campaigned for independence in the 1930s. Britain granted independence in 1957 and it became Malaysia in 1963.

In 1945, the Indonesian Republic (formerly the Dutch East Indies) declared independence. The Dutch tried to regain control but after four years of fighting, independence was gained in 1949.

The Dutch kept control of the western half of New Guinea until 1963, when it joined Indonesia.

KEY

Former colonies

- USA
- Dutch
- French
- British

Map labels

RUSSIA
Ulan Bator
MONGOLIA
Beijing
CHINA
NORTH KOREA
Pyongyang
Seoul
SOUTH KOREA
Tokyo
JAPAN
Pacific Ocean
TAIWAN
BHUTAN
INDIA
BANGLADESH
Dhaka
BURMA
Hanoi
Rangoon
THAILAND
LAOS
Bangkok
CAMBODIA
Phnom Penh
VIETNAM
Colombo
SRI LANKA
Manila
THE PHILIPPINES
Kuala Lumpur
MALAYSIA
BRUNEI
Singapore
Jakarta
INDONESIA
NEW GUINEA
Indian Ocean
AUSTRALIA

A NEW AFRICA

After World War Two, African colonies, like their fellow colonies in Asia, began to demand independence. Europe was devastated by the war and could not hold onto its possessions abroad.

This poster commemorates all the colonies that sent soldiers to fight on behalf of the Allies in World War Two.

Stamps celebrating the independence of Ghana, Gambia, Congo and Nigeria.

ALGERIA

The French colony of Algeria was promised that after the war it would be given a share in its own government. France, though, did not keep her promise on this. In 1952, oil was discovered in Algeria and French settlers grew even more determined to stay, hoping that the oil might bring wealth. In 1954, war broke out. After eight years of bitter guerilla fighting, France finally granted Algeria her independence in 1962.

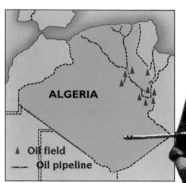

Algeria's oil fields. Pipelines take the oil from the desert to the coast for export.

An Algerian soldier. In the war of independence, women were required to fight.

EGYPT

In 1922, after nationalist protests, the British recognized Egypt as a constitutional monarchy but retained some powers, including control over Sudan. The British were keen to maintain some power in Egypt because of the Suez Canal. The canal (built between 1854 and 1869) is a vital short cut between the Mediterranean Sea and the Indian Ocean.

APARTHEID

After World War Two, South Africa's politics were dominated by the white minority – descendants of British and Dutch settlers who had colonized the area in past centuries.

In 1948, the National Party was in power. It introduced an official policy of apartheid, or "separateness". This meant that the different races, Asians, Africans and Europeans, were given different rights. In practice, whites were given more privileges and nonwhites had very little opportunity to improve their standard of living. Mixed marriages were forbidden and at first nonwhites were not allowed to vote or even share the same buses as whites. Anti-apartheid riots at Sharpeville in 1960 led to the death of 67 people.

Apartheid was internationally condemned. Protests from the British Commonwealth led to South Africa leaving it in 1961.

THE SUEZ CRISIS

In 1952, Colonel Nasser came to power in Egypt. In 1956, he brought the Suez Canal under Egyptian control, threatening British and French interests. Later that year Israel invaded Egypt, which gave Britain and France the opportunity to send troops on a pretence of restoring order. In reality, they wanted to restore control over the canal. Fierce protests, led by the United Nations, forced them to withdraw.

RHODESIA BECOMES ZIMBABWE

In Southern Rhodesia, the white Rhodesia Front Party wanted independence from Britain, but refused Britain's demands for the party to share power with the black Africans. In 1965, Southern Rhodesia made its Unilateral Declaration of Independence (UDI) from Britain. The white government ruled until 1979 when it was finally made to accept black majority rule. The country took the name Zimbabwe in 1980.

The canal is 162km (100 miles) long and 60m (197ft) wide. Before it was built, ships bound for Asia had to go around Africa.

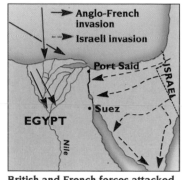

British and French forces attacked Egyptian bases, and paratroops landed around Port Said, the entrance to the canal.

British colonies in Africa in 1945. Southern Rhodesia was renamed Rhodesia on UDI – its break from Britain.

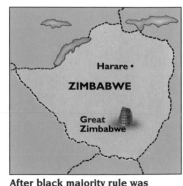

After black majority rule was brought in, Rhodesia was renamed Zimbabwe after the ancient stone ruins of Great Zimbabwe.

THE MAP OF AFRICA

Many borders of African countries are straight lines. This is because Africa was divided by its colonizers, without regard to traditional tribal borders. This has led to problems after independence, as many countries contain two or more peoples, with different languages and religions.

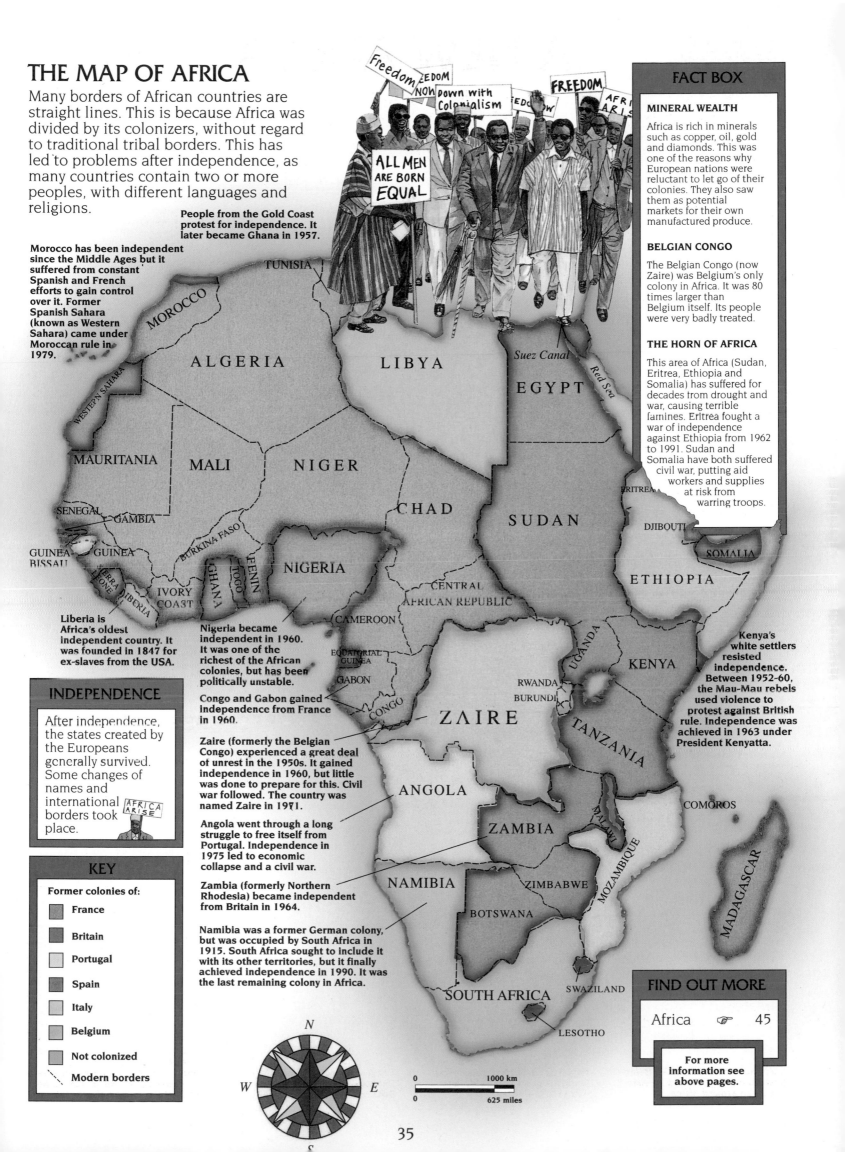

People from the Gold Coast protest for independence. It later became Ghana in 1957.

Morocco has been independent since the Middle Ages but it suffered from constant Spanish and French efforts to gain control over it. Former Spanish Sahara (known as Western Sahara) came under Moroccan rule in 1979.

Liberia is Africa's oldest independent country. It was founded in 1847 for ex-slaves from the USA.

FACT BOX

MINERAL WEALTH

Africa is rich in minerals such as copper, oil, gold and diamonds. This was one of the reasons why European nations were reluctant to let go of their colonies. They also saw them as potential markets for their own manufactured produce.

BELGIAN CONGO

The Belgian Congo (now Zaire) was Belgium's only colony in Africa. It was 80 times larger than Belgium itself. Its people were very badly treated.

THE HORN OF AFRICA

This area of Africa (Sudan, Eritrea, Ethiopia and Somalia) has suffered for decades from drought and war, causing terrible famines. Eritrea fought a war of independence against Ethiopia from 1962 to 1991. Sudan and Somalia have both suffered civil war, putting aid workers and supplies at risk from warring troops.

Nigeria became independent in 1960. It was one of the richest of the African colonies, but has been politically unstable.

Congo and Gabon gained independence from France in 1960.

Zaire (formerly the Belgian Congo) experienced a great deal of unrest in the 1950s. It gained independence in 1960, but little was done to prepare for this. Civil war followed. The country was named Zaire in 1971.

Angola went through a long struggle to free itself from Portugal. Independence in 1975 led to economic collapse and a civil war.

Zambia (formerly Northern Rhodesia) became independent from Britain in 1964.

Namibia was a former German colony, but was occupied by South Africa in 1915. South Africa sought to include it with its other territories, but it finally achieved independence in 1990. It was the last remaining colony in Africa.

Kenya's white settlers resisted independence. Between 1952-60, the Mau-Mau rebels used violence to protest against British rule. Independence was achieved in 1963 under President Kenyatta.

INDEPENDENCE

After independence, the states created by the Europeans generally survived. Some changes of names and international borders took place.

KEY

Former colonies of:

- France
- Britain
- Portugal
- Spain
- Italy
- Belgium
- Not colonized
- - - Modern borders

Map labels

TUNISIA
MOROCCO
ALGERIA
LIBYA
EGYPT
Suez Canal
Red Sea
WESTERN SAHARA
MAURITANIA
MALI
NIGER
CHAD
SUDAN
ERITREA
DJIBOUTI
SENEGAL
GAMBIA
GUINEA-BISSAU
GUINEA
BURKINA FASO
SIERRA LEONE
LIBERIA
IVORY COAST
GHANA
TOGO
BENIN
NIGERIA
CAMEROON
CENTRAL AFRICAN REPUBLIC
SOMALIA
ETHIOPIA
EQUATORIAL GUINEA
GABON
CONGO
ZAIRE
UGANDA
KENYA
RWANDA
BURUNDI
TANZANIA
ANGOLA
ZAMBIA
MALAWI
COMOROS
NAMIBIA
ZIMBABWE
MOZAMBIQUE
BOTSWANA
MADAGASCAR
SWAZILAND
SOUTH AFRICA
LESOTHO

N
W — E
S

0   1000 km
0   625 miles

FIND OUT MORE

Africa ☞ 45

For more information see above pages.

LATIN AMERICA

Latin America is the name given to Central and South America. Few of the countries in the region were involved in the two world wars, but they had plenty of conflicts of their own.

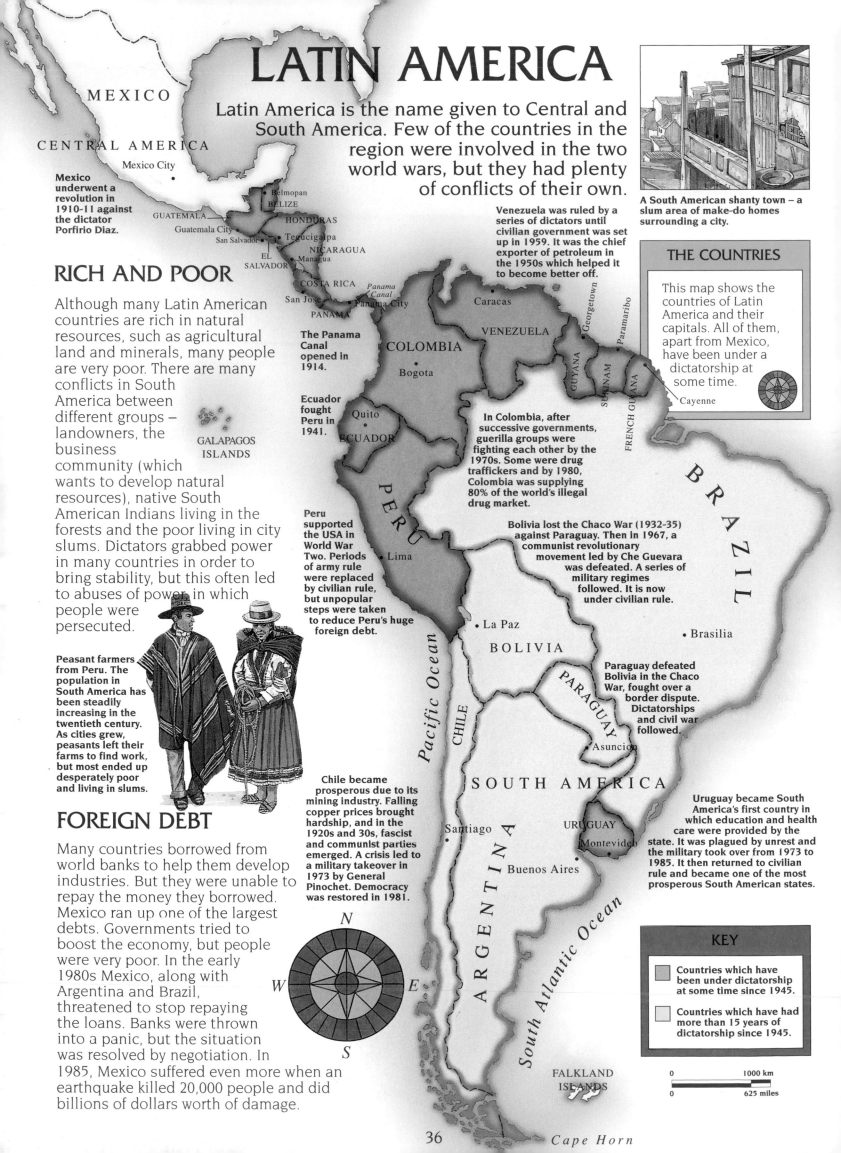

A South American shanty town – a slum area of make-do homes surrounding a city.

MEXICO

CENTRAL AMERICA

Mexico City

Mexico underwent a revolution in 1910-11 against the dictator Porfirio Diaz.

RICH AND POOR

Although many Latin American countries are rich in natural resources, such as agricultural land and minerals, many people are very poor. There are many conflicts in South America between different groups – landowners, the business community (which wants to develop natural resources), native South American Indians living in the forests and the poor living in city slums. Dictators grabbed power in many countries in order to bring stability, but this often led to abuses of power in which people were persecuted.

Peasant farmers from Peru. The population in South America has been steadily increasing in the twentieth century. As cities grew, peasants left their farms to find work, but most ended up desperately poor and living in slums.

FOREIGN DEBT

Many countries borrowed from world banks to help them develop industries. But they were unable to repay the money they borrowed. Mexico ran up one of the largest debts. Governments tried to boost the economy, but people were very poor. In the early 1980s Mexico, along with Argentina and Brazil, threatened to stop repaying the loans. Banks were thrown into a panic, but the situation was resolved by negotiation. In 1985, Mexico suffered even more when an earthquake killed 20,000 people and did billions of dollars worth of damage.

Belmopan
BELIZE
GUATEMALA
Guatemala City
San Salvador
EL SALVADOR
HONDURAS
Tegucigalpa
NICARAGUA
Managua
COSTA RICA
San José
PANAMA
Panama Canal
Panama City

The Panama Canal opened in 1914.

Ecuador fought Peru in 1941.

Quito
ECUADOR

GALAPAGOS ISLANDS

Peru supported the USA in World War Two. Periods of army rule were replaced by civilian rule, but unpopular steps were taken to reduce Peru's huge foreign debt.

Lima

PERU

Pacific Ocean

CHILE

Chile became prosperous due to its mining industry. Falling copper prices brought hardship, and in the 1920s and 30s, fascist and communist parties emerged. A crisis led to a military takeover in 1973 by General Pinochet. Democracy was restored in 1981.

Santiago

Venezuela was ruled by a series of dictators until civilian government was set up in 1959. It was the chief exporter of petroleum in the 1950s which helped it to become better off.

Caracas
VENEZUELA
COLOMBIA
Bogota
Georgetown
GUYANA
Paramaribo
SURINAM
FRENCH GUIANA
Cayenne

In Colombia, after successive governments, guerilla groups were fighting each other by the 1970s. Some were drug traffickers and by 1980, Colombia was supplying 80% of the world's illegal drug market.

Bolivia lost the Chaco War (1932-35) against Paraguay. Then in 1967, a communist revolutionary movement led by Che Guevara was defeated. A series of military regimes followed. It is now under civilian rule.

BRAZIL

• La Paz
BOLIVIA
• Brasilia

Paraguay defeated Bolivia in the Chaco War, fought over a border dispute. Dictatorships and civil war followed.

PARAGUAY
Asuncion

SOUTH AMERICA

URUGUAY
Montevideo
Buenos Aires

Uruguay became South America's first country in which education and health care were provided by the state. It was plagued by unrest and the military took over from 1973 to 1985. It then returned to civilian rule and became one of the most prosperous South American states.

ARGENTINA

South Atlantic Ocean

FALKLAND ISLANDS

Cape Horn

THE COUNTRIES

This map shows the countries of Latin America and their capitals. All of them, apart from Mexico, have been under a dictatorship at some time.

KEY

▢ Countries which have been under dictatorship at some time since 1945.

▢ Countries which have had more than 15 years of dictatorship since 1945.

| 0 | 1000 km |
| 0 | 625 miles |

N
W   E
S

REVOLUTION IN CUBA

In many Latin American countries, socialism or communism were seen as solutions to instability and poverty. From the 1930s, Cuba was governed by Gulgencio Batista, a corrupt, US-backed dictator. In 1956, a Cuban rebel, named Fidel Castro, joined forces with Che Guevara, an Argentinian

USA
CUBA
MEXICO

Cuba is only 150km (90 miles) from the USA.

communist who was experienced in guerilla warfare. Together they led rebels against Batista and in 1959 they overthrew him. Castro reformed the government and Cuban society along communist lines. His reforms, backed by the Soviet Union, were successful and brought stability.

Che Guevara became a popular symbol for socialist revolution. His face adorned T-shirts and posters.

ARGENTINA

Argentina earned its living by exporting grain and meat. Then, in the 1930s during the Great Depression, other countries could no longer afford to buy Argentina's produce.

In 1943, a military coup brought the army to power. One of its leaders, Juan Peron, was elected President in 1946. His strong nationalist style gained support from all sections of society. He was deposed in 1955, but returned to power in 1973. In 1976 a harsh new military dictatorship came to power, which lasted until 1983. During this period, in order to stamp out opposition, around 20,000 people were killed.

BRITAIN

→ Route of the British "task force" sent to defend the islands

ARGENTINA

FALKLAND ISLANDS

In 1982 Argentina invaded the Falkland Islands, which had been a British colony since 1833. The Argentine invasion force was defeated.

BRAZIL

In the early part of the century, Brazil's coffee exports brought stability and prosperity to the country. In the 1920s, however, social unrest grew and there was a revolt in 1930. In 1964 there was a military takeover, in response to the peasants demanding land reforms.

In 1985 there was a return to elected government, but Brazil still faces many problems. Like the rest of South America, it faces huge debts. There is much social unrest, and environmental problems have been caused by the cutting down of the rainforest.

☐ Areas of rainforest
■ Areas of severe deforestation

BRAZIL

The destruction of the rainforest. This is one of the world's great environmental problems.

NICARAGUA

In 1933, the wealthy Somoza family came to power in Nicaragua. The peasants were very poor and they supported an opposition group, called the Sandinistas, or FSLN. Frequent clashes led to civil war between 1976-79, in which around 50,000 people were killed.

One of the Sandinista rebels, guerilla fighters who overthrew the government in Nicaragua.

In 1979, the Sandinistas won. They accepted aid from communist countries, which worried the USA because of its business links in Nicaragua. The Contras, an anti-government group, invaded. The US government was later seriously embarrassed when it was revealed that illegal funds had been used to support the Contras. In 1990 peace was agreed, but unrest continued.

For more information see above pages.

THE COLD WAR

After World War Two, the superpowers grew wary of each other. Both stockpiled nuclear weapons in a "Cold War" – a war of threats and politics, rather than direct conflict.

This Soviet cartoon portrays the West as a ruthless thug.

US poster advertising an anti-communist film.

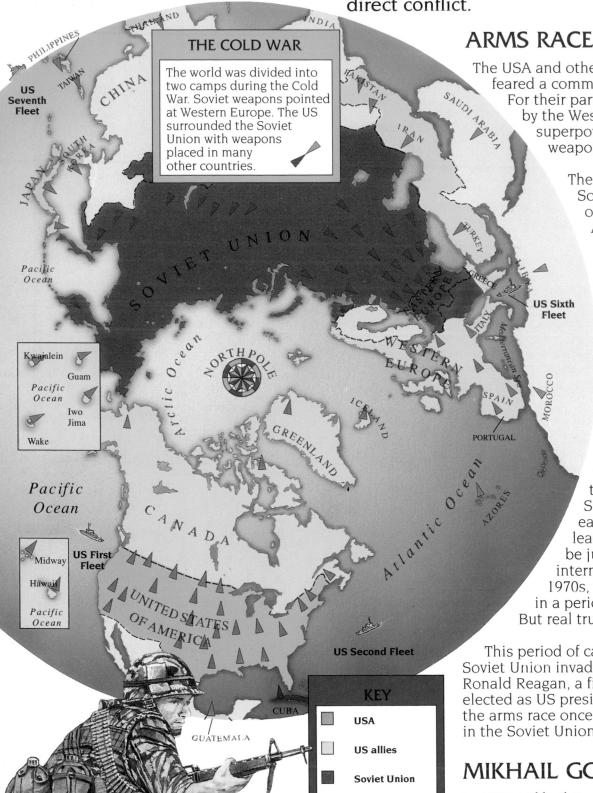

THE COLD WAR

The world was divided into two camps during the Cold War. Soviet weapons pointed at Western Europe. The US surrounded the Soviet Union with weapons placed in many other countries.

A heavily armed US soldier.

KEY

	USA
	US allies
	Soviet Union
	Soviet allies
	US missiles or airfields
	Soviet missiles or airfields
	US fleet

ARMS RACE

The USA and other Western capitalist nations feared a communist takeover of the world. For their part, the Soviets were alarmed by the West's military power. The superpowers set out to amass weapons in a vast global arms race.

The US wanted to encircle the Soviet Union. It persuaded other countries to allow American nuclear weapons onto their land, aimed at Soviet cities. The Soviets built up a larger force of troops, submarines and tanks, and they also built nuclear weapons. Soon, both sides had so many weapons that if either started global war, their own people would perish along with their enemies.

THAW AND FREEZE

There were hopes of a "thaw" in the Cold War when Stalin, the Soviet leader, died in 1953. But early hopes faded when the new leader, Khrushchev, turned out to be just as tough as Stalin on international matters. During the 1970s, world tensions eased a little, in a period of calm known as *détente*. But real trust never developed.

This period of calm came to an end when the Soviet Union invaded Afghanistan in 1979. Ronald Reagan, a fierce anti-communist, was elected as US president in 1981. He started up the arms race once again. But economic problems in the Soviet Union were to bring about change.

MIKHAIL GORBACHEV

In 1987 Mikhail Gorbachev, the new Soviet leader, signalled an end to the Cold War when he spoke of a "common European homeland". The Soviet Union could not afford the new weapons technology. She wanted peace with the US. Ironically, the superpowers' first act as allies was to fight side by side in another war – against Iraq in the Gulf War in 1991.

WORLD WAR OR LOCAL CONFLICT?

Despite their bluffing and threats, in reality the superpowers were
anxious to avoid global nuclear war. But each supplied arms to
their allies in the Cold War, and sent troops to fight in local
conflicts around the world. Often, guerilla fighters
outwitted the superpowers' troops, but the fighting
caused huge suffering among ordinary people.

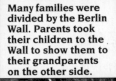

A US nuclear
missile. Anti-
nuclear protests
grew in Europe,
where many feared that
the superpowers would
use nuclear weapons.

KOREA

After Japan's surrender in World War Two, Korea was
divided into two halves – Soviet-occupied North Korea
and US-occupied South. But when the superpowers
withdrew their forces in 1950, both parts of Korea
claimed the right to rule the whole country. Border
clashes soon began. Communist North Korean troops
invaded the south. The US did not want to let Korea
become a communist state, so President Truman sent
American troops to support South Korean and United
Nations forces. After bloody fighting, a peace treaty
was agreed in 1953 – but Korea was left divided.

Communist troops invaded South Korea
from North Korea.

CUBA

Cuba's new communist leader, Fidel Castro, needed
allies. In 1959, the Soviet leader, Khrushchev, offered
aid to Cuba – in return for permission to build military
bases on the island. In 1963, US spy planes discovered
their plans. Swiftly, US President Kennedy ordered a
naval blockade of Cuba, threatening to sink any ships
which refused to be searched. For days the world
teetered on the brink of nuclear war. In the end,
Khrushchev backed down. After this terrifying scare, the
two superpowers avoided direct conflict. To increase
contact, a telephone hotline linked their leaders.

The US blockade of Cuba, where Soviet
bases would be too close for comfort.

VIETNAM

In 1963, North Vietnam's communist leader, Ho Chi
Minh, launched an invasion of South Vietnam. Worried
that nearby China would help to spread communism,
the US sent troops to support South Vietnam's dictator.
By 1968, 500,000 US troops were struggling in
unfamiliar jungle against guerilla fighters. Growing
desperate, the Americans sprayed deadly chemicals
over villages and farmland. Photos of the war horrified
millions in the US, and protests forced the government
to withdraw in defeat in 1973. In 1975, North Vietnam
united the country under communist rule.

Communist North Vietnam invaded
South Vietnam.

EASTERN EUROPE

Eastern Europe was dominated by the Soviet Union.
Puppet governments in many nations bowed to Stalin's
orders. Even after Stalin's death, Soviet troops crushed
a series of anti-communist uprisings in East Germany,
Poland, Hungary and Czechoslovakia. The city of Berlin
symbolized the East-West split, divided between the
Soviet Union and the West since World War Two. In
1961 Soviet and East German troops built the Berlin
Wall overnight, to divide the city and stop Eastern
Europeans crossing to the West. East German border
guards shot people trying to escape.

Revolts were crushed in Poland,
Hungary and Czechoslovakia.

Many families were
divided by the Berlin
Wall. Parents took
their children to the
Wall to show them to
their grandparents
on the other side.

FACT BOX

CHINA

At first, communist China
was an ally of the Soviet
Union. But by 1960
Chinese-Soviet relations
had cooled. After this
China followed an
independent path.

PROPAGANDA

Propaganda means
spreading opinions in a
one-sided way. Both
superpowers used
propaganda, such as films
and broadcasting, to
boost their own system
and undermine the
other's. Some US
politicians stirred up anti-
communism. In the 1950s,
US Senator Joe McCarthy
accused many famous
people, such as writers
and actors, of being
communists. Many people
lost their jobs as a result,
and some were even sent
to prison.

FIND OUT MORE

Berlin	☞	28
Gulf War	☞	43
Gorbachev	☞	46

For more
information see
above pages.

39

CHINA – "THE EAST IS RED"

Japan's defeat in World War Two freed China from the struggle between them. But civil war raged on until 1949, when the communists' peasant army, led by Mao Zedong, swept through the country. Across China, people flew the red flag of communism.

China's red flag. Red is a symbol both of China and of communism.

RUSSIA

Urumqi

Tarim

MONGOLIA

PAKISTAN

Western China is dry and mountainous. Most of the country's population lives in the fertile, crowded east.

The Chinese invaded Tibet in 1951, crushing the Tibetans' religion and culture. Their spiritual leader, the Dalai Lama, lives in exile in India.

Manchuria

RUSSIA

Japan had invaded Manchuria in 1933. The divided Chinese fought against them, but the Japanese occupied land as far south as the Yangtze River until the end of World War Two. This area now has many industrial cities.

Beijing

NORTH KOREA

Sea of Japan

Yellow River

Yenan

Xi'an

Zhengzhou

SOUTH KOREA

East China Sea

JAPAN

NEPAL

Himalaya Mountains

TIBET

INDIA

Lhasa

Mekong

CHINA

Chengdu

Wuhan

Shanghai

Yangtze

Hangzhou

BHUTAN

BANGLADESH

BURMA

Kunming

COMMUNIST CHINA

During the years of bitter civil war in 1946-49, the communists took control of the rest of China from their early strongholds in the east.

N W E S

VIETNAM

THAILAND

Nanning

Hainan

Guangzhou

HONG KONG

In 1997, Britain returns one of its last colonies, Hong Kong, to Chinese rule.

KEY

■ Communists' early strongholds

■ Communist conquests during the civil war 1946-49

⌒ China's border today

TAIWAN

0   300   600 km
0   300   miles

Taiwan was formerly Formosa.

THE NEW STATE

China's hundreds of millions of peasants were poor, overworked and hungry. They welcomed the communists, who offered them peace, land reform and education. In 1949, Mao and the communist government set about building up China's industry and economy,

中国

东方红

The communists simplified Chinese writing, to make it easier to learn to read and write. This says "China – the East is Red".

ravaged by decades of war. They took land away from the landlords and gave it to the peasants. The peasants were keen to work on their own small plots of land, but few wanted to live and work on the large collective farms planned by the communists.

FIVE YEAR PLAN

Mao's first Five Year Plan, begun in 1953, achieved mixed results. Factories met their vast orders – but produced shoddy goods. There was unrest in the countryside as peasants were forced onto collective farms, or communes.

In response, Mao launched a new campaign in 1957 inviting people to discuss the way forward. It was called "Let a Hundred Flowers Bloom". People entered the new debate with enthusiasm. But many who criticized the Communist Party were punished. Some thought they had been tricked into speaking out. Mao had shown himself to be a strong, ruthless leader.

GREAT LEAP FORWARD

In 1958, Mao announced the Great Leap Forward. He saw steel as the key to industrial growth. Tiny "backyard furnaces" were to double steel production every year. All peasants were to work on huge communes. But the results were disastrous. No crops were sown, and in the countryside millions died of famine. Mountains of brittle steel had to be scrapped.

"Backyard furnaces" like this one were powered by hand. To meet orders for steel, people melted down their own metal pots and pans.

CULTURAL REVOLUTION

Mao wanted permanent revolution, to stop people from growing complacent. In 1967 he launched the Cultural Revolution. He called on the young to rise up and criticize their elders, especially intellectuals and old-fashioned communist party members. Many pupils accused teachers of anti-revolutionary thoughts, and some children even reported their parents. Millions were beaten, tortured or driven to suicide. Schools were closed and factories stopped work. Normal life was impossible. Troops sent to calm the violence and chaos joined in the fighting. At last, by 1968, order was restored, but only by clamping down severely on people's freedom. Millions lost their education when Mao ordered young people to go to work in the fields, to learn from the peasants.

During the Cultural Revolution, young people answered Mao's call to arms. Battalions of fanatical teenagers, called Red Guards, terrorized the cities.

FINAL DAYS OF MAO

By the 1970s, Mao was growing old and sick. His wife and her supporters, known as the Gang of Four, plotted ruthlessly to hang onto power. But by 1973, Deng Xiaoping and Chou En Lai had taken over day to day governing. They started to dismantle the Cultural Revolution. When Mao died in 1976, the Gang of Four were tried and imprisoned for their brutal crimes.

Mao Zedong, China's leader from 1948 to 1976.

THE "NEW CHINA"

Deng wanted to reform China's economy and scrap the communes. He sought Western and Japanese help to modernize China's backward industry. This meant admitting that Mao had made disastrous mistakes in his later years.

Deng's reforms worked. By the early 1980s, factories were flourishing with the new investment, and farmers produced far more crops. Deng encouraged trade and built links with tiny, prosperous Hong Kong, in preparation for her return to Chinese rule.

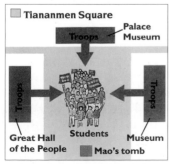

In 1989, democracy protests spread quickly across China. Demonstrations erupted in many cities, often led by students.

TIANANMEN SQUARE MASSACRE

By the late 1980s, the people grew impatient for change, especially after *glasnost* reforms in the Soviet Union. In April 1989, Beijing students began to demand democracy. Protests spread across China. In May, half a million people demonstrated in Beijing's Tiananmen Square to support the three thousand students on hunger strike there.

Deng's hardline prime minister, Li Peng, called in the army. On June 4th, 1989, troops massacred up to a thousand students in Tiananmen Square. Thousands more were imprisoned or executed. The Chinese people's call for democracy remains denied.

This young man bravely stood in front of a line of tanks to stop them from entering Tiananmen Square. He was taken away by police.

Troops surrounded the protestors camping in Tiananmen Square. Tanks drove through the capital's streets to enter the square.

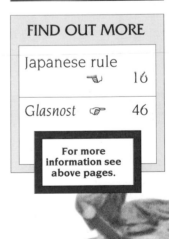

THE MIDDLE EAST

This extremist Palestinian poster says "Smash Israel".

After Israel was formed in 1948, conflict over land and religion exploded into war again and again in the Middle East. Rival Arab states, united by hatred of Israel, used oil wealth to buy arms and support terrorists. Islamic and Jewish extremists resisted peaceful compromise.

A supporter holds up a portrait of the *Ayatollah* Khomeini, Iran's Islamic leader from 1979-89.

ISRAEL

The new state of Israel was supported in 1948 by both the USA and the Soviet Union. In America, Jewish groups pressed the US government to send aid and arms to Israel. At first the Soviet Union was pleased to see Israel's new socialist government and the communist-style farms, or *kibbutzim*, which produced most of Israel's food. But gradually the Soviets turned against the new state. As the Cold War developed, they counter-balanced US support for Israel by sending tanks and fighter planes to several Arab nations.

Israel was tiny – only 15km (9 miles) across at her narrowest point – and surrounded by hostile nations. She felt vulnerable. But her defiant military response and treatment of the Palestinians led to criticism from the rest of the world.

ISRAEL AND THE ARAB STATES

Israel won extra land in the Six Day War of 1967. Many Palestinian Arabs lived in the areas taken by Israel. Since 1995 some of these Palestinian areas have won self-rule after lengthy peace negotiations.

ARAB-ISRAELI WARS

Between 1956 and 1973 Israel and the Arab nations fought three wars. The Arabs vowed to destroy the new state, force out the Jews and set up a Palestinian state in its place. Colonel Nasser, Egypt's strong new leader, united Arab nations behind him.

Israel was constantly on guard against attack. In a war lasting just six days, in 1967, the Israelis won strategically important land. This increased their feeling of security. Jewish extremists claimed that this land should always be part of Israel, and they built settlements there. But the many Palestinian Arabs in the area did not want to live under Israeli rule.

Golda Meir, Israel's Prime Minister from 1969 to 1974.

In October 1977, after months of secret talks, Egypt shocked the world when her next leader, President Sadat, signed a peace treaty with Israel. As part of the peace deal, Israel handed Sinai back to Egypt. Arab extremists assassinated Sadat in 1981.

THE OIL CRISIS

Middle Eastern countries exported oil to many Western nations, who came to rely upon it. In 1960, these countries, united by their religion (Islam), formed a trading group called OPEC*. OPEC was hostile to Israel. In 1973, the Arab nations lost the Yom Kippur War against Israel. OPEC members decided to reduce oil supplies to Israel's supporters, including the US, until they withdrew their support. The cost of oil increased by five times in a year, causing economic crisis in the West. But still Israel clung to the land she had won in 1967.

*Organization of Petroleum Exporting Countries

Map labels

LEBANON

Beirut

SYRIA

Damascus

Mediterranean Sea

Golan Heights

Nazareth

Even in peace time, Syria shelled Israel from the Golan Heights.

West Bank

Jordan

The West Bank of the Jordan river was part of Jordan until 1967, when Israel conquered it. 600,000 Palestinian Arabs lived there.

Tel Aviv

Jerusalem

Bethlehem

JORDAN

Jerusalem, once divided, was united under Israeli rule after 1967.

Gaza Strip

The Gaza Strip, home to many Palestinians.

ISRAEL

Port Said

Suez Canal

Sinai Desert

The Israelis took the Sinai Desert in 1967. But in 1977 they agreed to hand it back to Egypt as part of a peace deal.

Eilat

N
W   E
S

0   50   100   km
0   50   miles

KEY

- Israel in 1948
- Land taken by Israel in 1967
- Sinai Desert, now part of Egypt.
- Oil fields

SAUDI ARABIA

Saudi Arabia's enormous oil supplies are mainly in the east of the country.

Gulf of Suez

EGYPT

Egypt's oil fields are around the Gulf of Suez and in the north of the country.

The Sinai Desert is barely populated but it has valuable oil reserves.

Red Sea

PALESTINIAN ANGER

Since the formation of Israel, hundreds of thousands of Palestinians had lived in squalid refugee camps in Arab countries. There they were denied citizenship, homes and freedom. In 1964, a new movement was formed, called the Palestinian Liberation Organization, or PLO. Its leader was Yassir Arafat. In the 1970s, supported by Arab nations, the PLO carried out terrorist attacks to draw attention to their cause. In 1987, Palestinians inside Israel launched a violent uprising, or *Intifada*, to call for independence. Thousands of young men were exiled, imprisoned or killed in street fighting over the next few years.

THE LEBANON

Lebanon, on Israel's northern border, was home to many rival groups. Tensions exploded in a complex and bloody civil war in 1975 between different Islamic groups, Christians, Syrian fighters, and the PLO, whose headquarters were based there. The capital, Beirut, was reduced to rubble. In response to shelling over her borders, in 1982 Israel invaded southern Lebanon, hoping to drive out Palestinian terrorists and create a neutral buffer zone along her border. The world protested against Israeli aggression, and her troops withdrew in 1983. But this did not put an end to fighting in Lebanon.

IRAN, IRAQ AND KUWAIT

In 1979, the King or *Shah* of Iran was overthrown by a fiercely anti-Western group of Islamic religious leaders. In 1980, Iraq's dictator, Saddam Hussein, declared war on Iran. The West supplied Iraq with weapons, hoping to stop the spread of extremist Islamic feeling in the Middle East. The war dragged on for eight years, and millions died. Having failed to crush Iran, in 1990 Iraq invaded Kuwait. This threatened Saudi Arabia – and the West's oil supplies. The UN acted swiftly. In the Gulf War, as it was called, the Americans led international troops against Iraqi forces, bombing them into surrender.

SHALOM, SALAAM – PEACE

After the Gulf War, many Palestinians decided on a more moderate approach. Yasser Arafat led peace talks with Israel. These negotiations were long and difficult, and brought protests from both Jewish and Arab extremists. Spring 1996 saw the first elections for self-rule in Palestinian areas inside Israel. But doubts remain on both sides. In 1995, Israeli Prime Minister Rabin was assassinated by an extremist Jew.

Yitzhak Rabin (left) and Yasser Arafat (right) make peace in 1993. US President Clinton congratulates them.

Palestinian refugee camps were mostly in Lebanon and on the West Bank of the Jordan river. The West Bank became a part of Israel in 1967.

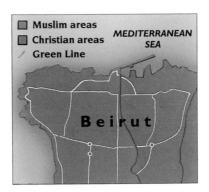

During the Lebanese civil war, a strip of wasteland called the "Green Line" divided the capital, Beirut, into the Muslim west and the Christian east.

Saddam Hussein's army, the fourth largest in the world, invaded Kuwait in 1990 – only two years after the long war with Iran ended without a clear winner.

FACT BOX

OIL AND LOANS

Many Arab nations – especially those with tiny populations – made so much money from oil that they could not spend it all. Instead they invested vast sums in the international banks. In the 1970s, this money was offered around the world as loans. Many developing countries grasped the chance to borrow, to finance large projects such as dam building. But interest on the loans now costs many of these nations half their spending each year, or even more – paid to some of the world's richest countries.

ISLAMIC FUNDAMENTALISM

In some Islamic countries, such as Iran, there has been a return to a very strict, traditional form of Islam. This is known as fundamentalism. It means that Islamic criminal and social laws are observed, for instance women must cover themselves with a long veil. But some extremists have used Islam to justify acts of terrorism, including suicide bombs – which fanatics believe will earn them a place in heaven.

ARAB-ISRAELI WARS

1948 Israel's War of Independence
1956 Suez Crisis
1967 Six Day War
1973 Yom Kippur War

 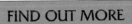

DEVELOPING WORLD

Simple wells like this can provide clean drinking water.

Most nations in Africa and Asia won independence from European rule in the years after World War Two. Many are now known as developing countries because their farming and industry are not yet as developed as those in the industrialized world.

Aung San Suu Kyi, elected as leader by the people of Burma.

FREEDOM AND HOPE

After independence, people had high hopes of freedom, democracy and wealth. In many countries, though, European rule left behind poverty, and recovery has been slow. Many new nations have been plagued by corrupt governments, civil wars, poverty and famine, so most people are no wealthier than they were before.

Richer countries sent aid but did little to tackle the causes of poverty in the developing world, such as trading disadvantages. Many developing countries still struggle to provide basic services such as health care and education for their fast-growing populations.

DICTATORS

One of the main problems to face many developing countries after independence was the rise of dictators – leaders who rule alone and have absolute control over people's lives.

A terrible example was Cambodia in the 1970s and 80s. By 1975, Pol Pot, leader of the Khmer Rouge (the Cambodian Communist Party), had taken control of the country. Around two and a half million Cambodians, nearly half the population, died during his reign of terror. In 1993, elections excluded the Khmer Rouge from power, but guerilla fighting continued after this.

PEOPLE'S HEROES

The struggle for freedom from dictatorship has brought forth some heroic leaders. One example is Aung San Suu Kyi of Burma. Since 1962, Burma has been in the grip of harsh military dictators who have renamed it Myanmar.

Even though Aung San Suu Kyi led the National League for Democracy to victory in elections in 1990, she has not been allowed to govern. Since then, she has lived under house arrest and has not been able to see her family. Each week, people gather outside her home, risking imprisonment to hear her speak.

AFTER THE EMPIRES FELL

Shared language or religion can bind people together into cultural groups. European rule had held varied cultural groups together, often ignoring their differences. After independence, many peoples wanted self-rule. Some have demanded the right to break away and form an independent state.

The Sikh flag. Sikhs want a homeland in the Punjab.

India is a country of many languages and religions. It has to work hard to create a feeling of national unity.

Sikhs want to make this area an independent homeland, Khalistan. The Punjab was first divided between India and Pakistan in 1948.

In 1948 the western part of Bengal joined India, and the east joined Pakistan, later becoming Bangladesh.

In India, there are 14 main languages, and 1,600 more are spoken. English is used as the official language, for convenience.

PAKISTAN
Islamabad
Jammu and Kashmir
Punjab
New Delhi
CHINA
NEPAL
BHUTAN
INDIA
BANGLADESH
Bengal
BURMA
Indian Ocean
INDIA
Lakshadweep
MALDIVES
Tamil Nadu
Tamil area
SRI LANKA
Colombo

| 0 | 500 km |
| 0 | 300 miles |

BREAKAWAY AREAS

This map shows some breakaway areas around India which have demanded or won self-rule.

KEY

- Breakaway provinces
- Cultural or language groups

In 1948, when India and the Islamic state of Pakistan won independence, the area of Bengal was divided between them. Many people fled from one side to the other. Eastern Bengal became East Pakistan and was ruled from the main part of Pakistan. In 1971, it won self-rule, and was renamed Bangladesh.

Jammu and Kashmir, one of India's few Islamic regions, wants its independence. India and Pakistan have fought for control of the area.

Thousands of Tamils, Hindu people originally from the province of Tamil Nadu in southern India, have lived in Sri Lanka for centuries. Now they want their own state. In northeast Sri Lanka, guerillas called the Tamil Tigers are fighting a bitter civil war.

FAMINE

Developing countries have suffered devastating famines, when severe drought causes crops to fail, and land turns into desert. Often famine is also caused by war. In Ethiopia in the 1980s, for instance, 800,000 people died in a terrible famine. Food was available, including aid sent from abroad, but soldiers fighting in the civil war stopped trucks from taking it to enemy parts of the country.

TRADE AND AID

In the 1960s and 70s, rich nations sent aid in the form of loans to developing countries, to help them build up their industry. Many developing countries are now struggling to repay the loans and the charges for borrowing. To earn cash, they have to grow crops to sell abroad, such as coffee or cotton, instead of food for their people. But developing countries are disadvantaged over trade, too. Industrialized countries keep down prices for the raw materials. Then they use these to manufacture goods such as instant coffee, which sell for more profit.

SMALL-SCALE AID

In 1985, during Ethiopia's famine, a huge televised pop concert called Live Aid raised $70,000,000 to send food to the starving. Aid organizations also support small-scale projects which help people to become self-sufficient and skilled. In the long term it is more useful to train people in tree planting to stop soil erosion, for instance, than to send food or fund high-tech projects which are hard to mend if they break down.

A NEW PATH

In 1991, Eritrea broke free from Ethiopia after 30 years of war. The new nation is determined to rebuild itself without using costly international loans. Instead, the people work by hand to clear fields and build roads, rather than using expensive machinery. Old trains, built by Italian colonizers in the 1930s, are being carefully restored and brought back into service.

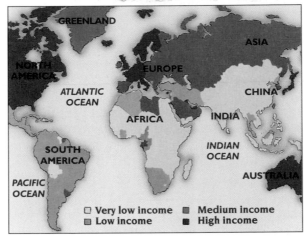

Deserts around the world are growing, increasing the risk of famine. One cause is overgrazing by cattle and goats, bred to try to produce more food for the rising population. This can leave the soil bare and in danger of blowing away, called soil erosion.

Average income per person around the world. The poorest countries are in Africa and Asia.

□ Very low income   ■ Medium income
■ Low income   ■ High income

FACT BOX

WHO GIVES TO WHOM?
Since the 1970s, charges for international loans have risen steeply. As a result, poor countries have paid thousands of millions of dollars to the rich nations – far more than they receive in aid. This means that there is less money to spend at home. Uganda, for instance, spends $17 per person per year on loan charges – five times more than it spends on health care. At last, after a quarter of a century, the rich countries are discussing ways to cancel the debts.

IDI AMIN (born 1926)
Idi Amin overthrew Uganda's first President, Milton Obote, in 1971. He then expelled all non-Africans from the country, and used torture and murder to keep his power. He was overthrown when Tanzania invaded in 1979.

THE GRAMEEN BANK
The Grameen Bank started in Bangladesh in the 1970s. It lends tiny amounts, mainly to women – just enough to buy cotton to weave or a cow to milk. Then the woman can set up her own small business, and pay back the loan in small instalments. In this way, a whole family may be able to escape from generations of poverty.

This woman has used a small loan from the Grameen Bank to buy a rickshaw and start her own business for her family.

COMMUNISM FALLS

Communist control in Eastern Europe ended with a peaceful revolution. Except in Romania, hardly a shot was fired. Many different peoples have won self-rule at last. But for some, the new freedom has brought uncertainty and chaos.

People waved the Romanian flag with the communist symbol ripped out.

Eastern Europeans driving to the West after the fall of communism.

GORBACHEV

Mikhail Gorbachev came to power in the Soviet Union in 1985. He admitted that the nation was facing industrial and economic failure, made worse by the long, unpopular war with Afghanistan. Gorbachev swiftly drew up plans for change, and withdrew from Afghanistan. He soon grabbed the goodwill of the public, as a young, energetic leader who wanted to improve people's lives.

Mikhail Gorbachev, the leader who dismantled the Soviet Union.

REFORM

Gorbachev launched a series of reforms, called *perestroika*. People could now vote in free elections, and set up their own businesses. *Glasnost*, or openness, meant more honest reporting of problems, such as the shortages of everyday goods in the shops. Past failings were revealed, including the horrors of Stalin's rule. At first, people were delighted with the new freedoms. But soon they became impatient for more change.

PERESTROIKA ABROAD

At the seventieth anniversary celebrations of the Russian Revolution, in 1987, Gorbachev encouraged other communist leaders to reform too. Some welcomed his message enthusiastically. More traditional leaders, such as East Germany's Erich Honecker, were furious. Gorbachev's words sent a signal that Soviet troops would not crush anti-communist protests as they had in the past. As a result, people all over Eastern Europe began to demand free elections. This encouraged an exciting new feeling of independence among peoples of many different cultures.

AFTER COMMUNISM

The vast communist empire broke up in the late 1980s. Many new nations rose out of it. Other peoples of the old Soviet Union joined together to form the Russian Federation.

In many regions, most of the population is not Russian, but belongs to other ethnic groups. Many now have self-rule, but still belong to the Russian Federation.

Conflict has arisen in many parts of the former Soviet Union. Control over valuable oil supplies in the southwest has triggered tension.

KEY

— **Boundary of the old Soviet Union**

Nations now independent of the Soviet Union

Areas of self-rule by ethnic groups within the Russian Federation

Formerly communist countries of Eastern Europe

** **Former Iron Curtain**

CANADA

Arctic Ocean

Lena

SIBERIA

GREENLAND

ICELAND

North Sea

Atlantic Ocean

NORWAY

SWEDEN

FINLAND

Ural Mountains

Ob

RUSSIAN FEDERATION

ESTONIA

KAZAKHSTAN

IRELAND

BRITAIN

DENMARK

LATVIA

LITHUANIA

Baltic Sea

NETHERLANDS

GERMANY

RUSSIAN FED.

BELARUS

BELGIUM

E U R O P E

POLAND

UKRAINE

KYRGYZSTAN

A S I A

SWITZERLAND

AUSTRIA

SLOVAKIA

CZECH REPUBLIC

FRANCE

HUNGARY

MOLDOVA

Aral Sea

TAJIKISTAN

UZBEKISTAN

Himalaya Mountains

ITALY

SLOVENIA

CROATIA

ROMANIA

SPAIN

BOSNIA

YUGOSLAVIA

Caspian Sea

TURKMENISTAN

Mediterranean Sea

MACEDONIA

ALBANIA

BULGARIA

Black Sea

GEORGIA

ARMENIA

AZERBAIJAN

GREECE

SOVIET DISUNION

In 1990 Lithuania, Latvia and Estonia declared themselves independent from the Soviet Union. The call for self-rule spread, bringing fighting in some places. People grew impatient for still more change. After a failed coup against him, Gorbachev stepped down, and Boris Yeltsin became president in his place. On December 31, 1991, the Soviet Union was declared at an end. In the new economic system, some have grown wealthy. But the cost of food and fuel has risen, and life is harder for many, especially old people with small pensions. Some people miss the old certainties of communism.

Many monuments to communist heroes, like this statue of Lenin, were demolished after communism fell.

This Soviet poster says "Long live peace among all the peoples". For decades, the Soviet Union had held together many different peoples, who split apart when the union broke up.

EASTERN EUROPE THROWS OFF COMMUNISM

East Germany was freed from communist control in May 1989 when Hungary opened its Austrian border. The East German leader, Erich Honecker, condemned this move, but thousands grasped the chance to go to the West. Many visited relatives they had not seen for decades. In November 1989, Germans on both sides of the hated Berlin Wall rejoiced as it was torn down. East Germans could now travel freely for the first time. The two Germanies were reunited less than a year later. Now Germans are working hard to make the poorer eastern regions as efficient and wealthy as the West.

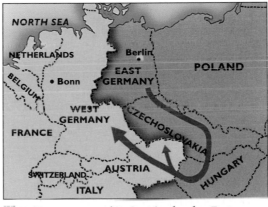

When Hungary opened its Austrian border, East Germans came through Czechoslovakia to the West.

Poland was the first to rise against communism. In 1979, striking ship workers formed an anti-communist trade union, Solidarity. Communist army leaders passed strict laws, but Solidarity continued to grow and in 1989 won a huge election victory.

In Czechoslovakia, the mass demonstrations that brought about change were so peaceful that they were known as the Velvet Revolution. In 1992 the country split peacefully into two independent halves – the Czech Republic and Slovakia.

Protests in Romania began in 1989, while Ceaucescu, the brutal dictator, was away. He returned to address a demonstration, but the people refused to hear him speak. He fled, but was captured and executed – the only communist leader to die.

National feeling grew in Poland when the new Polish Pope, John Paul II, visited the capital, Warsaw, in 1979. Major demonstrations took place at Gdansk, Poznan and Katowice.

Mass protests in Brno and the capital, Prague, in 1989 brought change in Czechoslovakia. The Czechs and Slovaks, thrown together after World War One, have now split.

Romanian protests started in Timisoara, after the arrest of a priest who stood up for the Hungarian minority. Unrest soon spread to the capital, Bucharest.

For more information see above pages.

WOMEN TODAY

During the twentieth century, women have fought for the right to vote and for education, careers and birth control. Many women today have more freedom than their mothers or grandmothers.

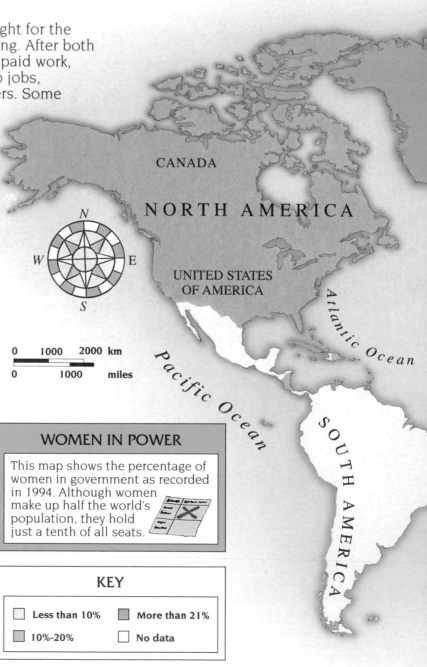

WOMEN OF BRITAIN COME INTO THE FACTORIES

During both world wars, governments asked women to take over men's jobs. This poster encouraged British women to do war work.

This suffragette is led away from a demonstration calling for votes for women in Britain before World War One.

SUFFRAGETTES

By 1900, women could vote in national elections only in New Zealand and Australia. In Britain and the USA, women protestors known as suffragettes organized huge demonstrations to demand the vote. Some even went to prison where they went on hunger strike to draw attention to their cause. During World War One, millions of women worked in the factories and fields. In 1918, in recognition of their work, British women over 30 won the vote. Two years later, so did women over 21 in the USA.

WOMEN AND WORK

Throughout the twentieth century, women have fought for the freedom and independence gained by earning a living. After both world wars, many women wanted to carry on doing paid work, rather than stay at home. Women began to gain top jobs, becoming managers, judges or government ministers. Some churches and synagogues now ordain women priests and rabbis. But progress is slow. Despite laws on equal pay, in many countries women still earn much less than men.

WOMEN'S CAMPAIGNS

Around the world, women in action groups and trade unions have campaigned for peace, justice and equal rights. Often they use peaceful, untraditional tactics to get their message across. In many developing countries, women took part in the struggle against colonial rule. They called for women's rights to be a part of the new freedom of independence.

A handful of women, such as Mrs. Sirimavo Bandaranaike of Sri Lanka, have been elected as prime ministers. But there is still a long way to go before women and men are elected to government in equal numbers.

In 1960, Mrs. Bandaranaike of Sri Lanka became the first woman in the world to be elected Prime Minister.

CANADA

NORTH AMERICA

UNITED STATES OF AMERICA

Atlantic Ocean

Pacific Ocean

SOUTH AMERICA

N
W E
S

| 0 | 1000 | 2000 km |
| 0 | 1000 | miles |

WOMEN IN POWER

This map shows the percentage of women in government as recorded in 1994. Although women make up half the world's population, they hold just a tenth of all seats.

KEY

| ☐ Less than 10% | ☐ More than 21% |
| ☐ 10%-20% | ☐ No data |

BIRTH CONTROL

Without birth control (which lets people plan if or when they have children) women might have up to a dozen children. This means that they would spend most of their time and energy caring for children. Improved methods of birth control let women choose to have a small family, leaving them more time for activities outside the home as well.

In developing countries with poor health care, many women continue to have large families because so many children die from malnutrition and disease. Until parents can be fairly sure that their children will survive, many will be reluctant to use birth control. Some Catholic and Islamic leaders discourage birth control for religious reasons.

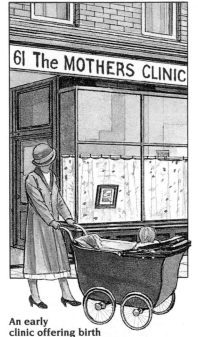

An early clinic offering birth control to mothers in the 1920s.

FEMINISM

Feminism is a movement which calls for women to have the same rights and freedom as men. The feminist movement grew up in Europe and the USA in the 1960s and 70s. It built on the achievements of the suffragettes and other women who campaigned early in the twentieth century for better education for girls, and improved working conditions for women.

Feminists now campaign for fair pay and working conditions, more childcare and for health care which meets women's needs. They also demand punishment for men who commit violent crimes against women and children.

WOMEN ACHIEVERS

IDA B. WELLS-BARNETT
Ida Wells-Barnett (1862-1931) campaigned in the USA for justice against vicious lynch mobs, who murdered black people. She helped to set up the National Association for the Advancement of Colored People in 1909.

MARIE STOPES
Marie Stopes (1880-1958) believed that women should be able to use birth control. Despite protests from doctors and Christian groups, she set up the first clinic in London offering birth control to women.

COCO CHANEL
Coco Chanel (1883-1971) was a fashion designer. Early in the twentieth century she designed comfortable, stylish dresses in soft fabrics such as wool and flannel, which liberated women from tight, painful corsets.

AMELIA EARHART
Amelia Earhart (1898-1937) was a pioneer American aviator. In 1932 she became the first woman to fly solo across the Atlantic. She died when her plane was lost without trace on the last leg of a trip around the world.

MOTHER TERESA
Mother Teresa, born in 1910, trained as a nun. She set up a worldwide charity caring for orphans, drug addicts and victims of famine and civil war.

VALENTINA TERESHKOVA
Valentina Tereshkova, born in 1937, was the first woman astronaut to fly in space. In 1963 she piloted Soviet spacecraft Vostok 6 for 48 orbits of the Earth.

In the 1980s, women set up peace camps outside US army bases in Europe, in protest at nuclear weapons stationed there.

At 39%, Finland has the highest proportion of women in parliament.

SCANDINAVIA

RUSSIA

EUROPE

ASIA

MIDDLE EAST

CHINA

Pacific Ocean

AFRICA

Mrs. Indira Gandhi was elected three times as Prime Minister of India, first of all in 1966.

A few small countries, such as Papua New Guinea, have no women yet in their governments.

Indian Ocean

In South Africa, women of all races fought against apartheid. They set up schools for black children and organized boycotts and strikes.

In some Islamic countries, for instance in the Middle East, spiritual leaders dictate how women dress, and whether or not they can work. Many women have argued that true Islam should not oppress women.

AUSTRALIA

NEW ZEALAND

In Argentina, in South America, the mothers of people murdered by the military government in the 1970s bravely protested every week in the capital. Up to 20,000 people were killed, known as "the Disappeared".

APARICION CON VIDA

Mothers of the Disappeared wearing white headscarves at a protest against the murder of their children. Their banner demands "openness" or truth about their fate.

RIGHTS FOR EVERYONE

One of the greatest changes to take place in the twentieth century is the rise in democracy (the right to vote). Kings and queens no longer have absolute say and great empires no longer rule the world.

A wheelchair athlete. In fairer societies, those with disabilities now have the chance of a freer life and to enjoy activities once denied them.

Democracy has inspired people to campaign for change. The organization Amnesty International campaigns for people imprisoned for their beliefs.

The Campaign for Nuclear Disarmament protested against nuclear weapons.

A RISE IN DEMOCRACY

In 1900, in most countries of the world, few men and even fewer women had the right to vote. Now, many countries of the world are democratic and more people than ever before are able to have a say in how their country is run. Even the old Soviet Union saw itself as democratic, because people could vote within the Communist Party. This is also true of modern day China. This rise in democracy has encouraged people to campaign against injustices that they feel are neglected by their governments.

UNICEF, a branch of the United Nations, works on behalf of child welfare around the world.

GREENPEACE

Greenpeace campaigns for the protection of endangered species and the environment.

THE JARROW MARCH

During the Great Depression, unemployment was desperately high in the industrialized world. Many popular protests took place against the poverty in which the working class found themselves. One such protest took place in 1936. Two hundred and seven unemployed men from Jarrow, a shipbuilding town in northeast England, went on a march to London. They carried a petition to the government protesting about unemployment in their town.

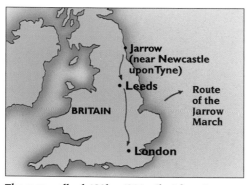

The men walked 480km (300 miles) from Jarrow to London with their petition in October 1936.

CIVIL RIGHTS IN THE USA

In the 1950s, a campaign for equal rights for black people, known as the Civil Rights Movement, surfaced in the USA. In 1954, after a legal battle, it was announced that segregated schools (in which the different races were taught separately) were against the law. Desegregation of schools followed, but in some areas, especially the southern states, there was fierce opposition.

Civil Rights Acts were passed to enforce equality, and peaceful protests were held to force desegregation. One of the leaders of the Civil Rights Movement was a Baptist minister called Martin Luther King. He was awarded the Nobel Peace Prize in 1964, but was assassinated four years later while on a civil rights mission in Memphis, Tennessee. Despite more Civil Rights Acts, many people believe that there is still widespread prejudice.

Martin Luther King, one of the leaders of the Civil Rights Movement in the USA.

In the 1960s, people in the United States protested against the Vietnam War. Here, peace demonstrators are held back by military police.

Major events in King's life. The southern states were traditionally against civil rights for blacks.

THE RIGHT TO LAND AND CULTURE

One of the major injustices in today's world is the situation of many of the indigenous peoples (original inhabitants) of Australasia and America. When white settlers arrived, they lost their land, culture and way of life and many found it impossible to fit into a new society. Their numbers fell rapidly and many were reduced to living in squalor and misery.

ABORIGINES

In Australia, many Aborigine people were killed by settlers, who regarded their culture as inferior. Since the 1930s there have been campaigns to give them more rights and they were granted the right to vote in 1967. Aborigines are determined to preserve their culture, history and land rights. They have made demands to share the wealth earned from mining in Aboriginal regions.

An Aborigine playing the didgeridoo – a traditional instrument.

MAORIS

In New Zealand, the indigenous people are the Maoris. In 1929, the Young Maori Party managed to win more rights with the Native Land Settlement Act. This provided Maoris with money and land to develop their traditional culture. The Ratana political movement and the New Zealand Labour Party have campaigned for reforms and promoted an awareness of Maori culture, although there are still disagreements over land ownership.

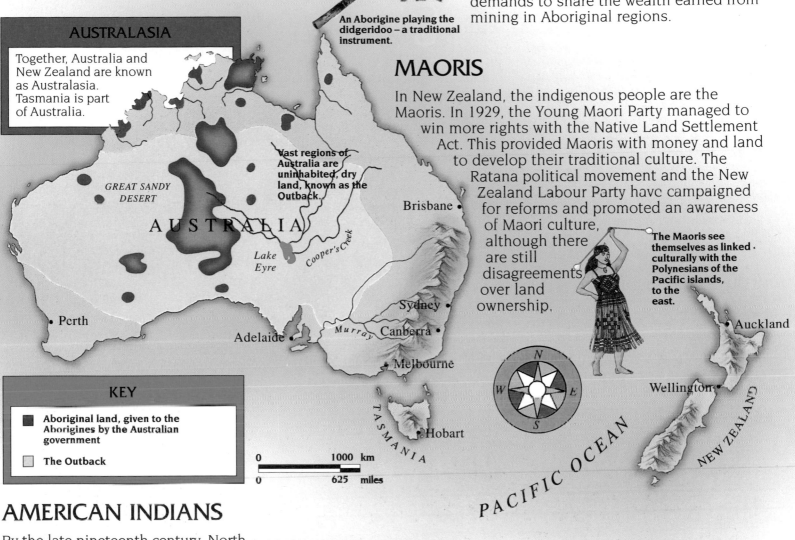

AUSTRALASIA

Together, Australia and New Zealand are known as Australasia. Tasmania is part of Australia.

GREAT SANDY DESERT

AUSTRALIA

Vast regions of Australia are uninhabited, dry land, known as the Outback.

Lake Eyre

Cooper's Creek

Brisbane

Sydney

Canberra

Melbourne

Perth

Adelaide

Murray

TASMANIA

Hobart

The Maoris see themselves as linked culturally with the Polynesians of the Pacific islands, to the east.

Auckland

Wellington

NEW ZEALAND

PACIFIC OCEAN

KEY

■ Aboriginal land, given to the Aborigines by the Australian government

□ The Outback

0   1000 km
0   625   miles

AMERICAN INDIANS

By the late nineteenth century, North American Indians were defeated by the US army and confined to areas called reservations. In 1924, they gained full citizenship, but their status in society was slow to improve.

To protect South American Indians from a similiar fate, people are campaigning to protect their way of life. But they are under constant threat from developers closing in on their rainforest homes.

CANADA

UNITED STATES OF AMERICA

■ Indian reservation

Reservations in North America. Many Indians still live there, but have protested about conditions.

■ Areas where South American Indians are still living their traditional way of life

SOUTH AMERICA

PACIFIC OCEAN

ATLANTIC OCEAN

Areas of South America where Indians live. Around 100 groups have been wiped out since 1900.

FACT BOX

"I HAVE A DREAM"

In 1963, Martin Luther King led over 200,000 people in a peaceful Civil Rights march through the streets of Washington. At the Lincoln Memorial, the march ended and King made a famous speech. He said, "I have a dream that my four little children will be judged not by the color of their skin, but by the content of their character."

CHILDREN'S RIGHTS

In many developing countries, young children work in conditions which are little better than slavery. Despite long hours and dangerous surroundings, they earn a pittance. In wealthy countries, the hours and conditions in which children work are strictly regulated, but some are still at risk from cruelty and abuse by adults.

FIND OUT MORE

For more information see above pages.

CENTURY OF SCIENCE

During the twentieth century, science and technology have transformed everyday life – in industrialized countries at least. They have also generated deadly weapons. Now the challenge for science is to bring peaceful progress to the whole planet.

Marie Curie (1867-1934) discovered radium, used to treat cancer.

The shuttle uses its robot arm to launch this satellite.

The satellite will carry out experiments in space.

MOTOR CAR

By the end of World War One, more motor cars were becoming available. Their engines were lighter than steam engines, and used fuel made from oil. The motor car and its new engine changed the world. Towns spread. Horses disappeared from the streets, and motorized buses carried people on long and short trips. The tractor revolutionized agriculture. There are now over 450 million cars worldwide, causing congestion in cities and producing harmful air pollution which may contribute to global warming.

This car is a Volkswagen Beetle. Over 20 million have been produced, more than any other type of car. *Volkswagen* is German for "people's car".

SHRINKING PLANET

Since powered flight began in 1903, the twentieth century has seen tremendous developments in flight technology. Planes transformed warfare. Bombers destroyed cities and battles raged in the skies. Military inventions, such as the faster jet engine, were used in peacetime too. Jet engines revolutionized travel in the 1950s. International air travel has become much cheaper. Now the planet seems to have shrunk, as millions of people take flights across continents each year for work or leisure. In 1976 Concorde became the first passenger plane to fly faster than the speed of sound. Computer technology now helps pilots to fly planes even more safely.

SPACE

In 1957, the Soviets launched the first object into space – Sputnik, an information-gathering satellite. The superpowers competed for the glory of conquering space. A Soviet astronaut, Yuri Gagarin, was the first person in space in 1961, but eight years later, an American, Neil Armstrong, first walked on the Moon. Since the end of the Cold War, space technology around the world has been shared for exploration and communications. Now space probes are visiting distant planets to gather information.

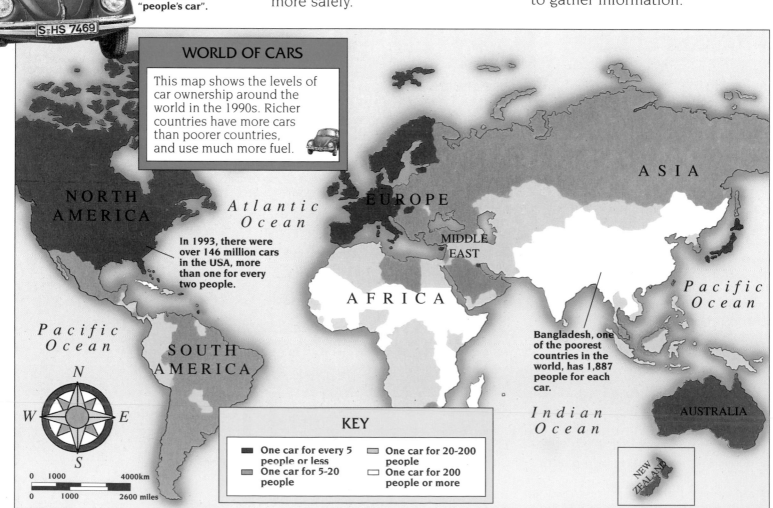

WORLD OF CARS

This map shows the levels of car ownership around the world in the 1990s. Richer countries have more cars than poorer countries, and use much more fuel.

NORTH AMERICA

Atlantic Ocean

EUROPE

ASIA

In 1993, there were over 146 million cars in the USA, more than one for every two people.

MIDDLE EAST

AFRICA

Pacific Ocean

Pacific Ocean

SOUTH AMERICA

Bangladesh, one of the poorest countries in the world, has 1,887 people for each car.

N
W E
S

0   1000   4000km
0   1000   2600 miles

Indian Ocean

AUSTRALIA

NEW ZEALAND

KEY

- One car for every 5 people or less
- One car for 5-20 people
- One car for 20-200 people
- One car for 200 people or more

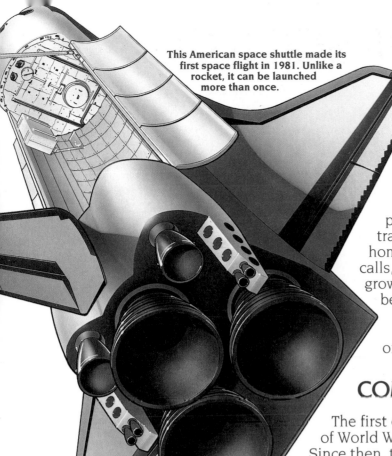

This American space shuttle made its first space flight in 1981. Unlike a rocket, it can be launched more than once.

Rocket engines power the shuttle in space. Its streamlined shape helps it to glide safely back to Earth.

COMMUNICATION

Before the twentieth century, people found out what was happening in other places from letters and newspapers. Now we can receive the news as it happens. First radio, then television and now solar-powered satellites started to transmit news directly into our homes. International telephone calls, once extremely expensive, are growing cheaper as optical cables below the Earth's surface each carry hundreds of thousands of calls and fax messages from one continent to another.

COMPUTER REVOLUTION

The first computers, built around the time of World War Two, were huge and slow. Since then, they have become smaller, cheaper and far more powerful. Computers, which store and process huge amounts of information, have transformed work in schools, offices and factories. Computerized robots can be programmed to do repetitive or dangerous tasks. All around the world, people can communicate with each other on the Internet, a giant computer network linked up using telephone lines.

MEDICINE

In the 1940s antibiotics, such as penicillin, came into use. Made from microscopic fungus, they stop the spread of bacteria. This made surgery much safer, and so did better painkillers, blood transfusions and X-rays. By the 1960s, surgeons could replace faulty organs such as kidneys with others from donors. Scientists tackle new challenges all the time, such as finding a cure for Aids, and developing artificial hearts and other organs.

Medicines are now produced industrially, and are much cheaper. But they are still unavailable to many in the developing world. Weakened by lack of food, millions of children die there each year from diseases which could be prevented or cured with cheap, simple medical care.

Nigerian children waiting to be vaccinated against illness. Diseases such as smallpox have disappeared as a result of vaccination.

FIND OUT MORE

Early transport	☞5
Developing World	☞44
Chernobyl	☞47
Environment	☞55

For more information see above pages.

ENERGY

New forms of energy became available in the twentieth century. By the 1930s, electricity powered an amazing variety of machines in the home and workplace. The first electricity generators burned coal, but later oil and gas were also used. Gradually, oil took over from coal as the major fuel. Regions rich in oil, such as the Middle East, grew in importance. Cheaper nuclear-generated electricity has been available since the 1950s, but it brings dangers such as the explosion at Chernobyl in 1986. In the twenty-first century, we will need to develop new environment-friendly energy sources.

In this 1950s advertisement, a family shows off its new electric refrigerator.

THE CENTURY ENDS

The last ten years of the twentieth century started in a spirit of hope. Peace talks were set up to tackle complex and bitter conflicts in Israel and South Africa. The threat of nuclear destruction faded. Governments took positive steps to protect the environment.

This ballot paper is from South Africa's first multiracial elections. It uses pictures and symbols to make sure all voters know who they are voting for.

THE WORLD TODAY

This map shows all the nations of the world at the end of the twentieth century. Throughout the century, borders shifted. Many new nations have won self-rule, often restoring ancient national territories.

POLITICAL CHANGE

Fifty years of rivalry between the superpowers melted away as the Soviet Union broke up. International conflicts have subsided. But peace is hard to maintain. Many bitter civil wars still fester within countries around the world. Terrorists from various extremist groups have bombed planes and other targets to get their message across.

NEW FORCES

In some areas, especially in some of the old communist nations, the quest for self-rule turned into a fanatical desire for unity and hatred of outsiders. Yugoslavia, a country which contained many different peoples, started to split up in 1990. A terrible civil war followed, and in regions such as Bosnia, minority groups were forced to leave their homes to create areas which were purely Christian or Muslim. This sinister process was known as "ethnic cleansing".

WORLD NEGOTIATIONS

Since the end of the Cold War, there has been a growing spirit of trust between countries. The United Nations, still the main organization for negotiation between nations, has achieved a great deal, especially in its work with children, refugees and on health issues. But while its peacekeeping troops try to stop the worst of the bloodshed in civil wars, its powers to get involved in internal conflicts are very limited. Non-political groups such as Oxfam can bring international pressure, for instance to ban the use of landmines (tiny buried bombs which make land uninhabitable even after a war ends). Governments are sharing information to combat the terrorist threat.

SOUTH AFRICA

South Africa has at last dismantled apartheid. In 1990 the black leader, Nelson Mandela, was freed after 27 years in prison for his beliefs. He was elected president in the first multiracial elections in 1994. The new government faces huge challenges – to provide education, employment and health care for everyone denied it under apartheid.

Throughout the century, millions of refugees have fled war or famine. Most go to countries nearby. Many countries in the West are now closing their doors to them.

Most Latin American countries are now democracies. Some are unstable.

Here Nelson Mandela (left), South Africa's first black prime minister, wears the team strip as he congratulates the nation's rugby captain on winning the World Cup. For decades, South Africa was banned from international sports

GREENLAND (DENMARK)

ALASKA (USA)

CANADA

UNITED STATES OF AMERICA

Pacific Ocean

HAWAII (USA)

MEXICO

BAHAMAS

CUBA

JAMAICA

HAITI

DOMINICAN REPUBLIC

BELIZE

HONDURAS

NICARAGUA

COSTA RICA

PANAMA

BARBADOS

TRINIDAD & TOBAGO

VENEZUELA

COLOMBIA

FRENCH GUIANA

ECUADOR

PERU

BRAZIL

BOLIVIA

PARAGUAY

CHILE

ARGENTINA

URUGUAY

Atlantic Ocean

N

W

E

S

0   1000   2000   km

0   1000   miles

ENVIRONMENT

The Earth's growing population needs more food and fuel. But many new industry and farming methods harm the environment. Rainforests are being cut down, and the rising number of cars causes air pollution. As a result, the Earth's protective ozone layer is shrinking, and the climate is heating up, known as global warming. More land is turning into desert, increasing the risk of famine in poor countries. In 1992, at the Earth Summit conference, world leaders agreed on steps to tackle these threats, such as banning harmful chemicals. Global teamwork is vital to protect our environment in the twenty-first century.

An area in Indonesia where rainforest has been cleared for timber. Without trees, soil is easily blown or washed away, and land can become barren.

SHIFT TO THE EAST

Europe and the USA are no longer the world's only great industrial regions. Instead, production is shifting to the east. Japan and other Asian nations on the Pacific coast lead the world's high-tech industry. They export cars, computers and electrical goods around the world. Australia and New Zealand are turning now to these countries for trade instead of their traditional markets in Europe and the USA.

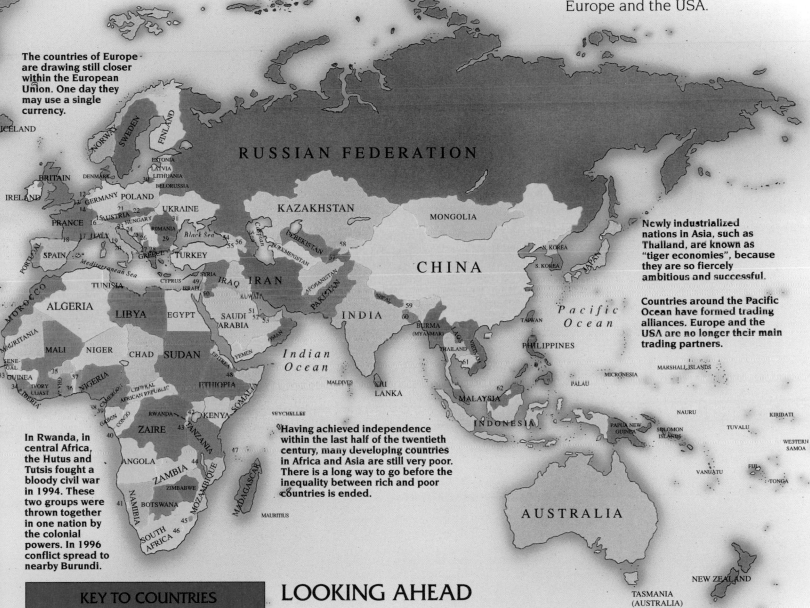

The countries of Europe are drawing still closer within the European Union. One day they may use a single currency.

Newly industrialized nations in Asia, such as Thailand, are known as "tiger economies", because they are so fiercely ambitious and successful.

Countries around the Pacific Ocean have formed trading alliances. Europe and the USA are no longer their main trading partners.

Having achieved independence within the last half of the twentieth century, many developing countries in Africa and Asia are still very poor. There is a long way to go before the inequality between rich and poor countries is ended.

In Rwanda, in central Africa, the Hutus and Tutsis fought a bloody civil war in 1994. These two groups were thrown together in one nation by the colonial powers. In 1996 conflict spread to nearby Burundi.

KEY TO COUNTRIES

1. GUATEMALA
2. EL SALVADOR
3. PUERTO RICO (USA)
4. ST. CHRISTOPHER & NEVIS
5. ANTIGUA & BARBUDA
6. DOMINICA
7. ST. LUCIA
8. ST. VINCENT & GRENADINES
9. GRENADA
10. GUYANA
11. SURINAM
12. NETHERLANDS
13. BELGIUM
14. LUXEMBOURG
15. LIECHTENSTEIN
16. SWITZERLAND
17. MONACO
18. ANDORRA
19. SAN MARINO
20. VATICAN CITY
21. CZECH REPUBLIC
22. SLOVAKIA
23. SLOVENIA
24. CROATIA
25. BOSNIA & HERZEGOVINA
26. YUGOSLAVIA
27. ALBANIA
28. MACEDONIA
29. BULGARIA
30. Part of RUSSIAN FEDERATION
31. MOLDAVIA
32. THE GAMBIA
33. GUINEA-BISSAU
34. SIERRA LEONE
35. BURKINA FASO
36. TOGO
37. BENIN
38. SAO TOME & PRINCIPE
39. EQUATORIAL GUINEA
40. CABINDA (ANGOLA)
41. WALVIS BAY (SOUTH AFRICA)
42. UGANDA
43. BURUNDI
44. MALAWI
45. SWAZILAND
46. LESOTHO
47. COMOROS
48. DJIBOUTI
49. LEBANON
50. JORDAN
51. BAHRAIN
52. QATAR
53. UNITED ARAB EMIRATES
54. GEORGIA
55. ARMENIA
56. AZERBAIJAN
57. TAJIKISTAN
58. KYRGYZSTAN
59. BHUTAN
60. BANGLADESH
61. CAMBODIA
62. BRUNEI

LOOKING AHEAD

The twentieth century has brought unimaginable advances in democracy, science and industry. New technology is developing so fast that it is hard to predict how people will live in the new century. But progress has not closed the gap between rich and poor countries. Nearly a fifth of the world's people have too little to eat, and millions cannot read or write. Around the world, people are campaigning for a safer and more economic use of resources, so that everyone has the chance of a better and fairer life.

FIND OUT MORE

Apartheid ☞	34
Developing countries ☞	44
European Union ☞	47

See above pages for more information.

GLOSSARY

Below is a list of important words used in this book. Words printed in bold type within a definition have their own separate entry.

aid Money or help given by one country to another that is poor or struck by disaster.

Allies The countries on the same side as Britain in the two world wars, including France and the USA.

ally An individual, group or country that gives help and support. An alliance is an agreement to support one another.

annex To occupy an area that was previously independent or under control of another country.

anti-Semitism Hatred and persecution of Jews.

apartheid The South African policy of keeping the different races apart, and not allowing nonwhite people the same rights as whites. The system was finally dismantled in 1994 by F. W. de Klerk and Nelson Mandela.

armistice An agreement between enemies at war to cease fighting and discuss peace terms.

assassination Murder, usually of someone famous or politically important.

atomic energy See **nuclear energy**.

Axis Powers The countries on the same side as Germany in World War Two, including Italy.

Bolshevik Originally a Russian **communist** and supporter of Lenin, working in order to cause revolution against the Czar of Russia. Later used as a general term to describe a communist.

capitalism An economic system, based on the private ownership of businesses and industry. Firms operate to make profit, and become efficient through competition.

Christianity The faith based on the teachings of Jesus Christ, set out in the New Testament. Christians believe Jesus is the son of God.

civil rights The rights of a citizen to personal freedom, including the right to vote, and legal and racial equality. The Civil Rights Movement campaigned for black people to have equal rights with whites in the USA in the 1960s.

civil war Fighting between rival groups or civilians within the same country.

cold war A struggle for power by all means short of fighting. The term is usually used to describe the struggle for supremacy in the 1950s and 60s between the **superpowers**, the USA and the Soviet Union.

colony An area and its people ruled from another country. For instance, Nigeria was a British colony until its **independence** in 1960.

communism A political system based on Karl Marx's writings, where the state owns all land and factories, and provides for people's needs. In the late 1980s, many countries in Eastern Europe rejected communism. China is now the world's largest communist country.

constitution The laws or political principles on which a state is ruled or governed.

constitutional monarchy A system of government by which a king or queen is head of state, but has no direct role in the decision-making of the government.

coup When one group uses force to take control of government away from another group.

culture The shared ideas, beliefs, values and traditions of a group of people.

Czar (or **tsar**) The Russian name for "Emperor". The word is a Slavonic form of the Latin "Caesar".

democracy A system of government where people can vote to elect representatives in the parliament or other governing body. There may be a **monarch**, but he or she has little real **constitutional** power. In Britain, for instance, the monarch is head of state but cannot overrule the elected government.

depose To remove someone (for instance a **dictator**) from power.

détente An improvement of relations between different nations, after a period of tension.

developing countries Countries, mostly in the southern hemisphere, that have not yet developed their full economic or industrial potential, often as a result of slavery or colonialism. Many are dependent on **aid** from richer nations.

dictator A ruler whose word is law, imposed by military force. Dictators often rule alone without the advice of a government.

economy The financial structure made up of all goods and services produced, sold and bought in a specific country or region.

election The selection by voting of a person or party to a position of power.

empire A large area of land, and its peoples, ruled by one powerful person or government. An example is the British Empire, which was at its height in the nineteenth century under Queen Victoria.

environment The surroundings in which humans, plants and animals live.

European Community An organization of European nations, originally formed for trade and **economic** purposes, but increasingly sharing financial, social and legal aims. Formerly known as the Common Market and now also known as the European Union.

Fascism The military form of government in Italy between 1922-43, led by the **dictator** Benito Mussolini, which was driven by **nationalism** and hostility to **communism**. The Fascists aimed to unify the country and, in an attempt to give it **economic** and military strength, put down all opposition. The name is also used for people or parties with similar views in other countries, such as Hitler's Germany.

feminism The movement that grew in the 1960s and 70s, campaigning for equal rights for women.

fundamentalism The strict following of a set of religious beliefs. In Christianity, it is the belief that the Bible is the source of all wisdom. In Islam, it is the strict observance of the teachings of the Ko'ran.

glasnost The Russian name for the policy of openness introduced in the **Soviet Union** in 1987 by Mikhail Gorbachev.

global warming The slow warming of the Earth's atmosphere, which is widely believed to be happening. It is thought to be caused by damage to the Earth's atmosphere, which in turn is caused by harmful gases (such as carbon dioxide) produced by industries and car exhausts.

Great Depression The period of worldwide unemployment and poverty, after the Wall Street Crash of 1929. The world's economy did not recover until the late 1930s.

guerillas A small band of fighters in combat with a larger army. Guerilla soldiers often fight for their strong political beliefs.

Hinduism The major faith in India. Hindus believe in reincarnation (rebirth in another form) and pray to many gods and goddesses. The Hindu caste system rigidly ranks groups in society according to their "purity" or importance, but the system is gradually losing its hold.

Holocaust The systematic murder of six million Jews by Nazi Germany between 1940 and 1945.

independence Self-rule, especially when it is achieved after a nation has been ruled by a foreign power. Many African and Asian countries achieved their independence after World War Two.

indigenous people The original inhabitants of a region. For example, the Aborigines of Australia or the Maoris of New Zealand are indigenous peoples.

inflation The rate of increase in prices of goods and services over a period of time.

Islam The religion of **Muslims**. Islam is based on the Ko'ran, the holy book which sets out the word of Allah (God) as revealed to prophet Muhammad (AD570-632).

isolationism A policy of non-participation in foreign affairs. The USA has followed this policy over several periods in its history, especially after World War One.

Judaism The religion of the Jews, based on worship of one God whose word is set down in the Torah (the first five books of the Old Testament). Jews do not worship Jesus, and believe the messiah (who will save the souls of humankind) has yet to come.

Kaiser The German name for "Emperor". The word comes from the Latin, "Caesar", after Julius Caesar.

majority rule Government by those who are politically or racially the same as most of their subjects.

mandates Former Axis colonies that the League of Nations put under control of one or other of the Allies, until they could be given independence. The term also means an official instruction.

Marxism Political theories following the teachings of Karl Marx (1818-83), that **communism** will overcome **capitalism**.

Middle East The Arabic-speaking region to the east of the Mediterranean Sea, and also including Turkey, Cyprus, Iran and most of North Africa.

monarch The head of state (king or queen) who inherits the crown. Few monarchs now have real power. The ruling of the state is entrusted to its government.

Muslim Someone who follows the faith of **Islam**.

nationalism The feeling of a common bond among people in a region who share a **culture**, language, history or religion. Nationalism often leads people to strive for unity and self-government.

natural resources Useful naturally-occurring materials, such as minerals, forests, fertile land, rivers and seas.

Nazism The **fascist** National Socialist movement in Germany, which grew out of the economic depression after World War One. In the 1920s and 30s, the Nazi Party was led by Adolf Hitler, whose policies caused World War Two to break out. The Nazis' fanatical **anti-Semitism** was also the cause of the **Holocaust**.

nuclear or atomic energy Energy created by splitting atoms. This releases a vast amount of energy which can be used in nuclear weapons or to make electricity.

pacifism The belief that all war is wrong, for whatever reasons. Pacifists believe that international tensions should be resolved by negotiation, not violence.

parliament An assembly of representatives, which meets for decision-making and law-giving.

perestroika The policies of restructuring and economic change in the Soviet Union which were begun in the 1980s under President Mikhail Gorbachev.

propaganda The organized distribution of information, such as on TV or in newspapers, in order to shape public opinion and discredit opposition.

protectorate A territory largely controlled by, but not **annexed** to, a more powerful nation.

rainforest Evergreen tropical forest, with very heavy rainfall, rich in plant and animal life. Rainforests, which are mainly in the southern hemisphere, contribute to global production of oxygen. Many are under threat from development for commercial purposes.

referendum A vote in which the electorate decides on an important single issue. For instance, some countries in Europe have had referendums on whether or not to agree to more controls under the **European Community**.

refugee Someone who flees from his or her home or country to seek safety. As well as from war or disaster, refugees flee from death threats or imprisonment for their beliefs.

republic A state where the people vote for their government in an **election**. A republic has no king or queen.

revolution The overthrow of a **monarch** or a government by mass action by the people.

revolutionaries People who try to cause revolutions or take part in them.

Russian Federation A state formed in 1992 from the alliance between Russia and parts of the old Soviet Union which now have self-rule.

Sikhism is based on the teachings of Guru Nanak. At their temple or *gurdwara*, Sikhs pray to one God and share food as a symbol of equality. All Sikhs share the surnames *Singh* for men and *Kaur* for women. Sikhs are campaigning for an independent homeland in northern India.

socialism A political system whereby every member of society has equal rights, all factories and farms are run by and for the people, and wealth is distributed equally between them.

Soviet Union The name given to the communist state formed in 1922 after the Russian Revolution of 1917. Also known as the USSR. It stretched from Eastern Europe to Asia. It broke up in 1991, when many of its republics gained independence.

suffragettes Women who campaigned for suffrage (the right to vote) at the end of the nineteenth and the beginning of the twentieth century. Suffragettes drew attention to their cause by getting arrested and going on hunger strike in prison.

superpower A very powerful state. The term is usually applied to the USA or the former **Soviet Union**.

terrorism Bomb attacks or other threats of violence used by extremist groups to try to force governments to meet their demands.

trade union An association of employees who band together in order to improve their pay and working conditions.

treaty A formal agreement between countries, usually relating to peace, trade or becoming **allies**.

unemployment Having no job and therefore not being able to earn money for oneself or one's dependents.

United Nations An international organization of independent states which aims to promote understanding and peace between nations of the world.

The West The capitalist countries of Western Europe and North America.

Zionism Political movement which campaigned for a Jewish homeland in Palestine.

MAP INDEX

This index lists all the place names shown on the maps. As well as page numbers, it gives the country or region for each place and alternative names through history, for example: Constantinople (now Istanbul).

A

Abu Dhabi United Arab Emirates 30
Adelaide Australia 51
Aden Protectorate (now part of Yemen) Middle East 13, 30
Adriatic Sea Europe 6, 26
Aegean Sea Europe 8
Afghanistan Asia 32, 55
Africa 4, 12, 19, 20, 24, 34, 45, 49, 52, 55
Agadir Morocco 4
Alaska USA 54
Albania Europe 5, 39, 46, 55
Albert France 7
Algeria Africa 4, 24, 30, 34, 35, 55
Algiers Algeria 24, 30
Amman Jordan 13, 30
Andorra Europe 55
Angola Africa 35, 55
Ankara Turkey 13
Antigua and Barbuda Central America 54
ANZAC Cove Turkey 8
Arabia 8, 19
Aral Sea 20, 46
Archangel Russia 10
Arctic Ocean 10, 20, 38, 46
Argentina South America 36, 37, 54
Armenia Europe 46, 55
Asia 20, 24, 25, 27, 32, 34, 45, 46, 49, 52, 55
Asia Minor 43
Astrakhan Russia 10
Asuncion Paraguay 36
Atlanta USA 14, 50
Atlantic Ocean 4, 14, 24, 38, 45, 46, 48, 51, 52, 54
Auckland New Zealand 51
Australia 33, 45, 49, 51, 52, 55
Austria Europe 12, 19, 22, 28, 29, 46, 47, 55
Austro-Hungarian Empire Europe 5, 6, 8
Azerbaijan Europe 46, 55
Azores islands Atlantic Ocean 38

B

Baghdad Iraq 13, 30
Bahamas Central America 54
Bahrain Middle East 55
Baku Azerbaijan 10
Baltic Sea Europe 10, 19, 25, 29, 46
Baltimore USA 14
Bangkok Thailand 33
Bangladesh (was East Pakistan) Asia 32, 33, 40, 44, 55
Bapaume France 7
Barbados Central America 54
Bayeux France 26
Bechuanaland (now Botswana) Africa 34
Beijing China 17, 33, 40, 41
Beirut Lebanon 13, 30, 42, 43
Belarus Europe 46, 55
Belgium Europe 6, 7, 22, 23, 28, 46, 47, 55
Belize Central America 36, 54
Belmopan Belize 36
Bengal India/Bangladesh 44
Benghazi Libya 24
Benin Africa 35, 55
Berlin Germany 22, 27, 28, 29, 39, 47
Bethlehem Israel 42
Bhutan Asia 16, 32, 33, 40, 44, 55
Black Sea Europe 10, 12, 13, 19, 20, 29, 46, 55
Bogota Colombia 36
Bolivia South America 36, 54
Bonn Germany 47
Bosnia-Herzegovina Europe 5, 6, 46, 55

Boston USA 14
Botswana (was Bechuanaland) Africa 34, 35, 55
Brasilia Brazil 36
Bratislava Slovakia 47
Brazil South America 36, 37, 54
Brest-Litovsk Belarus 10
Brisbane Australia 51
Britain Europe 6, 7, 12, 19, 23, 26, 28, 37, 46, 50, 55
Brno Czech Republic 47
Brunei Asia 33, 55
Bucharest Romania 47
Buenos Aires Argentina 36
Bulgaria Europe 5, 8, 19, 27, 29, 39, 46, 47, 55
Burkina Faso Africa 35, 55
Burma (Myanmar) Asia 16, 32, 33, 40, 44, 55
Burundi Africa 35

C

Cabinda Africa 55
Caen France 26
Cairo Egypt 13, 30
Cambodia (was part of French Indochina) Asia 33, 55
Cameroon (was Cameroons) Africa 12, 35, 55
Cameroons (now Cameroon) Africa 12
Canada North America 14, 38, 46, 48, 51, 54
Çanakkale Turkey 8
Canberra Australia 51
Canton (now Guangzhou) China 16, 17
Cape Helles Turkey 8
Cape Horn South America 36
Caracas Venezuela 36
Carentan France 26
Caribbean Sea Central America 14, 39
Caspian Sea Europe/Asia 10, 13, 20, 43, 46, 55
Cayenne French Guiana 36
Central African Republic Africa 35, 55
Central America 36
Ceylon (now Sri Lanka) Asia 32
Chad Africa 35, 55
Chengdu China 40, 41
Chicago USA 14
Chile South America 36, 54
China Asia 5, 16, 17, 21, 32, 33, 38, 39, 40, 41, 44, 45, 49, 54
Cleveland USA 14
Cologne Germany 28
Colombia Central America 36, 54
Colombo Sri Lanka 33, 44
Comoros Africa 35, 55
Congo Africa 35, 55
Congo river Africa 4
Constantinople (now Istanbul) Turkey 5, 10, 13
Cooper's Creek river Australia 51
Coral Sea battle Pacific Ocean 25
Costa Rica Central America 36, 54
Coventry Britain 28
Croatia Europe 46, 55
Cuba Central America 14, 38, 39, 54
Cyprus Middle East 13, 55
Cyrenaica region Libya 23
Czechoslovakia (now Czech Republic and Slovakia) Europe 12, 19, 22, 28, 29, 47
Czech Republic (see also Czechoslovakia) Europe 46, 47, 55

D

Dalstrop region Russia 21
Damascus Syria 8, 13, 30, 42
Danzig (now Gdansk) Poland 22

Dardanelles strait Turkey 8
Denmark Europe 9, 46, 55
De Panne Belgium 23
Detroit USA 14
Dhaka Bangladesh 33
Djibouti Africa 35, 55
Dominica Central America 54
Dominican Republic Central America 57
Dresden Germany 28
Dunkirk France 23
Dutch East Indies (now Indonesia) 32

E

East China Sea Asia 40
East Germany (now part of Germany) Europe 29, 39, 47
East Pakistan (now Bangladesh) 32
East Prussia (former German territory) Europe 22
Ecuador South America 36, 54
Egypt Africa 13, 24, 30, 31, 34, 35, 42, 43, 55
El Alamein battle Egypt 24
El Salvador Central America 36, 54
English Channel Europe 23, 26
Equatorial Guinea Africa 35, 55
Eritrea Africa 35
Essen Germany 28
Estonia Europe 12, 46, 55
Ethiopia Africa 19, 35, 55
Euphrates river 13
Europe 9, 20, 24, 28-29, 45, 46, 49, 52, 55
    Eastern Europe and Western Europe 38
Eyre, Lake Australia 51

F

Falkland Islands South Atlantic Ocean 36, 37
Fiji Pacific Ocean 55
Finland Europe 8, 12, 19, 46, 54
Formosa (now Taiwan) Asia 16
France Europe 6, 7, 12, 19, 23, 26, 28, 29, 46, 47, 55
Frankfurt Germany 28
French Guiana South America 36, 54
French Indochina (now Laos, Vietnam and Cambodia) Asia 16

G

Gabon Africa 35, 55
Galapagos Islands Pacific Ocean 36
Gallipoli Turkey 8
Gambia Africa 35, 55
Gdansk (was Danzig) Poland 22, 47
Georgetown Guyana 36
Georgia Europe 46, 55
German East Africa Africa 12
German Southwest Africa (now Namibia) Africa 4, 12
Germany Europe (see also East Germany and West Germany) 6, 8, 12, 19, 22, 23, 25, 27, 28, 46, 47, 54
Ghana Africa 35, 55
Golan Heights region Syria 42
Great Lakes USA/Canada 14
Great Sandy Desert Australia 51
Greece Europe 5, 8, 19, 29, 38, 46, 55
Greenland island Atlantic Ocean 38, 45, 46, 54
Grenada Central America 54
Guam island Pacific Ocean 38
Guangzhou (was Canton) China 16, 17, 40
Guatemala Central America 36, 38, 54
Guatemala City Guatemala 36
Guinea Africa 35, 55

MAP INDEX

Poland Europe 8, 12, 19, 22, 27, 29, 39, 46, 47, 55
Port Said Egypt 34, 42
Portugal Europe 19, 38, 54
Poznan Poland 47
Prague Czech Republic 22, 47
Puerto Rico Central America 54
Punjab India/Pakistan 44
Pyongyang North Korea 33, 39

Q

Qatar Middle East 55
Quito Ecuador 36

R

Rabat Morocco 30
Rangoon Burma 33
Red Sea Middle East 19, 30, 35
Rhineland Germany 11, 19, 22
Rio Grande *river* North America 14
Riyadh Saudi Arabia 13
Rocky Mountains North America 14
Romania Europe 5, 12, 19, 25, 29, 39, 46, 47, 55
Rome Italy 26
Russia (see also Russian Empire and Soviet Union) Europe/Asia 33, 40, 46, 49, 55
Russian Empire Europe/Asia 5, 6, 8, 10
Rwanda Africa 35, 55

S

Sahara Desert Africa 4
Saigon (now Ho Chi Minh City) Vietnam 39
St. Christopher and Nevis Central America 54
St. Louis USA 14
St. Lucia Central America 54
St. Petersburg (was Petrograd, also Leningrad) Russia 10, 20
St. Vincent and the Grenadines Central America 54
San'a Yemen 13, 30
San Francisco USA 14
San Jose Costa Rica 36
San Marino Europe 55
San Salvador El Salvador 36
Santiago Chile 36
São Tomé & Príncipe Africa 55
Sarajevo Bosnia-Herzegovina 6
Sardinia *island* Italy 24
Saudi Arabia Middle East 13, 30, 38, 42, 43, 55
Scandinavia Europe 20, 49
Seine *river* Europe 6
Senegal Africa 35, 55
Seoul South Korea 33, 39
Serbia Europe 5, 6
Seychelles Indian Ocean 55
Shanghai China 17, 40
Siam (now Thailand) Asia 16
Siberia *region* Russia 10, 46
Sicily *island* Italy 24, 25
Sierra Leone Africa 35, 55
Simbirsk Russia 10
Sinai Desert Egypt 42
Singapore Asia 33
Slovakia (see also Czechoslovakia) Europe 25, 46, 47, 55
Slovenia Europe 46, 55
Solomon Islands Pacific Ocean 55
Somalia Africa 35, 55
Somme *river* Europe 7
South Africa Africa 4, 35, 55

South America 20, 24, 25, 36, 45, 48, 51, 52, 54
South Atlantic Ocean 36
South China Sea Asia 16, 17
Southeast Asia 39
Southern Rhodesia (now Zimbabwe) Africa 34
South Korea (see also Korea) Asia 33, 38, 39, 40, 55
South Vietnam (now part of Vietnam) Asia 33, 39
Soviet Union (see also Russia) Europe/Asia 12, 19, 20-21, 25, 29, 38, 39, 47
Spain Europe 12, 19, 38, 46, 55
Sri Lanka (was Ceylon) 32, 33, 44, 55
Stalingrad (now Volgograd) Russia 20
Sudan Africa 35, 55
Sudetenland *region* Europe 22
Suez Egypt 34
Suez Canal Egypt 19, 24, 34, 35, 42
Surinam South America 36, 54
Suvla Bay Turkey 8
Swaziland Africa 35, 55
Sweden Europe 12, 19, 25, 46, 55
Switzerland Europe 6, 28, 29, 46, 47, 55
Sydney Australia 51
Syria Middle East 13, 30, 31, 42, 43, 55

T

Taiwan (was Formosa) Asia 16, 33, 38, 40
Tajikistan Asia 46, 55
Tamil Nadu *region* India 44
Tanganyika (now Tanzania) Africa 34
Tanganyika, Lake Africa 4
Tanzania (was Tanganyika) Africa 34, 35, 55
Tarim *river* Asia 40
Tasmania *island* Pacific Ocean 51
Tegucigalpa Honduras 36
Tehran Iran 13
Tel Aviv Israel 42
Tennessee *river* North America 14
Thailand (was Siam) 16, 33, 38, 40, 55
Thailand, Gulf of Asia 16, 39
Tibet Asia 32, 40
Tigris *river* Middle East 13
Timisoara Romania 47
Tobruk Libya 24
Togo (was Togoland) Africa 12, 35, 55
Togoland (now Togo) Africa 12
Tokyo Japan 33
Tonga Pacific Ocean 55
Transjordan (now Jordan) Middle East 13, 30
Trinidad and Tobago Central America 54
Tripoli Libya 24, 30
Trucial Coast (now United Arab Emirates) 13
Trucial States (now United Arab Emirates) 30
Tunis Tunisia 24, 30
Tunisia Africa 4, 24, 30, 35, 55
Turkey Europe/Asia 13, 19, 20, 38, 55
Turkmenistan Asia 46, 55
Tuvalu Pacific Ocean 55

U

Uganda Africa 34, 35, 55
Ukraine Europe 46, 55
Ulan Bator Mongolia 33
United Arab Emirates (was Trucial States) Middle East 13, 30, 55
United States of America North America 14, 38, 39, 48, 50, 51, 54
Ural Mountains Russia 10, 20, 46
Uruguay South America 36, 54
Urumqui China 40
Uzbekistan Asia 46, 55

V

Vanuatu Pacific Ocean 55
Vatican City Europe 55
Venezuela South America 36, 54
Vichy France 23
Victoria, Lake Africa 4
Vienna Austria 22
Vietnam (see also North Vietnam and South Vietnam) Asia 32, 33, 39, 40, 55
Vladivostock Russia 11
Volgograd (was Stalingrad) Russia 20

W

Wake *island* Pacific Ocean 38
Walvis Bay Africa 55
Warsaw Poland 10, 22, 29, 47
Washington USA 39, 50
Wellington New Zealand 51
West Bank *region* Middle East 42
Western Sahara *region* Morocco 35
Western Samoa Pacific Ocean 55
West Germany (now part of Germany) Europe 29, 39, 47
Wuhan China 40, 41

X Y

Xi'an China 40, 41
Yangtze *river* Asia 16, 17, 40
Yekaterinburg Russia 10
Yellow River *river* Asia 16, 17, 40
Yellow Sea Asia 16, 17, 39
Yemen Middle East 13, 30, 55
Yenan China 17, 40
Ypres *battle* Belgium 6
Yugoslavia Europe 12, 19, 29, 39, 46, 47, 55

Z

Zaire Africa 35, 55
Zambezi *river* Africa 4
Zambia (was Northern Rhodesia) Africa 34, 35, 55
Zhengzhou China 40
Zimbabwe (was Southern Rhodesia) Africa 34, 35, 55

INDEX

Main entries for subjects are shown in bold type.

INDEX

INDEX

LINE FOR
1¢ RESTAURANT

20 MEALS FOR 1¢

DONATIONS WANTED
HELP FEED THE HUNGRY
I WILL FEED 20
1¢ RESTAURANT
107 W 43ᴿᴰ ST

ACKNOWLEDGMENTS

The publishers would like to thank the
following for permission to use their
photographs in this book:

AKG London (28 left, 29 bottom);
Arhivo Fotografico Oronoz (19);
Associated Press/Topham (41 bottom);
Corbis UK (50 bottom); David King
Collection (38 left, 41 middle, 47 left);
Hulton Getty (9, 10, 12, 13, 16, 18, 21, 22
bottom, 24 bottom, 25, 26, 28 right, 30,
32, 34 right, 37 top, 41 top, 52); Imperial
War Museum (34 left, 48 top right); Sir
David Low/Evening Standard/Cartoon
Study Centre, University of Kent,
Canterbury (22 middle bottom); Mrs. P.
Miles (22 top; 23); Panos Pictures (37
bottom; 44, 45, 55); Popperfoto (cover,
5, 8, 22 middle top, 24 top, 31, 42
bottom, 43, 46, 47 right, 48 top left, 48
bottom, 50 top, 54); Topham
Picturepoint (15, 29 top; 39, 42 top, 53
top, 53 bottom).

Additional illustrations by:
Philip Argent, Andrew Beckett, Andy Burton,
Peter Dennis, Nicholas Hewetson, Janos
Marffy, Radhi Parekh, Qui Kai Jun
and Ross Watton.

Figures for the map on car ownership on
page 52 is based on *World Road Statistics* supplied by
the International Road Federation, Geneva.

Every effort has been made to trace and
acknowledge ownership of copyright.
The publishers will be glad to make suitable
arrangements with any copyright holder whom it
has not been possible to contact.

First published in 1996 by Usborne Publishing Ltd,
Usborne House, 83-85 Saffron Hill, London, EC1N 8RT, England.
Copyright © Usborne Publishing Ltd 1996 UE
First published in America March 1997

Great Gifts using Scrapbook Materials

A Tweety Jill Publication

Featuring: Nikki Cleary • Mindy Carpenter • Claudine Hellmuth • Dawne Renee Pitts
Amy Wellenstein • Karen Hamad, M.D. • Roben-Marie Smith • Sara White
Denise Merrill • Janet Klien • Jill Haglund

Tweety Jill
PUBLICATIONS
makes you creative!

Published and created by:

TweetyJill Publications

5824 Bee Ridge Road

PMB 412

Sarasota, FL 34233

For information about wholesale, please contact Customer Service at www.tweetyjill.com or 1-800-595-5497. Ask for free brochure detailing all books.

Printed in China

ISBN 1-891898-10-8

Artists: Nikki Cleary • Mindy Carpenter
Claudine Hellmuth • Dawne Renee Pitts
Amy Wellenstein • Karen Hamad, M.D.
Roben-Marie Smith • Sara White
Denise Merrill • Janet Klien • Jill Haglund

Book Design: Laurie Doherty

Graphic Designer: Michelle Glines

Book Layout: Jill Haglund

Editor: Lisa Codianne Fowler

Photography: Herb Booth
of Herb Booth Studios, Inc., Sarasota, FL

Additional Photo Credits: Teresa Henson

TABLE OF CONTENTS

Note: Most materials are available at your local craft, scrapbook or fabric store. If you cannot find them there, check the websites in the Resource Guide on page 111 for the closest retail store near you selling the items you are looking for.

Great Gift Ideas using Scrapbook Materials

What a concept! Use your scrapbook papers, embellishments and more to make fabulous gifts. It is almost like putting money in the bank! No longer do you need to buy presents for your friends; just make them. Today more than ever before, family and friends appreciate your handmade items. I know this is true because I make many of the gifts I give, especially at Christmas. I don't know who gets more excited actually, me, while I am thinking of the person as I create their special gift, or them when they see that time and effort has been put aside especially for them!

Regardless of who gets the most warm fuzzies, the creator or receiver, crafting is relaxing and enjoyable and it's one of the most rewarding pastimes for most women today.

Here's proof: more than 4.3 million women in America started scrapbooking just this past year. That means millions of us have all the supplies on hand to create fabulous gift items as well as make delicious scrapbook layouts. Now you can go into your local scrapbook store and look at materials with new eyes. Think paint cans, clocks, CD gift boxes, fun frames, wonderful tins with stationary, gift jars, even a ribbon box for your craft studio and so much more.

These fresh ideas are just the beginning of new and inspiring ways to use your scrapbook materials! It won't be long until you're having cropping and gift-making parties with your girlfriends!

When the time comes for a present for the next person on your list, I hope you will create something special from Great Gifts using Scrapbook Materials... a gift using your hands and from your heart.

Creatively Yours,

Jill

Boxes, Drawers & CD Holders

I Keep Your Letters Keepsake Box
Mindy Carpenter

MATERIALS

Rubber Stamps: Stampington & Co., Ephemera Designs

Dye Inkpads: Dark Brown

Papers: Carte Postale and Wrap by Cavallini & Co.

Ribbons: Local Craft Store

Adhesives: Matte Gel Medium by Golden

Other: Cigar Box; Assorted Vintage Buttons and Ephemera

Tools: Sponges; Embossing Gun; Brayers; Scissors; Cutters; Bone Folder

INSTRUCTIONS

Please see instructions for "You & Me" Decorated Cigar Box Below

Mindy's Note:
Keep it simple, keep it true to your aesthetic, and if it helps, think of the person who will most likely be keeping your letters... it's sure to inspire.

You & Me Decorated Cigar Box
Mindy Carpenter

MATERIALS

Rubber Stamps: Stampington & Co.; Ephemera Designs

Dye Inkpads: Dark Brown

Papers: Carte Postale by Cavallini & Co.

Paints: Acrylic Paints

Ribbons: Local Craft Store

Adhesives: Matte Gel Medium by Golden

Other: Cigar Box; Assorted Vintage Buttons and Ephemera

Tools: Paintbrush

INSTRUCTIONS

1. Paint inside of cigar box. Let dry.

2. Wrap wide ribbon around edge of cigar box and glue.

3. Mount desired papers on top of box with consideration to your theme.

4. Embellish with desired ephemera.

5. Rubber stamp message or quote.

Mindy's Note:
Think about your theme and color palette. Remember, less is usually more with decorated boxes.

FANCY DECORATED BOXES AND DRAWERS *give you a three-dimensional canvas for creating! Let your imagination run wild. Classic or whimsical, colorful or subdued, these tastefully decorated gifts are functional works of art. They provide fantastic storage for personal belongings such as mementos, letters and ephemera. They also present a most clever solution for organizing photographs, recipes, a myriad of craft embellishments, even mini scrapbooks.*

Special sizes and shapes are surprisingly conducive to all kinds of great gifts; Nikki Cleary unexpectedly discovered that a CD fits perfectly in a large Brie cheese box. You'll find wonderful new twists on those great old standbys — cigar boxes. They are incredibly versatile and can be creatively designed as gifts to make anyone happy for any occasion. Little drawers can house such items as jewelry, hair clips and scrunchies. Use them to hold small puzzles, cards or games for kids.

The possibilities are endless. Get ready to think "outside the box!"

Travel Memories Box

Nikki Cleary

MATERIALS

Papers: K&Company; 7gypsies

Words, Letters or Stickers: Real Life Strips Twill Tape by Pebbles Inc.; Self-Adhesive Chipboard by Marah Johnson for Creative Imaginations

Tags: Local Office Supply (Tea-Dyed)

Ribbons: Local Craft Store

Adhesives: Decoupage Finish by Plaid; Glue Lines by Glue Dots International

Other: Transparency Negative Strip; Envelopes; Mini Album; Arrow Tabs by Karen Russell for Creative Imaginations

Tools: Paintbrush; Scissors; Xacto Knife; Stapler

INSTRUCTIONS

1. Cover the top, sides, and inside cover of cigar box with travel papers, adhering with decoupage medium. Trim where needed with Xacto knife.

2. Embellish the cover, sides and inside lid as shown.

3. Write a special message on tag, staple on ribbon and slide into envelope.

Nikki's Note: I made this box as a gift for my mom and dad's 37th wedding anniversary. My husband Sean and I wanted to send them on a special weekend vacation. Sean and I had just gotten back from this great antiquing town Mount Dora, FL and we thought it would be the perfect place. So while we were there I collected every brochure and menu imaginable. Instead of just handing them the money and brochures, I wanted mom and dad to have a special place they could keep memorabilia, and pictures of their trip, and that is how the "Travel Memories" box was born. What a special gift it was to them.

Nikki's Note: This box was made to give my husband, Sean, on Valentine's Day. He likes to save the cards he receives from me, but most of the time they get thrown in a drawer somewhere. Now, he will have the perfect keepsake box to store them in.

Love Letters Box

Nikki Cleary

MATERIALS

Rubber Stamps: Kissing Lips by Hampton Art

Inkpads: Red

Papers: Rusty Pickle; K&Company; Creative Imaginations; 7gypsies

Paints: Deep Red

Words, Letters or Stickers: Pebbles Inc.; Making Memories; Narratives and Art Warehouse by Creative Imaginations; Wordsworth; DieCuts with a View

Tags: I Kandee by Pebbles Inc.

Metal Items: Creative Imaginations

Ribbons and Rick Rack: Local Craft Store

Fabrics: Dyeable Trims by Making Memories

Adhesives: Decoupage Finish by Plaid, FABRI-TAC by Beacon Adhesives

Other: Chipboard Words and Shapes by Li'l Davis Designs; Narratives Love Envelope and Arrow Tabs by Creative Imaginations

Tools: Makeup Sponge; Scissors; Stapler; Paintbrush

INSTRUCTIONS

1. Using a small bowl, mix a color wash slightly diluted with water. Apply it to the cigar box by dipping a makeup sponge into the mixture to apply to surface. Allow to dry.

2. Cover the top and sides of the box with decoupage medium. Adhere all paper and slickers to top and sides. Cover with decoupage medium again. Allow to dry.

3. Apply the chipboard, epoxy 3-D stickers, flower and tag to the top of the box.

4. Cut two coordinating papers to the size of the inside of your cigar box and adhere with FABRI-TAC.

5. Embellish and adhere the inside top cover with ribbon, trim, chipboard and the envelope using FABRI-TAC adhesive. Add letters.

6. Embellish the bottom inside of the box with metal blossoms, adhering with FABRI-TAC

7. Take letters/cards and tie them together with a strip of torn fabric, long enough to wrap around twice and tie a bow. Before tying the bow, attach the market tags.

Pink Shabby Ribbon Box
Jill Haglund

Jill's Note: *For a shabby look, use five coordinating papers to match your paint for the interior sides and bottom of the box. Once full of bright, patterned ribbons, this fun little box adds instant color to your studio. What a wonderful touch of inspiration.*

MATERIALS

Papers: Deja Views

Paints: Brown and Pink Acrylic

Ribbons: Local Craft Store

Adhesives: Matte Mod Podge by Plaid

Other: Original White Ribbon Box with Keyholes by Melissa Francis; Clear Matte Finish Spray by Krylon

Tools: Foam-Sponge Brush; Medium (1" wide) Acrylic Paintbrush; Small Watercolor Paintbrush; Sandpaper; Tack Cloth

INSTRUCTIONS

1. Choose several coordinating patterns of scrapbook papers. Cut papers to size for covering inside of box as shown. Set aside.

2. Paint entire box brown. Use a small paintbrush to paint around the keyholes. Let dry completely.

3. Paint entire box with one coat of pink. Let partially dry and wipe off edges and areas to allow for a distressed or shabby look. Allow to dry completely. Sand areas and edges lightly. Clean box completely with tack cloth.

4. Use foam brush and Mod Podge to adhere pre-cut pieces of paper into box. Smooth paper and let dry overnight.

5. Fill box with ribbons by snipping edges and pulling through keyholes.

Green Shabby Ribbon Box

Amy Wellenstein

MATERIALS

Papers: Chatterbox; Lasting Impressions for Paper, Inc.; FoofaLa

Paint: Brown, White and Green Acrylic

Adhesives: Matte Mod Podge by Plaid

Other: Original White Ribbon Box with Keyholes by Melissa Francis; Petroleum Jelly

Tools: Foam-Sponge Brush; Medium (1" wide) Acrylic Paintbrush; Small Watercolor Paintbrush

INSTRUCTIONS

1. Choose several coordinating patterns of scrapbook papers. Cut papers to size for covering inside of box as shown. Set aside.

2. Smear petroleum jelly on the unpainted ribbon box where normal wear would occur. Paint entire box brown. Let dry. Rub off the areas that were treated with petroleum jelly.

3. Apply more petroleum jelly in the same areas (this time covering a little more surface). Paint entire box with one coat of green. Let dry. Rub off the areas that were treated with petroleum jelly.

4. Use foam brush and Mod Podge to adhere pre-cut pieces of paper into box. Smooth paper and let dry overnight.

5. Use a small paintbrush to paint over the keyholes with a watered down wash of white paint, wiping off any excess, for a distressed look.

Love Keepsake Drawer Set

Karen Hamad, M.D.

MATERIALS

Papers: Twitterpated Collection by SEI

Words, Letters or Stickers: Acrylic Letters by Treehouse Memories

Metal Items: Love Locket by Around The Block; Pink Heart Brads; Jump Ring

Ribbons: Twitterpated Collection by SEI

Adhesives: Scrappy Tape by Magic Scraps; Glue Dots; Mod Podge by Plaid; Memory Mount Liquid Adhesive by Crafter's Pick; GLOO by KI Memories

Other: Adorn It Two-Drawer Set by Carolee's Creations; Chipboard Flowers by Heidi Swapp; Rhinestones

Tools: Sponge Brush; Hole Punch

INSTRUCTIONS

1. Take out drawers and separate all pieces to begin. Measure patterned papers to fit all around box, including inside and out and both sections of each drawer. Save the front of drawers for last and do not cover until step 6.

2. Use Mod Podge to cover box and drawer, and also to line drawer, working on one piece at a time.

3. Measure and cut ribbons. Line the edge of box and frame edge of drawers as shown.

4. Glue on rhinestones randomly.

5. Use liquid GLOO to adhere clear acrylic letters on top of first box.

6. Punch holes in front of drawer inserts, cover with paper and attach heart eyelets.

7. Cut length of ribbon and thread through eyelets to make handles. Tie knot and attach locket onto bottom drawer with a jump ring.

8. Apply Mod Podge to entire outside surface of drawers to make keepsake sturdy. Let dry completely before reassembling box.

Karen's Note:
Choose fun and bright papers to make this wonderful keepsake, and fill it with love letters, special treasures, jewelry, wishes and dreams... whatever strikes your fancy!

A Special CD for You

Nikki Cleary

MATERIALS

Pigment Inkpads: Pink

Chalk Inkpads: Brown

Papers: Pink Velvet Paper by SEI; Textured Cardstock by DieCuts with a View

Paints: Pink Acrylic

Words, Letters or Stickers: K&Company; Arctic Frog; Pebbles Inc.; Creative Imaginations; Making Memories

Tags: SEI

Metal Items: Extreme Eyelets by Creative Imaginations; Pink Safety Pins by Li'l Davis Designs

Ribbons: Local Craft Store

Fabrics: Pink Tulle

Adhesives: Decoupage Finish by Delta

Other: Brie Cheese Box; Heart Tokens by Doodlebug Design; Black Marker

Tools: Circle Cutter; Hole Punch; Eyelet Setter; Paintbrush; Scissors

INSTRUCTIONS

1. Use a circle cutter to cut a circle the size of the cover of the top of the Brie cheese box. Cut paper to fit inside; adhere to top of box and the inside of box with decoupage medium, trim off excess where necessary.

2. Cut two strips of paper to wrap around the box; adhere with decoupage medium.

3. Attach stickers and sayings on the top and sides of the box. Seal with a coat of decoupage medium. Let dry.

4. Cut two circles from pink cardstock and one circle from velvet paper the same size as the CD. Stack the large velvet circle over one of the cardstock circles, punch a hole and set eyelet in the middle. Place the CD on top. Tie a ribbon through the eyelet and around the CD as shown.

5. Cut the other circle of pink cardstock, ink the edges in brown. Place the smaller velvet circle off center as shown. Adhere SEI tag on top. Punch a hole and set eyelet through all pieces. Tie a piece of tulle through eyelet.

6. Attach the Doodlebug heart token with a safety pin. Add all embellishments to box.

Cherish Box
Nikki Cleary

MATERIALS

Papers: Pink Cardstock; Pink and White Striped Paper

Paints: Satin Cream Acrylic

Words, Letters or Stickers: Real Life by Pebbles Inc.; Making Memories; Li'l Davis Designs; Labels: Melissa Francis

Metal Items: Bottle Caps by Li'l Davis Designs; Antique Brass Metal Frames and ID Plates from Art Warehouse by Creative Imaginations

Adhesives: Decoupage Finish by Plaid; Wood Glue by Elmer's; FABRI-TAC by Beacon Adhesives

Other: Flower; Jewels; Wooden Box and Knobs from Local Craft Store

Tools: Paintbrush; Hammer; Paper Cutter; Circle Cutter

INSTRUCTIONS

1. Glue knobs securely to bottom of box for the legs, and to front of box for handle.

2. Paint box with two coats of Satin Cream acrylic paint.

3. Cover box in decoupage finish.

4. Cut strips of striped paper to fit side and top (as shown) and adhere to box with decoupage finish.

5. Adhere all flat embellishments and apply two more coats of decoupage finish.

6. Use FABRIC-TAC to adhere jewels, a bottle cap that has been hammered flat, all embellishments and ephemera.

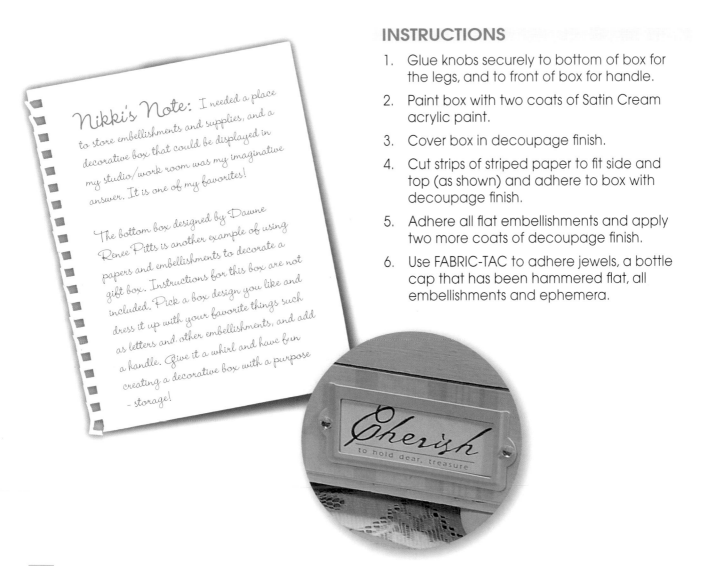

Nikki's Note: I needed a place to store embellishments and supplies, and a decorative box that could be displayed in my studio/work room was my imaginative answer. It is one of my favorites!

The bottom box designed by Dawne Renee Pitts is another example of using papers and embellishments to decorate a gift box. Instructions for this box are not included. Pick a box design you like and dress it up with your favorite things such as letters and other embellishments, and add a handle. Give it a whirl and have fun creating a decorative box with a purpose - storage!

CAMELLIA
BATH SOAP

Rose's HATS

ROSE'S GLYCERIN SOAP

b r i c

b a c

wish (wish) 1. want or long for something 2. expressing a true desire 3. a secret hope or desire

Cherish
to hold dear, treasure

TREASURES

K

SPECIAL
Handling

Hello Friends Tall Box

Kelly Lunceford

MATERIALS

Papers: Sixth Avenue by American Crafts

Words, Letters or Stickers: Stickers by American Crafts

Metal Items: Rob and Bob Studio Clipease by Provo Craft

Ribbons: Local Craft Store

Adhesives: Foam Squares by Making Memories; Mono Permanent Adhesive by Tombow; Glue Lines by Glue Dots International

Tools: Bone Folder; Paper Trimmer; Rob and Bob Studio Clipease Tool by Provo Craft

Kelly's Note:
These are terrific little gift boxes intended for lightweight presents. Consider them for hostess gifts, showers, birthdays, graduations and other special occasions when you want to give a little extra something.

INSTRUCTIONS

1. Score a 12" x 12" piece of patterned paper at 2 ¾" intervals. When you are finished there will be a small strip left over. Use this strip to secure sides of box base.

2. Choose a 12" x 12" coordinating paper for the top of the box and score at 2 $\frac{7}{8}$" intervals. You can choose how far you want the top to go down.

3. Wrap two patterned ribbons around bottom of box base, tie and cut to extend 1" as shown.

4. Mount "hello" sticker on a scrap of paper and adhere with foam square. Add Clipease to the top. Finish box with more stickers or embellishments of choice.

Smile and Laugh Box

Kelly Lunceford

MATERIALS

Papers: Wild Asparagus by My Mind's Eye

Words, Stickers or Letters: Typewriter Key Stickers by Nostalgiques by EK Success; Labels and Definitions by Wild Asparagus by My Mind's Eye

Metal Items: Photo Anchors and Brads

Ribbons: Local Craft Store

Adhesives: Mono Permanent Adhesive by Tombow; Glue Lines and Mini Glue Dots by Glue Dots International; Foam Squares by Making Memories

Tools: Bone Folder; Paper Trimmer

INSTRUCTIONS

1. Score a 12" x 12" piece of patterned paper at 2 ¾" intervals. When you are finished you will have a small strip left. Use this strip as a tab to glue box together. Score up from the bottom at 2 ¾".

2. Cut up along each score mark just until you reach the bottom score mark. This will create the tabs to fold in for the bottom of the box. Secure with adhesive.

3. Fold in the sides like a paper bag and tie a ribbon around the box.

4. Apply paper labels with foam squares; use adhesive to add definitions.

5. Attach photo anchors with Mini Glue Dots.

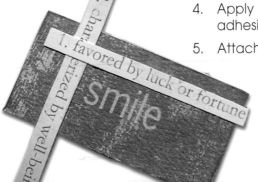

hello

hi

smile

2. char...
1. favored by luck or fortune
...erized by well-being and c...

A
N
D

laugh

happy

Friends Forever
Kelly Lunceford

MATERIALS

Papers: Wild Asparagus by My Mind's Eye

Words, Letters or Stickers: Typewriter Keys Sticker by Nostalgiques by EK Success; "Be Original" Sticker by K&Company; Descriptives Stickers and Tag by Making Memories; Friends Label by Wild Asparagus by My Mind's Eye

Metal Items: Bookplate, Brad and Metal Word by Making Memories

Ribbons: Local Craft Store

Adhesives: Mono Permanent Adhesive by Tombow; Glue Lines and Mini Glue Dots by Glue Dots International

Other: Clock Button; Pin; Blossom by Making Memories

Tools: Bone Folder; Paper Trimmer

INSTRUCTIONS

1. Follow instructions for Hello Friends Tall Box on page 16.

2. Apply sticker embellishments.

3. Thread ribbon through bookplate and around box; secure by tying in a knot at the side.

4. Add blossom with brad through the center; attach tag with the pin through the petals of the blossom. Secure "fun" metal word and clock button with Mini Glue Dots.

5. Apply "enjoy" Descriptives sticker under bookplate.

6. Place gift inside box and add box top.

Kelly's Note: These beautiful boxes are ideal for presenting thoughtful treats such as gift certificates for a movie, lunch or dinner for two; theater or symphony tickets; candles; favorite hard candy or specialty chocolates; vintage hankies or a silk scarf.

Delight Box
Kelly Lunceford

MATERIALS

Papers: Wild Asparagus by My Mind's Eye

Worlds, Letters or Stickers: Making Memories

Metal Items: Metal Frame, Brads and Key by Making Memories

Ribbons: Local Craft Store

Adhesives: Glue Dots; E-6000

Other: Blossom by Making Memories

INSTRUCTIONS

1. Follow instructions for Hello Friends Tall Box on page 16.

2. Apply both "delight" sticker embellishments.

3. Place a sweet photo in frame and adhere with E-6000. Let dry.

4. Pierce two small holes in top of box and thread ribbon; tie in bow.

5. Insert brads in blossom and glue to box with glue dots.

6. Tie ribbon through key and adhere both to box with E-6000. Let dry.

7. Place gift inside box and add box top.

Decorated Paint Cans

Beach Party in a Can

Nikki Cleary

MATERIALS

Papers: Coral Avenue Collection by Making Memories; Aqua Cardstock

Words, Letters or Stickers: Art Warehouse and Narratives Epoxy Stickers by Creative Imaginations

Metal Items: Paint Can: Local Hardware Store

Ribbons and Fibers: Local Craft Store

Adhesives: FABRI-TAC by Beacon Adhesives; Glue Dots; Glue Stick

Other: Pink Paper Flowers by Prima by Martin/F. Weber Co.; "Summer" Tokens by Doodlebug Design; Rhinestones

Tools: Paper Trimmer; Circle Cutter; Xacto Knife

INSTRUCTIONS

Can:

1. Trace paint can lid on aqua paper and cut circle to fit inside top of lid as shown; adhere with glue dots. Embellish lid with ribbons and rick rack, adhering with FABRI-TAC. Add "Bring on the Sun" epoxy sticker.

2. Cut a piece of paper to fit the bottom two-thirds of the can; cut another coordinating paper for the top one-third. Papers need to overlap slightly on all seams. Adhere to can with glue dots. Cut out a half-circle on both pieces of paper where the handle comes out of the can.

3. Use FABRI-TAC to adhere ribbon and rick rack to top, middle and bottom of can. Adhere flowers and rhinestone embellishments with the FABRI-TAC. Press all adhesive epoxy stickers to can.

4. Tie assorted bright colored ribbons to the handle.

Journal:

1. Using the same paper that you used for the can, cut two pieces the size of the front and back of the journal and adhere with glue stick. Trim the corners or excess with an Xacto knife.

2. Adhere three pieces of ribbon to the back of the binding with FABRI-TAC to use as bookmarks. Cut a piece of paper to cover the binding of the journal, allowing it to overlap the front and back cover. Adhere with glue stick.

3. Tie orange fiber through token. Use FABRI-TAC to adhere token, ribbon and rick rack to cover. Add epoxy sticker.

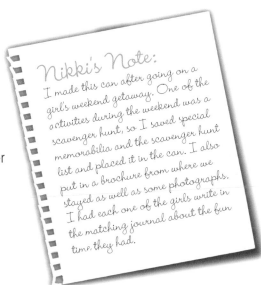

Nikki's Note:
I made this can after going on a girl's weekend getaway. One of the activities during the weekend was a scavenger hunt, so I saved special memorabilia and the scavenger hunt list and placed it in the can. I also put in a brochure from where we stayed as well as some photographs. I had each one of the girls write in the matching journal about the fun time they had.

Need to give a present? CAN it! Decorate a can in a fabulous theme, fill it with tissue, fabric or tulle, and place the present inside. Whether the gift is for birthday, bridal shower, Mother's or Father's Day, graduation or even Christmas, give it in a can!

Beach parties, hostess gifts and even Texas Barbeque... if you've got a reason to celebrate, put a lid on it! Give your host or hostess at the Texas Barbeque a paint can decorated with western and cowboy scrapbook papers and stickers; include barbeque and specialty hot sauces wrapped in bandanas along with a gift certificate to a fav barbeque restaurant. Wrap and adhere twine around a metal handle and you've got a taste of Texas in one colorful can.

Inspiration overflows in the next few pages...check out the beach-themed scavenger hunt "Beach Party in a Can" or "Born to Shop" for storing shopping addicts' receipts. And your little goblin will love the colorful "Trick or Treat" can for gathering Halloween goodies.

Think theme, event, and the recipient's favorite things. Most of all ENJOY making GREAT GIFTS WITH PAINT CANS AND SCRAPBOOK MATERIALS!

21

Shabby Chic Paint Can

Karen Hamad, M.D.

MATERIALS

Papers: Autumn Leaves Collection by FoofaLa

Words, Letters or Stickers: Bottle Cap Stickers by Design Originals; Vintage Stickers by Rusty Pickle

Tags: Evidence Tags by 7gypsies

Metal Items: Paint Can: Local Hardware Store

Ribbons: Local Craft Store

Adhesives: Memory Mount Liquid Adhesive by Crafter's Pick; Glue Dots

Other: Silk Flowers; Assorted Fabric Strips; Personal Ephemera

Tools: 1" Circle Punch; Circle Cutter

INSTRUCTIONS

1. Cut 12" x 12" piece of patterned paper in half horizontally, and using 1" circular punch, punch semi-circle out of each side where paper will fit against handle. Repeat for other half of paper. Tear a strip off of the piece designated for the bottom half of the paint can. Use liquid adhesive to glue paper around paint can.

2. Measure appropriate size circle for paint can lid, and cut out of contrasting paper. Use liquid adhesive to glue to lid.

3. Cut generous amount of matching ribbon and torn fabric strips and tie along handle.

4. Embellish can with theme-related doodads and stickers.

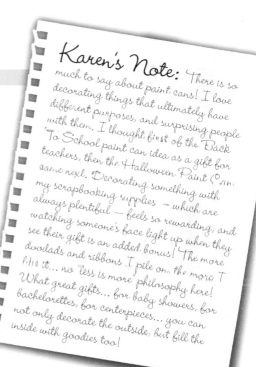

Karen's Note: There is so much to say about paint cans! I love decorating things that ultimately have different purposes, and surprising people with them. I thought first of the Back 'To School paint can idea as a gift for teachers, then the Halloween Paint Can came next. Decorating something with my scrapbooking supplies — which are always plentiful — feels so rewarding, and watching someone's face light up when they see their gift is an added bonus! The more doodads and ribbons I pile on, the more I like it... no "less is more" philosophy here! What great gifts... for baby showers, for bachelorettes, for centerpieces... you can not only decorate the outside, but fill the inside with goodies too!

Halloween Paint Can

Karen Hamad, M.D.

MATERIALS

Papers: Halloween Collection by Pebbles Inc.

Words, Letters or Stickers: Halloween Stickers by EK Success

Tags: Halloween-Themed Metallic Tag by Creation Dance Championships

Metal Items: Paint Can: Local Hardware Store

Ribbons and Fabric Strips: Local Craft Store

Adhesives: Memory Mount Liquid Adhesive by Crafter's Pick; Glue Dots

Other: Twist Ties by Pebbles Inc.

Tools: 1" Circle Punch; Circle Cutter

INSTRUCTIONS

1. Cut 12" x 12" piece of patterned paper in half horizontally, and using 1" circle punch, punch semi-circle out of each side where paper will fit against handle. Repeat for other half of paper to fit handle. Tear a strip off of the piece designated for the bottom half of the paint can. Use liquid adhesive to glue paper around paint can.

2. Measure appropriate size circle for paint can lid, and cut out of contrasting paper. Use liquid adhesive to glue to lid.

3. Cut generous amount of matching ribbon and tie in short strips along handle.

4. Embellish can with theme-related doodads and stickers.

Karen's Note:
Use as much ribbon as you can stand to tie on the handle... although tedious, the effect is a robust one! Try inking the torn edges of your paper before you adhere to the can. Use fabric strips torn to match your papers if you like! Fill the cans with appropriate goodies and give as gift containers or use as centerpieces for holiday tables!

Girly Girl Paint Can

Karen Hamad, M.D.

MATERIALS

Papers: Dirty Laundry by KMA

Words, Letters or Stickers: Epoxy Letters by Li'l Davis Designs

Tags: Metal-Rimmed Tags by Making Memories; Laser Cut Tags by EZ Laser Designs

Metal Items: Paint Can: Local Hardware Store

Ribbons and Fibers: Local Craft Store

Adhesives: Memory Mount Liquid Adhesive by Crafter's Pick; Glue Dots

Other: Safety Pin; Ball Chain

Tools: Circle Punch; Circle Cutter

INSTRUCTIONS

1. Cut 12" x 12" piece of patterned paper in half horizontally. Using 1" circle punch, punch semicircles out of each side where paper will fit against handle. Repeat for other half of paper. Tear a strip off of the piece designated to be the bottom half of the paint can. Use liquid adhesive to glue paper around paint can.

2. Measure appropriate size circle for paint can lid, and cut out of contrasting paper. Use liquid adhesive to glue to lid.

3. Cut generous amount of matching ribbon and fibers and tie in short strips along handle.

4. Embellish can with theme-related doodads and stickers.

Nikki's Note:
I wanted to make a time capsule for my son that he could display and admire. When's he's older I can tell him the story of how, in the first year of his life, Mommy, Daddy, family and friends wrote letters to him and collected special photos, articles from the paper and other mementos to put inside. On his 16th birthday, he can open it and experience what life was like for both him and us in 2004, the year he was born.

From the time you were 1 day old till you turned 1 year old your mom, dad, family & friends wrote letters to you, Took pictures of what the city you were born in looked like, Saved newspaper clipping of world news & amazing stories, Saved momentos of special places & We placed them in this can for you to open on your 16th Birthday!

FaMILY FaMILY FaMILY
FUN

MEM-O-RIES

Time
Capsule

Time

Southwest Florida International Airport continues to expand so too does the commercial office and warehouse development surrounding the airport.

Time Capsule Paint Can
Nikki Cleary

MATERIALS

Rubber Stamps: Foam Stamps by Creative Imaginations

Chalk Inkpad: Yellow

Papers: Scenic Route Paper Company

Paints: Blue Acrylic

Markers: Blue Size .05

Words, Stickers or Letters: Art Warehouse by Creative Imaginations; Real Life by Pebbles Inc.

Tags: Local Craft Store

Metal Items: Staples and Metal Ring

Ribbons and Rick Rack: Local Craft Store

Adhesives: FABRI-TAC by Beacon Adhesives; Glue Dots

Other: Decorative Tape in Green, Brown and Yellow (assorted widths) by Rainbow Tape

Tools: Stapler; 12" Paper Trimmer; Circle Cutter; Pinking Shears

Nikki's Note: This time capsule makes a wonderful baby gift, but also can be used for many other occasions. You can make a wedding time capsule for a bride and groom, let them add special wedding and honeymoon mementos, and have them wait until their tenth anniversary to open it again. You can make a senior class time capsule and have class members put small items inside. When they open it at a reunion five or ten years later, they will all have a good laugh. The possibilities are endless.

INSTRUCTIONS

1. Using a circle cutter, cut a circle the size of paint can lid to fit inside the rim as shown. Adhere with glue dots. Use FABRI-TAC to embellish lid with ribbons and rick rack. Apply decorative tape, epoxy stickers and "fun" plaque.

2. For the bottom half of can, cut two pieces of paper 5" long by 12" wide to go around entire can. Overlap the pieces on the sides; adhere to can with glue dots.

3. For the top half of the can, cut two strips 3" long by 12" wide, allowing pieces to overlap slightly where they meet. Cut or punch with 1" punch for the hole in paper for handle. Position paper and adhere, overlapping slightly.

4. Embellish the can with ribbon, trim, letter stickers and epoxy stickers. Adhere the ribbon and trim with FABRI-TAC.

5. Ink edges of two tags in yellow. Stamp "T" and "C" on the tag; allow to dry. On the first tag, write "time capsule" with the date it should be opened. On the second tag, write the instructions for what should be included in the can.

4. Embellish can with theme-related doodads and stickers.

Friendship Correspondence Can

Janet Klein

MATERIALS

Rubber Stamps: Three Little Girls and Friend Stamp by Stampotique Originals; Miniature Postcard Stamp by Stampcraft; Miniature Letter Stamp

Inkpads: Green, Black and Brown

Papers: Paisley Print, Red Script on Cream, Cranberry with Script Papers by 7gypsies; White, Ivory and Sage Cardstock; Scrap Paper

Colored Pencils: Red

Ribbons: Cream and Wine Satin Finish

Metal Items: One-Gallon Paint Can with Handle: Local Hardware Store

Adhesive: Glue Stick

Other: 2" x 3" Glassine Envelope

Tools: Old Credit Card; 1" Circle Cutter; Paper Cutter

INSTRUCTIONS

1. For the bottom of the can, cut a 12" x 12" sheet of cranberry paper 4" high. Adhere the first piece by centering on the front section of the can, applying adhesive and burnishing the sides with an old credit card.

2. Measure the remaining space and cut additional paper to finish bottom layer.

3. For top of can, use scrap paper to create a template. Measure top paper for template 3" high. Measure for holes and punch with 1" circle cutter to accommodate handle anchors. Once you have adjusted your templates, repeat process with paisley print paper. Snip edge of paper to hole to allow slipping over the handle anchors.

4. Glue top pieces in place; burnish with credit card.

5. Cut red script/cream paper to 1 ½" high for center strip. Evenly apply a thin layer of glue to the back. Glue in place, overlapping the top and bottom papers.

6. Stamp "Friend" with green ink on sage cardstock and trim.

7. Prepare ivory paper by rubbing it with brown inkpad. Stamp miniature letter and miniature postcard with black ink. Accent with red color pencil and trim.

8. Tuck the stamped papers into the glassine envelope. Glue to the center of the can, overlapping the center strip.

9. Trim ribbon snippets to 5 ½ - 6" pieces. Tie around handle and fluff to desired fullness.

10. Punch 1" holes of contrasting papers and glue to center strip to create contrast and balance.

Janet's Note:
For a finishing touch, create a small gift tag with matching scraps. Hole punch corner of the card and attach desired ribbon cord. Tie to side of handle.

Jill's Note:
Everyone has created their paint cans not only a little differently in design and function but also in how they assembled them and with what adhesives. We thought you would be interested to learn how each artist worked through their individual paint can projects. I particularly like the idea of using templates because they can be used again and again as you change designs and papers!

Born to Shop
Janet Klein

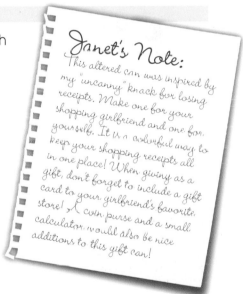

MATERIALS

Rubber Stamps: Shopping Shoes by Janet Klein for Stampotique Originals

Inkpads: Black (bleed-proof for use with watercolors)

Papers: Green Floral Plaid and Aqua Mod from Brenda Walton's Neapolitan Collection for K&Company; White Cover Paper (80 lb weight); Crimson Red and Lavender Cardstock; Scrap Paper

Paints: Watercolors

Ribbons: Local Craft Store

Metal Items: One-Gallon Paint Can with Handle: Local Hardware Store; Aqua Eyelets

Adhesives: Large Glue Stick

Tools: Old Credit Card; 1" Circle Punch; Corner Punch; Measuring Tape; Eyelet Setter; 1/8" Hole Punch; 1/4" Hole Punch; Watercolor Brush; Paper Cutter

INSTRUCTIONS

1. Use scrap paper to create templates. Measure top paper 3" high and measure for hole for templates; punch with 1" circle punch to accommodate handle anchors. Once you have adjusted templates, repeat process with green floral plaid paper.

2. Apply a thick layer of glue stick to paper and burnish in place using old credit card.

3. Repeat the process for the bottom portion. Piece together papers that are 4 ½" high to fit the circumference of the can. Use Aqua Mod for bottom paper.

4. Create the center paper by selecting a coordinating paper and cut into a 1 1/4" strip to fit around can.

5. Select an accent color from the papers. Red-orange was chosen here. Select font of choice and computer-generate "Born to Shop" in 22-point size on sturdy white cover paper.

6. Trim "Born to Shop" copy and round corners. Glue to red scrap paper. Trim red paper to provide a 1/16" accent border.

7. Align the copy in the center of the 1 1/4" strip. Punch holes 1/8" on each end. Set eyelets as shown on label. Adhere to can.

8. Use paper scraps to create a decorated "pieced look" for can lid.

9. Use bleed-proof black ink to stamp "shopping shoes" on white cover stock. Hand-paint with watercolors as desired. In this sample, elements of the paper were repeated in the background to create a uniform look.

10. Trim to tag shape. Glue to lavender scrap paper and re-trim contours. Use ¼" hole punch at top. Snip to accommodate ribbon.

11. Tie a solid and a dotted ribbon to each side of the can. Slip the "shopping shoes" tag over one side of the ribbons. Write your message on the other side of the tag.

Janet's Note:
This altered can was inspired by my "uncanny" knack for losing receipts. Make one for your shopping girlfriend and one for yourself. It is a colorful way to keep your shopping receipts all in one place! When giving as a gift, don't forget to include a gift card to your girlfriend's favorite store! A coin purse and a small calculator would also be nice additions to this gift can!

Chocolate Lovers (Valentine) Can

Janet Klein

MATERIALS

Papers: Paper Wishes by Hot Off the Press; Anna Griffin; DieCuts with a View; Scrap of Gold Metallic Paper

Paints: Brown, Red and White Acrylic Paints

Metal Items: Small Paint Can: Local Hardware Store

Ribbons: Scarlet Red; Pink

Adhesives: Large Glue Stick; E-6000; Gloss Gel Medium by Golden; Mod Podge by Plaid

Other: Wooden Button; Wooden Knob; 20" Black Waxed Linen; Assorted Pink Beads; Silver Accent Beads

Tools: Old Credit Card; ¼" Flat Brush; Paper Cutter; Scallop Edge Scissors

INSTRUCTIONS

1. For base, cut two 12" x 12" pieces of paper 4 ⅝" high. Apply thin layer of glue stick to back of center paper. Glue in place; gently rub over surface with old credit card to burnish.

2. Align contrasting papers with the edge of the front paper and glue in same manner.

3. Glue the final piece in the back of the can.

4. Cut scarlet ribbon into four ⅝" pieces. Back each with glue and cover all four of the joining seams.

5. Cut two pieces of pink ribbon approximately 14" in length. Glue one side of each ribbon and press in place along the top and bottom rim, trimming to fit.

6. For lid, cut a 3 ¼" diameter circle out of scrap paper of choice. Adhere with Mod Podge and allow to dry. Apply a second layer of Mod Podge and let dry.

7. Paint the wooden button with brown acrylic and a white "icing" detail. Paint the knob red. Allow to dry.

8. Trace a circle on the back of the metallic paper. Cut with scallop edge scissors.

9. Apply gloss medium to faux chocolate and to knob. Allow to dry.

10. Use E-6000 to attach the chocolate piece to wrapper then to the side of the can. Let dry. Use E-600 for adhering brown knob to lid as well.

11. Tie a knot about 5" from one end of the linen thread; string beads in desired pattern and knot off the other end.

12. Wrap the beaded cord around the knob and let hang.

Janet's Note:
Fill a clear cellophane bag with chocolates to place in the can. Tie off top of bag with coordinating ribbon. Papers can be changed for that "anytime of year" chocolate lover! Make lots of them – as it turns out, chocolate is good for you!

Trim and Clip Sewing Can

Janet Klein

MATERIALS

Rubber Stamps: "Trim and Clip" by Janet Klein for Stampotique Originals

Inkpads: Brown

Papers: Old Rose by Life's Journey by K&Company; Mesurement by 7gypsies; Ivory Cardstock

Paints: Watercolors

Metal Items: One-Quart Paint Can with Handle: Local Hardware Store

Adhesives: Large Glue Stick; Scotch Tape; E-6000; Mod Podge by Plaid

Other: Embroidery Floss (assorted colors); Blue Tape Measure; Assorted Buttons; Wooden Spool

Tools: 1" Circle Punch; ¼" Punch; Old Credit Card; Ruler; Paper Cutter

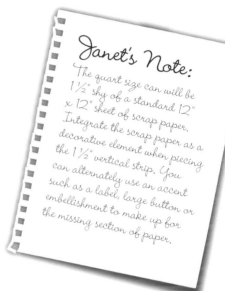

Janet's Note:
The quart size can will be 1½" shy of a standard 12" x 12" sheet of scrap paper. Integrate the scrap paper as a decorative element when piecing the 1½" vertical strip. You can alternately use an accent such as a label, large button or embellishment to make up for the missing section of paper.

Jill's Note:
This cute can will allow you to remember where you store that emergency needle and thread! It can also make a thoughtful accessory for a student going away to college, a housewarming gift, a fun and useful present for bride, sister, girlfriend ... I can't think of anyone that wouldn't love this little special little gift can! Fill it with the essentials: needles, thread, buttons, small scissors, measuring tape and a seam ripper.

INSTRUCTIONS

1. Trim Mesurement paper to 2 ½" high for top of can. Carefully wrap embroidery floss around paper, about every 2 ½". Be careful not to pucker paper. Glue or tape ends of threads to back of paper.

2. Apply a thin layer of glue to the back of the paper. Align paper with top of the can. Burnish in place with old credit card.

3. Apply a thin layer of glue to the Old Rose paper. Align with the bottom edge of the can, glue in place. There should be a 1 ½" gap in the back of the can. Cut additional paper to 1 ½" x 4 ½" and adhere to fill in gap.

4. Measure the circumference of the can and trim a portion of tape measure to border the bottom. Glue as shown.

5. Use E-6000 to adhere buttons around the can as desired.

6. Apply Mod Podge to top of lid. Place pre-cut circle in lid and add more Mod Podge to top. Allow to dry thoroughly.

7. Wrap wooden spool with embroidery floss. Glue down floss to prevent unraveling.

8. Punch a 1" circle of desired scrap and punch in center with ¼" punch. Glue punched paper to top of spool.

9. Center spool on lid with E-6000 adhesive. Tuck a blunt needle through thread in spool as shown.

10. To make a gift card, stamp "Trim and Clip" in brown ink on scrap of ivory cardstock. Apply a light brownish-yellow watercolor wash. Hole-punch corner, add a cord and slip over spool on lid.

CHAPTER 3

Creative Notebooks & Journals

My Creative Journal
Nikki Cleary

MATERIALS

Papers: Garden Party Collection by Arctic Frog

Words, Letters or Stickers: Life's Journey by K&Company; Arctic Frog; Real Life by Pebbles Inc.

Metal Items: Colored Staples by Making Memories; Frame by Li'l Davis Designs

Ribbons: Rick Rack and Pom Poms: Local Craft Store

Adhesives: Glue Stick, FABRI-TAC by Beacon Adhesives

Other: Composition Notebook

Tools: Paper Cutter; Stapler; Xacto Knife

Nikki's Note:

If you're like me, you need a place to write down all your ideas for scrapbooking page layouts, paper crafts, sewing, wood projects and so on. I also needed a place to keep track of all the products I used when I created those items. This journal seems a perfect fit for the task. Before this book existed, many of my ideas never became a reality. Instead I had scraps of paper floating in pockets, my purse and kitchen drawers that eventually were thrown away. Now, every time a new idea surfaces I know exactly where to write it down. Whenever I need inspiration, I just flip through the pages and my creative juices begin to flow.

INSTRUCTIONS

1. Cut two coordinating pieces of paper to the approximate size of front/back cover and adhere with glue stick. Cut and adhere a strip of corresponding paper 3-4" wide for the binding. Let dry completely. Trim all edges with Xacto knife.

2. Use FABRI-TAC to glue pom pom trim over seam where the two pieces of paper meet.

3. Tie ribbons to frame and adhere frame to cover.

4. Adhere buttons to envelope and envelope to cover.

5. Apply all stickers.

6. Staple the rick rack and glue all buttons down the right edge of cover as shown.

Everyone keeps notes, dates and tabs on things to remember. We scribble daily reminders and make "to do" lists. We jot down birthdays, baseball games, dance rehearsals, fundraisers...with our busy lives we would go crazy without a place to document our schedules. Perhaps you've got tiny pieces of papers tucked here and there, or a jumble of calendars you can't keep track of. Now you can clear the clutter from your home and your head!

This chapter is brimming with ideas for beautiful books that inspire organization! From a mini journal for babysitter phone number storage to a birthday reminder book, from diaries to prayer journals, you'll relish recording special numbers, dates and thoughts.

You'll also discover you can judge a book by its cover... and these are simply fabulous. So get out your fancy scrapbooking papers and embellishments and PLAY! Make some for yourself or as gifts for your friends. They won't need to "read between the lines" to see how much you care.

Siena Journal
Roben-Marie Smith

MATERIALS

Rubber Stamps: Fleur by Paperbag Studios

Dye Inkpads: Black

Papers: Jade Pattern by BasicGrey; Map Maze and Black Floral by Li'l Davis Designs; Ledger by K&Company

Paints: White and Black Acrylic Paints

Metal Items: Metal Word Charm and Baroque Moulding Strips by Making Memories; Bar Brad by Karen Foster Design

Ribbons: Local Craft Store

Adhesives: Glue Dots; Glue Stick

Other: Mini Journal by 7gypsies, Black Alphabet Tabs by Autumn Leaves; Photograph; Vintage Button; Small Black Buttons

Tools: Paintbrush, 1/8" Hole Punch; Stapler; Sponge

INSTRUCTIONS

1. Remove covers from mini journal and cover with assorted torn papers.

2. Apply a small amount of paint to a dry 1/2" wide paintbrush; add white paint to cover as shown.

3. Punch two holes in photo, adhere bar brad and glue to cover.

4. Paint moulding strip with a light coat of black and white paint. Adhere to bottom of cover.

5. Using black ink, stamp Fleur onto scrap paper, cut out and glue to cover.

6. Adhere vintage button, metal word charm and buttons to cover with glue dots.

7. Re-assemble book and tie ribbons to coils.

8. Tear pieces of scrapbook paper, fold in half and staple word tabs to top of each. Create one for each letter in "Siena". Staple them to the inside pages along the edge so the word can be read at the side when the book is closed.

9. Sponge the edges of the pages with black ink.

Friends Journal
Kelly Lunceford

MATERIALS

Papers: Bo Bunny Press

Words, Letters or Stickers: Bo Bunny Press

Ribbons: Local Craft Store

Adhesives: Mono Permanent Adhesive by Tombow; Foam Squares by Making Memories

Other: Stenographer's Notebook

Tools: Paper Cutter

INSTRUCTIONS

1. Cut cherry patterned paper 6" x 5" and adhere to steno pad. Add the red polka dot paper to left side and striped paper to right side.

2. Add "Friends" sticker to center.

3. Place "You", "Me" and ribbon stickers as shown onto bottom left of journal. Mount quote sticker to a scrap of red patterned paper and adhere with foam squares.

4. Cut lengths of coordinating ribbons and tie onto each spiral of the top binding.

Memories Journal
Kelly Lunceford

MATERIALS

Papers: Tim Coffey Collection for K&Company; Vellum

Words, Letters or Stickers: "Young Girl" Grand Adhesions and Clearly Yours Letter Stickers by Tim Coffey for K&Company

Metal Items: "Young Girl" Metal Tags and Cap Embellishment by Tim Coffey for K&Company

Ribbons: Local Craft Store

Adhesives: E-6000

Other: Stenographer's Notebook

INSTRUCTIONS

1. Cut paper to 6" x 5" as shown.

2. Adhere tall papers to front of stenographers notebook.

3. Add letters and flower embellishments to top left.

4. Adhere lavender ribbon or paper strip to center; add cap and quote.

5. Cut lengths of coordinating ribbon and tie onto each spiral of the top binding.

6. Thread metal tags with ribbons and tie. Lay notebook flat and use E-6000 to glue metal tags and ribbon to bottom of journal as shown. Let dry overnight.

Funky Ribbon Journals
Jill Haglund

MATERIALS

Papers: FoofaLa; K&Company

Words, Letters or Stickers: Initial "J" and "Two Cherries" Epoxy Sticker by FoofaLa

Metal Items: "Cherish" Charm by K&Company; Colored Brads

Ribbons: Local Craft Store

Other: Stenographer's Notebook; Silk Flowers; Rick Rack

Adhesives: Glue Stick; Sobo Fabric Glue by Delta; Foam Squares by Making Memories; Glue Dots

Tools: Paper Cutter

Jill's Note:
These ingenious little journals are the original conceptions of Kelly Lunceford. Once I saw them I just had to use my favorite papers and make a few; needless to say I got addicted! As you can see, simply changing papers, ribbons and embellishments make each one unique and fun to create.

INSTRUCTIONS

1. Cut patterned paper 6" wide by 7" long for top section of the cover of notebook. Cut paper 6" wide by 4" long for bottom section of the cover. Adhere both to front cover of notebook with Glue Stick, meeting papers as shown. Adhere a coordinating piece of patterned paper to back of notebook that matches the front cover pattern. Trim all as necessary.

2. Adhere coordinating rick rack with Glue Stick or Sobo Fabric Glue where the paper seams meet on cover.

On front of K&Company notebook cover:

3. Add colored brads in flower centers. Slip ribbon through charm piece.

4. Use glue dots to adhere flowers, buttons, embellishments and charm to notebook cover as shown.

On front of FoofaLa notebook cover:

5. Mount FoofaLa initial and the cherry epoxy sticker onto coordinating patterned paper and then to cardstock for sturdiness. Use foam squares to adhere to notebook front as shown.

6. Cut ribbon lengths and tie at least one coordinating ribbon in a double knot in each of the spirals across the top of the notebook.

Address Book

Nikki Cleary

MATERIALS

Papers: Garden Party Collection by Arctic Frog

Words, Letters or Stickers: Li'l Davis Designs

Tags: Creative Imaginations

Metal Items: Circle Clips by Li'l Davis Designs; Star Cookie Cutter by Melissa Francis; Eyelets

Ribbons: Rick Rack and Fibers: Local Craft Store

Adhesives: Glue Stick; FABRIC-TAC by Beacon Adhesives

Other: Composition Notebook; Reversible Tabs in Green, Red and Pink by Melissa Francis; Chipboard Words and Clay Phrases by Li'l Davis Designs; silk flower

Tools: Paper Cutter; Xacto Knife; Eyelet Setter; Hammer

Nikki's Note:
Tie at least three ribbons and or fibers through each eyelet for a nice full look. If your composition notebook cover is glossy, rough it up a bit first. Sand it for a few minutes before applying glue; your papers will adhere much better. These address books make great gift ideas for housewarming, college students or newlyweds.

INSTRUCTIONS

1. Cut two coordinating papers the approximate size of front and back cover and adhere with glue stick. Cut a matching strip of paper 3-4" wide for the cover binding and glue to spine. Once completely dry, trim the edges with Xacto knife.

2. Use FABRI-TAC to adhere rick rack on the seam where the two pieces of paper meet.

3. Set eyelets down right side of cover and tie perky-colored fibers and ribbon snippets through them, leaving the center eyelet for the fabric tag. Adhere clay phrase to fabric tag.

4. Staple a reversible tab on every four to five sheets of paper. Apply the letters for your address book to the tabs.

5. Add additional embellishments as desired.

Coffee Ministry Journal

Nikki Cleary

MATERIALS

Fluid Chalk Inkpads: Yellow and Brown

Papers: K&Company

Words, Letters or Stickers: Real Life by Pebbles Inc.

Tags: Local Craft Store or Office Supply

Metal Items: Creative Imaginations

Ribbons: Local Craft Store

Adhesives: Glue Stick, FABRI-TAC by Beacon Adhesives

Other: Composition Notebook; Library Pocket

Tools: Paper Cutter; Xacto Knife; Scissors; Paper Piercer

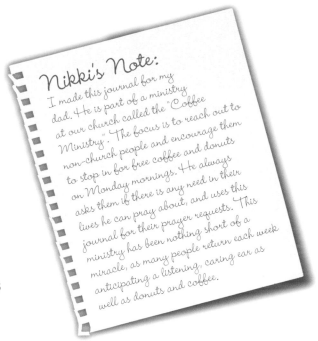

Nikki's Note:
I made this journal for my dad. He is part of a ministry at our church called the "Coffee Ministry". The focus is to reach out to non-church people and encourage them to stop in for free coffee and donuts on Monday mornings. He always asks them if there is any need in their lives he can pray about, and uses this journal for their prayer requests. This ministry has been nothing short of a miracle, as many people return each week anticipating a listening, caring ear as well as donuts and coffee.

INSTRUCTIONS

1. Cut two coordinating pieces of paper to the approximate size of front/back cover and adhere with glue stick. Cut a matching strip of paper 3-4" wide for covering the binding.

2. Before the glue dries on the binding, open the journal and drop a ribbon (with FABRI-TAC on the end) between the binding and the paper for a bookmark.

3. Once completely dry, trim the excess with Xacto knife.

4. Ink the edge of the journal with yellow and brown fluid chalk ink.

5. Adhere the brown ribbon to paper seam on front cover as shown.

6. Adhere library pocket to front cover. Journal on tag, staple ribbon and slip into pocket.

7. Apply "coffee ministry" or sticker letters of choice.

8. Pierce holes through cover and insert brads.

9. Use FABRI-TAC to adhere envelope on inside cover for additional notes.

These Mini Composition Notebooks are easy and versatile. Notice there is basically one set of instructions for all three. Just change out the materials, the occasion and the inspiration, and you've got a limitless number of gift ideas!

Birthday Mini Organizer
Karen Hamad, MD

MATERIALS

Rubber Stamps: Magnetic Date Stamp Set by Making Memories

Words, Letters or Stickers: Tiered Cake Sticker by Rob and Bob Studio for Provo Craft; Birthday Hat Sticker by Pebbles Inc.

Inkpads: Black

Papers: Mara Mi

Tags: Local Craft Store or Office Supply

Ribbons: Local Craft Store

Adhesives: Glue Stick

Other: Index Tabs; Mini Composition Notebook

Tools: Stapler; Paper Cutter

Babysitter's Log
Karen Hamad, MD

MATERIALS

Papers: Christina Cole for Provo Craft

Words, Stickers or Letters: Monogram Sticker by Kimberly Hodges for K&Company

Markers: Black

Tags: Mini Tag Letters by Doodlebug Design

Ribbons: Local Craft Store

Adhesives: Glue Stick

Other: Index Tabs; Mini Composition Notebook; Prima Flowers by Martin/F. Weber Co.; Mini Buttons; Domino; Ladybug Clip

Tools: Stapler; Paper Cutter

Optional: Alphabet Stamps

Summer Reading List Journal
Karen Hamad, MD

MATERIALS

Papers: American Traditional

Markers: Black

Ribbons: Local Craft Store

Adhesives: Glue Stick

Other: Index Tabs; Mini Composition Notebook; Acrylic Letters ("read") by Pebbles Inc.

Tools: Stapler; Paper Cutter

Optional: Alphabet Stamps

INSTRUCTIONS

1. Choose your theme and appropriately patterned paper. Cut to measure front, back and inside covers of mini composition book.

2. Before attaching paper to back cover, cut snippets of assorted ribbons and staple to bottom of inside back cover as shown.

3. Using gluestick cover inside and outside back covers with papers.

4. **Birthday Mini Organizer:** Stamp months of the year on index tab inserts.

   Babysitters Log: On index tabs write or stamp categories such as: schedules, contact and emergency numbers, favorite foods, books and TV shows; bedtime, etc.

   Summer Reading List Journal: Write or stamp categories of books on index tab inserts.

5. Attach index tabs to sections of composition book and insert the tabs.

6. Embellish front and back of cover as desired with stickers and ephemera.

Karen's Note:
I fell in love with the miniature aspect of these projects. I brainstormed one night and came up with five or six different themes that could work with this concept and stayed up all night playing and making mini-books. Use your imagination ...New Year's resolutions, Christmas gift lists, sketch books, portable journals for scrapbooking ideas, the possibilities are endless! And what great gift ideas they are! Plus you can use all the little scraps and doodads you have hidden at home that you haven't used in years!

CHAPTER 4

Decorated Frames

Miracle Frame

Kelly Lunceford

MATERIALS

Pigment Inkpads: Gold Metallic

Papers: Sisters Floral and Polka Dot by Wild Asparagus by My Mind's Eye

Words, Letters or Stickers: Miracle Sticker and Baby Definitions by Making Memories; Baby Stickers by 7gypsies; Treasure by Wild Asparagus by My Mind's Eye; Baby Carriage Vintage Cutouts by Melissa Francis

Tags: Mini Paper Tags by Making Memories

Metal Items: Book Plate by Li'l Davis Designs; Washer Words and Brad by Making Memories; Large Skeleton Key by Paper Bliss by Westrim Crafts; Paper Clip by Karen Foster Design; Small

Skeleton Key by K&Company; Brads

Ribbons: Local Craft Store

Adhesives: Mono Permanent Adhesive by Tombow; Scotch Tape by 3M; Glue Dots

Other: Frame by Melissa Francis; Paper Flower by Making Memories; Pin

Tools: Paper Cutter; Pencil; Xacto Knife

INSTRUCTIONS

1. Mat picture on polka dot paper and trim leaving ½" margin all around.

2. Trim polka dot and floral paper to fit the front of the frame as shown. Turn paper upside down, position frame on top. Use a pencil to mark placement of matted picture. Use Xacto knife to cut out area slightly smaller than marked.

3. Adhere picture and paper together, then to frame, with Mono Permanent Adhesive. Distress edges with gold metallic pigment ink. Add a length of polka dot ribbon at the bottom with scotch tape secured to the back of the paper.

4. Take the back off the frame and wrap ribbons around the right side, adding embellishments as you go. Place back onto frame for security.

5. Attach baby definition. Add ribbons to paper clip and attach to frame.

6. Carefully stick "miracle" definition to frame. Secure skeleton key with glue dots. Slip brad through washer words then flower. Attach with glue dots. Distress paper tag with metallic ink and add to frame with glue dot.

Jill's Note:
Frames are a personal and sentimental gift for anyone on your list. Pick up wood frame bases at your local craft store or use one like this from the Melissa Francis collection. They come in all sizes and shapes to fit different size photos. Simply add your favorite scrapbook materials!

Decked out, decorated frames make for long lasting treasured keepsakes. Spice up your creations up by adding the latest papers, ribbons and embellishments and don't forget foam shapes! Use all your extra doodads, like buttons, charms, tabs and tags. Collect your special scraps and convert them into an enduring masterpiece. Frames are a gift "staple" because everyone cherishes displaying their photos!

You'll discover you can make attractive, all-occasion frames as well as design fun, themed frames to showcase photos of pets, baby, family, best friends, vacation highlights and more. Can't you just picture it?!

Eternity Frame
Nikki Cleary

MATERIALS

Papers: Black and White Print by DieCuts with a View

Paints: Burgundy

Words, Letters or Stickers: "Eternity Headline" from Art Warehouse by Creative Imaginations

Tags: Market Tags by Pebbles Inc.

Metal Items: Brad

Ribbons: Rick Rack

Adhesives: FABRI-TAC by Beacon Adhesives

Other: Tailored Tabs by Scrapworks; Twist Ties by Pebbles Inc.; Faux Jewels

Tools: Paintbrush; 12" Paper Cutter; Scissors

INSTRUCTIONS

1. Paint frame with two coats of burgundy and let dry.

2. Tear two strips of black/white paper and adhere to top and bottom of frame.

3. Run rick rack through "Eternity Headline" and adhere to back of frame.

4. Twist and tie market tags and add all other embellishments as shown.

Nikki's Note: I was inspired to make this frame when I saw this picture of my mom and dad kissing. They have been married for 36 years and are still "in love". I wanted to capture this special moment in a frame they might like to display. The black and white photo is accented by black and white paper, a simple color scheme that makes the embellishments "pop".

Best Buds
Nikki Cleary

MATERIALS

Papers: Spring Collection by SEI; Cobblestone Textured Paper by Fibermark

Paints: Green Acrylic

Words, Letters or Stickers: Spring Collection Alphabet Stickers and Rub-Ons by SEI; Groovy Daisies Foam Stickers by Creative Hands

Tags: Spring Collection by SEI; Tag in a Bag by Paperbilities by Westrim Crafts

Ribbons and Rick Rack: Local Craft Store

Adhesives: Glue Dots; FABRI-TAC by Beacon Adhesives

Other: Frame by Maple Lane Press by EK Success; Buttons; Rhinestones

Tools: Paintbrush; Pinking Shears; 12" Paper Trimmer; Tweezers; Popsicle Stick

Nikki's Note: My best friend Sherry lives in Guam and I only get to see her once a year. The last time she visited, someone snapped this fabulous photo of us. It deserved a special frame and this is what evolved. I absolutely love it and keep it in my craft studio.

INSTRUCTIONS

1. Paint frame green as shown and allow to dry.

2. Cut purple and blue Fibermark textured paper as shown; adhere to top and bottom of frame.

3. Cut, layer and adhere striped and polka dot papers.

4. Embellish top left corner of frame with foam flowers, buttons and rhinestones.

5. Rub on "we're best buds".

6. Layer tag to the Tag in a Bag and embellish with "B" sticker, foam flower, rhinestone and button. Tie a ribbon to the striped spring tag, write a special message and slip it in the "bag" or pocket. Adhere both to frame.

7. Use FABRI-TAC to add rick rack to Tag in a Bag, and up the right side of frame as shown.

8. Embellish bottom of frame as desired with buttons, foam flower and rhinestone.

9. Tie short white ribbon snippets through three buttons. Tie, trim and adhere to top right of frame with glue dots.

Hawaiian Vacation

Nikki Cleary

MATERIALS

Papers: Scrapworks

Words, Letters or Stickers: Monogram Bubble Type by Li'l Davis Designs

Metal Items: Tropical Bottlecaps and Circle Frames by Li'l Davis Designs; Letter "D" by Making Memories

Ribbons: Local Craft Store

Adhesives: Scotch Packing Tape by 3M; FABRI-TAC by Beacon Adhesives

Other: Wood Boards; Mini Clothespins; Flower; Tailored Tabs by Scrapworks; Buttons

Tools: Paper Trimmer

INSTRUCTIONS

1. Wrap boards with scrapbook papers and secure with packing tape to back of board.

2. Layer additional strips of coordinating papers and again secure with clear packing tape to back of board.

3. Cut ribbon to size and adhere with FABRI-TAC on back of board.

4. Tie rick rack or ribbon on clothespin(s) and secure to board with FABRI-TAC and clip on picture(s).

5. Adhere tags and desired embellishments as shown.

Aloha Frame

Nikki Cleary

MATERIALS

Papers: Li'l Davis Designs; Creative Imaginations

Paints: Bright Yellow Acrylic

Metal Items: Plates from Art Warehouse by Creative Imaginations; Flower Brads by Alison Connors for Creative Imaginations

Fibers: Local Craft Store

Adhesives: FABRI-TAC by Beacon Adhesives

Other: Narratives File Tabs by Creative Imaginations; Frames by Maple Lane Press by EK Success

Tools: Paper Cutter; Pinking Shears; Paintbrush

INSTRUCTIONS

1. Paint frame yellow and allow to dry.

2. Cut paper with paper cutter and pinking shears to fit right side of frame. Cut desired paper for top of frame; roll edges slightly as shown. Cut paper for bottom of frame and roll edges. Adhere all paper to frame with FABRI-TAC.

3. Cut out the words "souvenir" and "explore" from the Creative Imaginations paper and adhere to frame.

4. Use FABRI-TAC to attach the metal flower brads.

5. Run fibers through the Aloha plate and tie to frame, do the same for the 2C Hawaii plate.

6. Adhere file tabs to right side as shown.

Bone Frame
Kim Henkel

MATERIALS

Rubber Stamps: Watch Face and Fussy Numbers by Postmodern Design; Tag by Inkadinkado Rubber Stamps; Fleur de Lis

Pigment Inkpads: Black

Dye Inkpads: Light, Medium and Dark Brown; White

Papers: 7gypsies; K&Company; Cardstock by Bazzill Basics; Postage Stamp Paper by 100 Proof Press

Words, Letters or Stickers: "WP" by Sticker Studio

Metal Items: Metal Plate and Bottle Cap by Li'l Davis Designs; Brads

Ribbons and Lace: Local Antique Store

Fabrics: Homespun by Moda for United Notions

Adhesives: Mod Podge and Stiffy Fabric Stiffener by Plaid; Glue by Magic Scraps

Other: Cardboard; Buttons; Key; Large and Mini Clothespins; Linen Thread

Tools: Dymo Label Maker and Tape; Foam Brush by Making Memories

INSTRUCTIONS

1. Cut a piece of cardboard into dog bone shape and a free standing stand for the frame (or display on an easel).

2. Use Mod Podge to adhere papers to the front of bone shape.

3. Add photo of dog to frame and Mod Podge over frame with foam brush.

4. Place brads in metal plate for decoration.

5. Add a fabric strip to bottom of metal plate.

6. Adhere the metal plate on top of photo using glue by Magic Scraps.

7. Using alphabet stickers to add dog's initials.

8. Decorate postage stamp paper using stamps and ink. Adhere it to frame using foam brush and Mod Podge.

9. Add red embossed Dymo tape.

10. Cut out heart from homespun fabric and use Stiffy to stiffen (may take up to 24 hours to dry).

11. Stamp images onto cardstock. Attach stamped images to frame using clothespins. Tie on a string of buttons.

12. Tie small key to clothespin using linen thread. Tie a piece of lace to top of clothespin.

13. Slip smashed bottle cap under mini clothespin.

14. Attach cardboard stand to frame using glue by Magic Scraps.

We Remember Moments Frame

Roben-Marie Smith

MATERIALS

Papers: Basic Grey; K&Company; 7gypsies

Paints: White Acrylic

Words, Letters or Stickers: Rub-On Words by Making Memories

Metal Items: Metal Flower Photo Corners, Decorative Brad and Black Mini Brad by Making Memories; Bulldog Clip

Ribbons: Printed Twill by 7gypsies

Adhesives: Glue Dots; Glue Stick

Other: Frame by Melissa Francis; Artificial Flowers; Photograph; Buttons

Tools: Paintbrush; Black Pen

Roben-Marie's Note: There are so many creative ways to showcase our treasured photographs. If you have a photo that you love, why not show it off by treating a photo frame like you would a scrapbook page? Add papers, paint and embellishments to create a unique art piece in which to feature your special photo!

INSTRUCTIONS

1. Trim Alpha Berry paper to fit onto front of frame.

2. Tear and layer papers onto front of frame as shown.

3. Using a dry brush technique, paint white acrylic paint onto the front of the frame. (For the "dry brush technique" apply only a little paint to a 1/2" to 1" bristle or regular paintbrush. The brush is almost dry before applying to project.)

4. Wrap printed twill around the top of the frame, tie in a knot with checked ribbon and add bulldog clip near knot.

5. Glue on small tags and write words on them with a black pen.

6. Add brads and buttons to artificial flowers and adhere to frame with glue dots.

7. Adhere buttons to the top of the frame with glue dots.

8. Attach metal flower photo corners to opening edges of frame with glue dots.

9. Apply rub-on word to bottom right of frame.

10. Place photo into frame.

Love Chalkboard

Kelly Lunceford

MATERIALS

Rubber Stamps: Foam Stamps by Making Memories

Papers: Vintage Hip Collection by Making Memories

Paints: Pink and White Acrylic

Words, Letters or Stickers: Epoxy Stickers by Creative Imaginations; "love" tab by 7gypsies; Descriptives by Making Memories

Tags: Small Tag by Making Memories

Metal Items: Vintage Hip Frame, Ribbon Charms, Love Charm

and Pewter Brad by Making Memories; Key by K&Company

Ribbons, Rick Rack and Trims: Vintage Hip Collection by Making Memories

Adhesives: Mono Permanent Adhesive by Tombow; Glue Dots

Other: Chalkboard by Provo Craft; Flower Blossoms by Making Memories; Pin

Tools: Paper Cutter; Stapler; Foam Paintbrush

Kelly's Note:
The Love Chalkboard is a perfect gift idea for writing the kitchen grocery list. Use papers to match the décor add a photo to personalize it. Your special friend is sure to be delighted!

INSTRUCTIONS

1. Paint the frame of the chalkboard white and let dry.

2. Apply paint to foam stamps and stamp corners and "LOVE" to chalkboard and let dry. Distress edges of chalkboard with pink paint. Let Dry.

3. Add epoxy stickers to corner of chalkboard frame. Attach Love metal charm with glue dots over the stamped word "Love".

4. Cut strips of polka dot paper to frame inside edges of the bottom chalkboard portion as shown.

5. Cut and adhere a square of floral paper to fit the inside of the top. Cut photo to fit inside of metal frame and layer onto red paper, then to polka dot paper.

6. Staple "love" tab to right corner and attach metal frame piece to chalkboard. Cut a strip of calico paper and add to the bottom under the frame. Add "beautiful" definition sticker.

7. Adhere trim. Cut a small strip of striped paper and attach to right side of chalkboard. Add the blossom with glue dot.

8. Thread ribbon charm with velvet trim and secure to chalkboard with glue dots.

9. Tie a length of velvet ribbon to key and attach to metal frame. Secure tag with a pin through the knot of the ribbon.

ADORE

LOVE

LOVE

Buddies Frame
Dawne Renee Pitts

MATERIALS

Rubber Stamps: Antique Uppercase and Lowercase Alphabets by Hero Arts

Inkpads: Brown and Burnt Orange

Papers: Various Autumn-Colored Patterned Papers; Off White Cardstock

Words, Letters or Stickers: Definitions by FoofaLa

Metal Items: Bookplate by 7gypsies

Adhesives: Mod Podge by Plaid

Other: Tiny Buttons by Hero Arts; Chipboard

Tools: Stippler

Jill's Note: Imagine creating a frame for subjects other than people or pets... a fiery sunset at the beach, a fluffy powder-white ski slope, the mist off a lake at dawn's first blush, even a fresh bloom peeking out from your garden. These simple, yet stunning images not only bring to mind special moments and memories, but also provide infinite inspiration! Let your frame mirror your mindset at the time of your natural discoveries.

INSTRUCTIONS

1. Cut frame from chipboard.

2. Cut various fall-colored pieces of patterned paper to cover the frame. Cover with Mod Podge and allow to dry.

3. Stamp "buddies" with brown ink using a mix of upper and lower case stamps on off white cardstock. Age the cardstock by stippling with the burnt orange ink.

4. Cut out various fall-themed definitions and age those with the brown and burnt orange inks.

5. Trim and set the stamped "buddies" cardstock under the bookplate on the lower right side of the frame. Adhere two tiny buttons over the bookplate holes. Cover the entire bookplate, buttons and cardstock with a light coat of Mod Podge.

6. Place the definitions on the frame and cover with another light coat of Mod Podge.

7. Cut out a back, from cardboard or chipboard, to fit the frame and attach a fall-themed photo.

Beyond Scrapbooks

Family Mini Album

Kelly Lunceford

MATERIALS

Rubber Stamps: Express It by Making Memories

Dye Inkpads: Tan

Papers: Reading Poppies by Chatterbox; Kraft Cardstock

Words, Letters or Stickers: Typewriter Key Letters and Measuring Tape by Nostalgiques by EK Success

Metal Items: Metal Quote and Photo Turns by Making Memories; Brads; Eyelets

Ribbons: Local Craft Store

Adhesives: Mono Permanent Adhesive by Tombow; Glue Dots

Other: Chipboard

Tools: Sewing Machine; Paper Cutter; Eyelet Hole Punch and Setter; Bone Folder; Sanding Block; Makeup Sponge

INSTRUCTIONS

1. Cut chipboard 5 1/2" x 12" and score in 5 1/2" on both sides. Using a bone folder, crease score marks and fold.

2. Cover the front and the back of the album with the poppy paper, leaving enough overlap to wrap around to the inside. Add a piece of red paper to binding, centering it on both sides. Wrap around to inside.

3. To cover the inside you will need three pieces of paper again, just SLIGHTLY smaller than the album. This will cover the raw edges and create a finished look. Use red with the binding and two pieces of poppy paper for each side, just as was done on the outside.

4. Keep the album flat and sew along the outside with a straight stitch. Use a zigzag stitch to sew the seam where the two patterns come together (front and back). Re-fold the album on the original score marks. Distress the edges with tan ink. Set a row of three eyelets on the top of the binding and three on the bottom to secure the pages.

5. For the pages, cut cardstock into six 10 1/2" x 5 1/4" pieces and fold each in half. Put one piece inside another; repeat three times. Measure placement with the eyelets on the binding and punch holes. Thread ribbon through pages and album and secure with bows. For a distressed look, sand the cover's edges, then use makeup sponge to rub tan ink lightly here and there.

6. Add stickers and metal embellishments to front. Stamp meaningful words on the cover.

Jill's Note:

Machine-stiched hand-made albums jazzed up with embellishments are a gift truly from the heart.

Instructions for the togetherness album are basically the same except change measurements to desired length; add embellishments of choice.

My Year of Wonder Scrapbook

Roben-Marie Smith

MATERIALS

Papers: Black Script Paper by 7gypsies; Green Crackled Paper by K&Company; Corrugated Paper by Graphic Products; Pink Paper by Autumn Leaves; Black Cardstock

Paints: White and Black Acrylic

Words, Letters or Stickers: Wood Chip Letters and Bubble Word by Li'l Davis Designs; Sticker Word by Creative Imaginations

Tags: She Tag by Making Memories; Round Tag

Metal Items: Colored Staples by Making Memories; Cameo Spiral by 7gypsies; Binder Clip; Safety Pin

Ribbons: Local Craft Store; Printed Twill by 7gypsies

Adhesives: Glue Stick; Glue Dots

Other: Buttons; Ivory Fabric; Beads; Photocopy of Dictionary Page

Tools: Paintbrush; Stapler

Roben-Marie's Note:
When I am working on a project like this, I find it best to lay everything out and work the design until I am happy with it. I don't glue anything in place until I have reached this point. I have also been known to snap a photo of the design before securing everything down so I don't forget how everything was placed.

INSTRUCTIONS

1. Using white and then black acrylic paint, apply paint with a dry brush technique to edges of scrapbook cover and torn piece of corrugated paper. Let dry.

2. Tear black script paper. Fold cut pieces of ribbon around the edge of the paper and staple in place. Set aside.

3. Cut a scrap piece of fabric and glue to the right edge of the book.

4. Cut and glue two pieces of ribbon to right edge of book near fabric.

5. Tear scrap pieces of pink and green papers.

6. Glue all papers to cover. Adhere buttons to top of two pieces of ribbon with glue dots.

7. Adhere photo to cover and embellish the side with scrap paper and button.

8. Adhere chip letters, word definition, tag and bubble word to bottom of cover.

9. Attach clip to top of cover and add ribbon, cameo spiral, button, pin and tag.

10. Adhere small beads to the bottom of the fabric with glue dots.

11. Cut and fold twelve small pieces of card stock and glue printed twill months to each. Fold each one, in sequence, over the pages in the book and staple in place.

Happy House Journal
Janet Klein

MATERIALS

Rubber Stamps: No. 4 Stamp by Stampotique Originals

Inkpads: Sage and Lapis Blue

Papers: Patterned Paper by DieCuts With a View; Cover Stock (5" x 30")

Paints: Blue and Lilac Acrylic

Colored Pencils: Prismacolor Indigo by Sanford

Adhesives: Aleene's Tacky Glue by Duncan Enterprises; Glue Stick

Other: Thin Cording; Small Wire Nail; Photo Corners; Three Beads; Twine; Poplar Wood, Mat Board or Foam Core

Tools: 1/16" Drill Bit and Drill or Book Awl; Scroll Saw; Xacto knife; Cutting Mat; 1/2" Flat Brush; Sanding Block; Scallop Edge Scissors; Bone Folder

INSTRUCTIONS

1. Create house and mini door pattern and trace to desired surface: poplar wood, mat board or foam core. Cut out, lightly sand and paint mini door and house. Paint edges as well.

2. Apply glue to all surfaces to be adhered with papers. Apply paper and use a bone folder to burnish in place.

3. Use a 1/2" flat brush to sweep strokes of acrylic paint accent color along the contour of book covers.

4. When dry, use Prismacolor indigo pencil to draw on accent lines.

Janet's Note:
The sample was used to celebrate a child's birthday. The inside is a concertina fold, perfect for photographs, illustrations, recipes, and more. Use your imagination — completely alter the look with the diverse papers available today!

5. Turn paper-covered wood pieces upside down on cutting mat. Carefully trim away excess paper close to contour of house and door shape with Xacto knife.

6. Use a $1/16$" drill bit to drill holes at the sides of both house pieces, as shown (approximately midway), for cording. (If you use mat board or foam core instead of wood, you can accomplish steps 6 and 7 with a book awl.)

7. Drill through the door to accommodate the wire nail with bead.

INSIDE:

8. Prepare 30" x 5" paper into a concertina fold by folding eight sections, $3 \, 3/4$" in width by 5" in height.

9. Decorate pages to your liking. Notice the page in this sample has a pocket created with scrap paper for notes or mementos.

10. Once pages are finished, position the drilled house pieces with the paper side down on your table.

11. Apply glue stick to back of concertina ends. Align with the bottom of the house form and use bone folder to burnish the endpapers to the inside.

12. Slip bead on nail. Align with pre-drilled hole. Use tacky glue to adhere nail and bead to mini door and door to house front.

13. String twine through the holes to tie if desired. Knot thread. Add small bead and string twine through holes. Cord can wrap several times around the book to tie closed around the beaded doorknob.

CHIC Vintage Album
Amy Wellenstein

MATERIALS

Papers: Red Floral by Anna Griffin; Scarlet Dots by Chatterbox; Script by 7gypsies; Pintuck (Garnet) by Moda for Daisy D's Paper Co.

Paints: Pale Yellow; Red

Words, Letters or Stickers: My Fair Lady Buckle Sticker from Nostalgiques by EK Success; Misunderstood Alphabet Rub-Ons in White by Making Memories

Metal Items: Life's Journey Metal Art Circle by K&Company

Adhesives: Xyron; The Ultimate! Glue by Crafter's Pick

Other: Chipboard; Rhinestone; Wooden Letters; Vintage Record Album; Photo

Tools: Die Cuts by Sizzix; Sandpaper

INSTRUCTIONS

Cover

1. Paint the cover of a vintage record album using pale yellow paint. Let dry, then sand the edges.

2. Cover a piece of chipboard with Pintuck paper. Adhere to the front cover.

3. Paint wooden letters with red paint. Let dry. Next, paint letters with pale yellow paint. Let dry again, then sand the surface lightly.

4. Glue the wooden letters to the front cover.

5. Adhere red floral paper to the inside of the cover.

Inside Page

1. Use Sizzix machine to die-cut a medium flower from script paper and a large flower from scarlet dot paper.

2. Crumple the flowers, smooth out, layer and glue to the top right corner of the page.

3. Glue a rhinestone into a round metal setting and adhere to the center of the flower.

4. Use rub-on letters to spell out the word "PHOTOS" across the bottom of the page.

5. Adhere a vintage buckle sticker to the left side of the page.

6. Insert photos into the album sleeves.

Jill's Note:
Look for vintage albums at flea markets, garage sales, antique stores or even in your mother's attic. These make unique and endearing gifts for anyone on your list!

Family Lunch Pail Photo Keeper

Karen Hamad M.D.

MATERIALS

Pigment Inkpads: Gold; Platinum; Black

Papers: Fusion Collection by BasicGrey

Paints: Purple; Orange

Words, Letters or Stickers: Monogram Letters from Fusion Collection by BasicGrey

Metal Items: Lunch Pail Album by BasicGrey; Brads; Circular Clips

Ribbons: Local Craft Store

Fabrics: Assorted Fabric Strips

Adhesives: GLOO by KI Memories; Scrappy Tape by Magic Scraps; Cheetah Tape Runner; Hermafix Tabs; Pop Dots by All Night Media/Plaid

Other: Alphabet Soup Acrylic Letters by KI Memories; Silk Flowers and Leaves

Tools: Paper Cutter

Karen's Note:
I found that using sepia or black and white photos really made these album pages stand out. A large focal point photo on the index page of each section, with smaller ones to add interest and detail on the pages to follow, helped flesh out the story of each special person in our family. My biggest problem now is having to choose who gets to keep the album and I want it for myself!

INSTRUCTIONS

1. Choose several patterns of coordinating papers and cut into 2" x 2 ½" rectangles. Adhere with liquid GLOO adhesive around base in a pleasing, random fashion as shown. Use Scrappy Tape to secure papers to the rounded areas of the lunch pail.

2. Cut a 2" coordinating paper strip and adhere above rectangle strip, as indicated in photo, using GLOO.

3. Ink Monogram letter for title and use Pop Dot to adhere it to bottom left corner of box. Adhere rest of title letters with liquid glue.

4. Embellish remainder of album with silk flowers, leaves and doodads of choice, leaving some of metal pail showing.

5. Tie strips of torn fabric along handle as desired.

6. Decorate each page insert and tabbed page with patterned paper and photographs as shown.

7. Paint blank chipboard embellishments to match and use as focal points on pages of album.

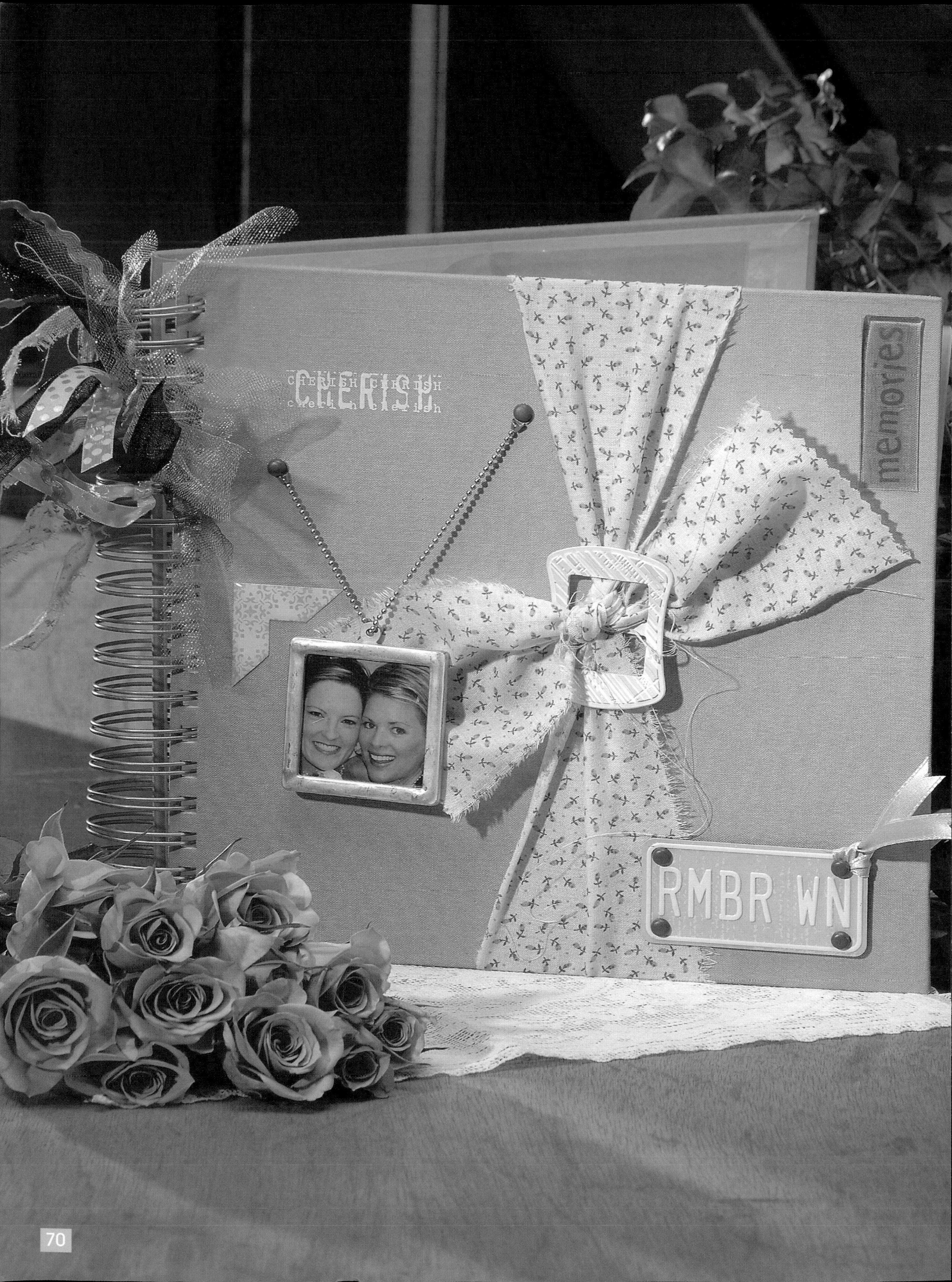
CHERISH
memories
RMBR WN

Remember When Album Cover

Nikki Cleary

MATERIALS

Words, Stickers or Letters: Graffiti from Art Warehouse by Creative Imaginations; Narratives Epoxy Stickers by Karen Russell for Creative Imaginations; "Cherish" Impress-On by Creative Imaginations

Metal Items: Large Keepsake Frame and Brushed Silver Chain by Pebbles Inc.

Ribbons, Rick Rack and Tulle: Local Craft Store

Fabrics: Small Blue Flower Fabric

Adhesives: FABRI-TAC by Beacon Adhesives

Other: 9" x 9" Album by Heidi Swapp; Art Warehouse Hardware Buckles and Plates by Creative Imaginations

Tools: Popsicle Stick; Scissors; Hole Punch

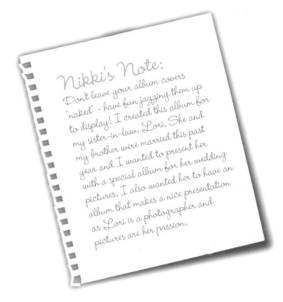

Nikki's Note:
Don't leave your album covers "naked" - have fun jazzing them up to display! I created this album for my sister-in-law, Lori. She and my brother were married this past year and I wanted to present her with a special album for her wedding pictures. I also wanted her to have an album that makes a nice presentation as Lori is a photographer and pictures are her passion.

INSTRUCTIONS

1. Tear a strip of fabric 3-4" wide and to desired length. Tie around album and through hardware buckle.

2. Place picture in frame. Cut chain to desired length. Punch holes in album cover where brads will go as shown. Attach frame to cover.

3. Embellish plate with brads and ribbon. Attach it to cover with FABRI-TAC. Add other embellishments.

4. Tie ribbons, rick rack, fabric strips and tulle to spiral. Keep all fabric scraps. You can tear them into strips and use them with or in place of ribbons.

Baby Album

Kim Henkel

MATERIALS

Inkpads: Brown

Paints: Yellow

Ribbons: Local Craft Store

Fabrics: Yoyo Quilt Pieces

Adhesives: Wet Glue by Magic Scraps

Other: Album by DieCuts with a View; Chipboard Letters by Heidi Swapp; Buttons, Safety Pin; Small Frame; Page from Vintage Children's Book; Linen Thread

Tools: Nail File; Makeup Sponge

Jill's Note:
Design a baby book to be displayed! This sweet baby album would look adorable in your baby's room or on your coffee table for all to see and enjoy.

INSTRUCTIONS

1. Tear a page out of a vintage children's book that has an illustration. Adhere to front of album.

2. Tie a ribbon around the right side of frame.

3. String several antique buttons on a piece of linen thread.

4. Attach string of buttons to ribbon using a safety pin.

5. Use Wet Glue to adhere small frame to album, framing the illustration from book page.

6. Glue yoyo quilt piece on bottom of album.

7. Using nail file, sand chipboard letters here and there.

8. Randomly apply paint on top of letters.

9. When paint is dry, distress sanded, painted letters using brown stamp ink and makeup sponge.

10. Glue letters on top of quilt pieces with Wet Glue.

LITTLE BO-PEEP AND
LITTLE BOY BLUE

"What have you done with your sheep,
    Little Bo-Peep?
What have you done with your sheep,
    Bo-Peep?"
"Little Boy Blue, what fun!
I've lost them, every one!"
"Oh, what a thing to have done,
    Little Bo-Peep!"

"What have you done with your sheep,
    Little Boy Blue?

BABY

Forever Family Mini Album

Kelly Lunceford

MATERIALS

Rubber Stamps: Express it by Making Memories

Dye Inkpads: Red; Black

Papers: Lollipop Shop by BasicGrey, Cardstock by Bazzill Basics

Paints: Tan

Words, Letters or Stickers: Defined by Making Memories

Metal Items: Ribbon Charm, "family" Metal Word and Colored Staples by Making Memories; Mini Brad by Close to My Heart; Eyelets by Stampin' Up! and Close to My Heart

Ribbons: Making Memories and Local Craft Store

Adhesives: Mono Permanent Adhesive by Tombow; Mini Glue Dots by Glue Dots International

Other: Silk Flower; Chipboard; Alphabet Mosaic Tiles by Westrim Crafts

Tools: Bone Folder; Scoring Blade; Sewing Machine; Eyelet Hole Punch and Setter; Paintbrush

INSTRUCTIONS

1. Cut chipboard 5 ½" x 12". Score in 5 ½" from each end. Fold score marks with a bone folder. Cut two pieces of floral patterned paper into 5 ½"x 6 ½" pieces, and one piece of striped paper into a 4" piece.

2. Apply adhesive to the two pieces of floral paper and apply to the outside edges of chipboard, smoothing it flat with a bone folder. There will be overlapping edges; fold into the inside, paying attention to give them mitered corners.

3. Apply adhesive to the striped piece and center it carefully over the "binding" area of the chipboard. Fold over edges.

4. Cut two pieces of floral patterned paper 5 $^3/_8$" x 4 ¾" and one piece of striped paper 5 $^3/_8$" x 4".

5. Apply adhesive to the striped paper and press it into place on the INSIDE of the book, then repeat with the two pieces of patterned paper.

6. Using a ¼" seam allowance, sew around entire album. Use a zigzag stitch along the seam where the stripes and floral meet.

7. Using a bone folder, re-fold your marks, making them crisp and clean. Set three eyelets at the top of the binding and three at the bottom. Using a direct-to-paper technique, rub the red inkpad on all of the outside edges of the album.

8. To create your albums pages, cut colored cardstock into six 10 ½" x 5 ¼" pieces and fold in half. Measure the pages next to the eyelets for hole punching placement. Mark and punch. Put two pieces together and thread ribbon through holes and out of binding, tying in a bow or knot. Repeat until entire book is assembled.

9. Paint "family" embellishment and let dry. Add ribbon and charm. Add mosaic alphabet, sticker, flower. and "family" embellishment.

ADDITIONAL INSTRUCTIONS ON PAGE 110

Paper Bag Album
Nikki Cleary

MATERIALS

Pigment Inkpads: Pink

Papers: Pink Cardstock by DieCuts with a View; Nick by Melissa Francis; Tweed Business Casual by Arctic Frog; Butterflies Coral Diamonds, Brianna Roses, Sommerset Engraving, Emma Blocks, Emma Botanical Blocks, Blue Roses and Pink Gingham by K&Company

Paints: Pink; Brown

Ribbons: Local Craft Store

Adhesives: FABRI-TAC by Beacon Adhesives; Glue Stick

Other: Paper Lunch Bags; Chipboard Heart by Heidi Swapp; Chipboard Numbers by Making Memories

Tools: 12" Paper Cutter; Paintbrush; Scissors

INSTRUCTIONS

1. Decide how many pages you want in your paper bag album. This is the number of lunch sacks you will need. Seven lunch sacks or paper bags were used in this particular project.

2. Fold a strip of cardstock accordion style, so as to have as many valleys as bags.

3. Glue the bottom of each bag into the valley folds.

4. Cut two pieces of mat board the size of the bottom of the first flat folded bag. Cover mat board with paper. Paint the edges lightly with very little paint on a dry paintbrush (dry brush technique). Once dry, adhere piece to the bottom of the bags on the front and back of the album, as shown, for more support.

5. Cover page spreads (or both sides of paper bags) inside the album with coordinating papers. Ink the edges of the paper and bags for a distressed effect.

6. Paint chipboard numbers brown, write the number on front, dry brush edge with pink paint. Tie ribbon around number. Adhere numbers to spread by years or months depending on photo.

7. Tie end of bag with ribbons and adhere chipboard heart to front.

8. Embellish with pictures and fill bags with memorabilia.

Nikki's Note:
Use a small paper
shopping bag to wrap
this album as a gift.
Just embellish the
shopping bag handles
with ribbons.

Unique Wire & Tin Creations

Sitting Relatives
Claudine Hellmuth

MATERIALS

Paints: Titan Buff and White Gesso by Golden

Markers: Black and Red Marking Pens

Fabrics: Polka Dotted and Striped in Quarter Flats (or use scrapbook papers)

Adhesives: Matte Gel Medium by Golden

Other: Photograph; Metal Roof Flashing from Local Hardware Store

Tools: Scissors; Paintbrushes; Sandpaper

Jill's Note:

Want to create a not-so-ordinary, whimsical present for that "hard-to-find a gift for" person? These little bendable people fit the bill. Make them holding signs that say "Happy Birthday", or make them for your hubby on your anniversary – make one man, one woman, and add a key to the painted heart with a note saying "you hold the key to my heart". Or how about one for your bunny crafty friend with whom you go antiquing or craft shopping? Just add the appropriate photos for the head for your very own custom piece.

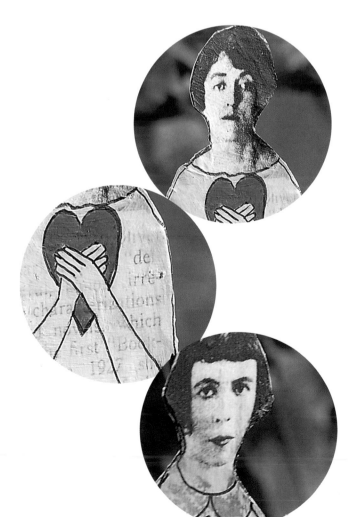

INSTRUCTIONS

1. Photocopy a picture of your relative's head.

2. Lay photocopy and body template down on metal roof flashing.

3. Use a permanent marker to trace around.

4. Cut out figure using scissors – be careful! Edges are sharp.

5. Lightly sand figure and then gesso to prime.

6. Glue photocopy on primed metal.

7. Cut out skirt material from fabric or paper and adhere.

8. Use red marker to color in shoes and add black lines to finish.

9. Bend figure at waist and knees so that it is sitting.

10. Sit your figure on a mantle and enjoy!

Welcome to the wonderful world of wire and tin! This intriguing genre lends itself to a myriad of dazzling creations. Bend, twist, assemble and cover... just use your imagination, experiment and play. The unique ideas presented on the next few pages are sure to inspire. You'll quickly discover that anyone can make magic from metal!

Ribbons Sap Bucket

Kim Henkel

MATERIALS

Rubber Stamps: Swirls and Large Flower by Stampotique Originals; Button by Savvy Stamps; Heart in Hand

Dye Inkpads: Assorted Colors

Papers: Cross My Heart; Doodlebug Design; Anna Griffin; KI Memories; BasicGrey; Chatterbox; My Mind's Eye; Fontwerks; Treehouse Memories; Li'l Davis Designs; Cardstock by Bazzill Basics

Words, Letters or Stickers: Alphabet Rub-Ons by KI Memories; Alphabet Rub-Ons and Cardstock Tags by Doodlebug Design; Stickers by Chatterbox

Ribbons: Doodlebug Design; Strano Designs, Beaux Regards and May Arts; Rick Rack by Doodlebug Design

Adhesives: Mod Podge by Plaid; Glue Dots

Other: Sap Bucket; Pom Poms

Tools: Sponge Brush; Scissors; Pinking Shears

Jill's Note:
These colorful ribbon, fabric and embellishment "catch-alls" look fabulous in your studio. And I can't imagine anything more fun to make!

INSTRUCTIONS

1. Cut a piece of your fabric papers and regular papers using straight edge scissors and pinking shears.

2. Stamp images on cardstock.

3. Randomly attach papers and stamped images to sap bucket with Mod Podge and sponge brush.

4. Add rub-ons and stickers to papers and again coat with a layer of Mod Podge.

5. Use Mod Podge to attach pieces of ribbon and rick rack to top of papers.

6. Add pom poms to top of tin with glue dots.

Jill's Note:
The bucket with a handle is a papier mache piece from a local craft store, covered with scraps and stamped images and trimmed out in pom poms. The large "D" wrapped in ribbon and tulle is for "Dawne" — Kim's friend; Kim made this as a gift for her. These are both gifts anyone would cherish!

Pink Floral Picture Clip

Amy Wellenstein

MATERIALS

Rubber Stamps: "Imagine Yourself Here" by Catslife Press

Dye Inkpads: Black

Papers: Black Tie Matteo by BasicGrey

Words, Letters or Stickers: GinX Express Ons Rub-On Alphabet by Imagination Project

Tags: Metal-Rimmed Tag

Metal Items: Alligator Clip by Darice

Adhesives: Xyron; The Ultimate! Glue by Crafter's Pick

Other: Heavy Wire; Photograph; Silk Flowers

Tools: Wire Snips; Round Nose Pliers

INSTRUCTIONS

1. Use pliers to bend wire into a spiral shape, tapering as you near the top. Snip to desired size. Two to three spirals are plenty, allowing it stand flat and steady.

2. Crimp an alligator clip to the top of the coil and use a dab of glue to hold in place.

3. Line a metal-rimmed tag with decorative papers.

4. Use rub-ons to transfer the word "Photos" to one side.

5. Stamp "Imagine Yourself Here" on the other side using black ink.

6. Hang the tag inside the alligator clip.

7. Glue a silk flower to the front of the clip.

8. Insert a photo in the clip.

Lilac Floral Picture Clip

Amy Wellenstein

MATERIALS

Rubber Stamps: "Love" by Stampotique Originals

Dye Inkpads: Black

Papers: The Paper Loft

Paints: Purple

Tags: Metal-Rimmed Tags

Metal Items: Alligator Clip by Darice

Adhesives: Xyron; The Ultimate! Glue by Crafter's Pick

Other: Heavy Wire; Photograph; Silk Flowers; Button; Dyeable Blossoms Paper Flowers by Making Memories; Rhinestones by Darice

Tools: Wire Snips; Round Nose Pliers

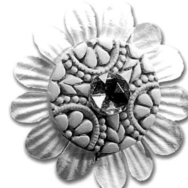

INSTRUCTIONS

1. Bend wire into a spiral shape, tapering as you near the top.

2. Crimp an alligator clip to the top of the coil and use a dab of glue to hold in place.

3. Line a rectangular metal-rimmed tag with decorative papers. Stamp the word "Love" on both sides using black ink.

4. Rub purple paint on a square metal-rimmed tag. Glue a heart-shaped rhinestone on both sides.

5. Hang the tags inside the alligator clip.

6. Glue a silk flower to the front of the clip.

7. Rub purple paint on a textured button, then glue it to the flower.

8. Glue a small round rhinestone in the center of the button.

9. Insert a photo in the clip.

Pink Striped "Thank You" Tin with Cards

Amy Wellenstein

MATERIALS

Rubber Stamps: Magnetic Alphabet Stamps (Providence) by Making Memories

Dye Inkpads: Black

Papers: Cosmopolitan Workweek Pink Stripe by Making Memories; Savvy Sloane Tan with Black Dots by Imagination Project; Black Licorice Dots by Lasting Impressions for Paper, Inc.; Licorice Stripe by Bo-Bunny Press; Pink Mini Grid by Paperfever; Bristol Vellum

Ribbons: Rick Rack

Adhesives: Xyron; The Ultimate! Glue by Crafter's Pick; Scotch Foam Tape by 3M; Glue Stick

Other: Small Round Rhinestones by Darice; Rhinestone Strand; Artisan Labels (Simply Basic) by Making Memories; Chipboard; Recycled Tin

Tools: Sandpaper

"Just a Note" Tin with Cards

Amy Wellenstein

MATERIALS

Rubber Stamps: Magnetic Alphabet Stamps (Rummage) and Foam Alphabet Stamps (Misunderstood Upper Case) by Making Memories

Dye Inkpads: Black

Papers: Ashton Plaid, Ventana, Saville and Black Tie Monograms by BasicGrey; School Paper Black Dots by Sandylion Sticker Designs; Bristol Vellum

Words, Letters or Stickers: Simply Stated Rub-On Alphabets (Rummage Large Lower Case and Misunderstood XL White) by Making Memories

Adhesives: Xyron; The Ultimate! Glue by Crafter's Pick; Glue Stick

Other: Recycled Tin; Chipboard

Tools: Sandpaper

COMBINED INSTRUCTIONS FOR TINS:

1. Use Xyron to cover the lid and bottom of a recycled tin with decorative paper. Sand the edges to distress.

2. Embellish the lid with various rub-on letters, cardstock monograms, rhinestones, labels, stamped sentiments, etc.

3. Use the base of the tin as a template to make three cards (from bristol vellum paper or heavy cardstock).

4. Embellish each card with a strip of coordinating paper, rick rack, and/or rhinestones.

5. Stamp sentiment vertically on each card. For the "Hello" cards, also stamp a large letter "H" in the upper left corner of each card using foam alphabet stamps.

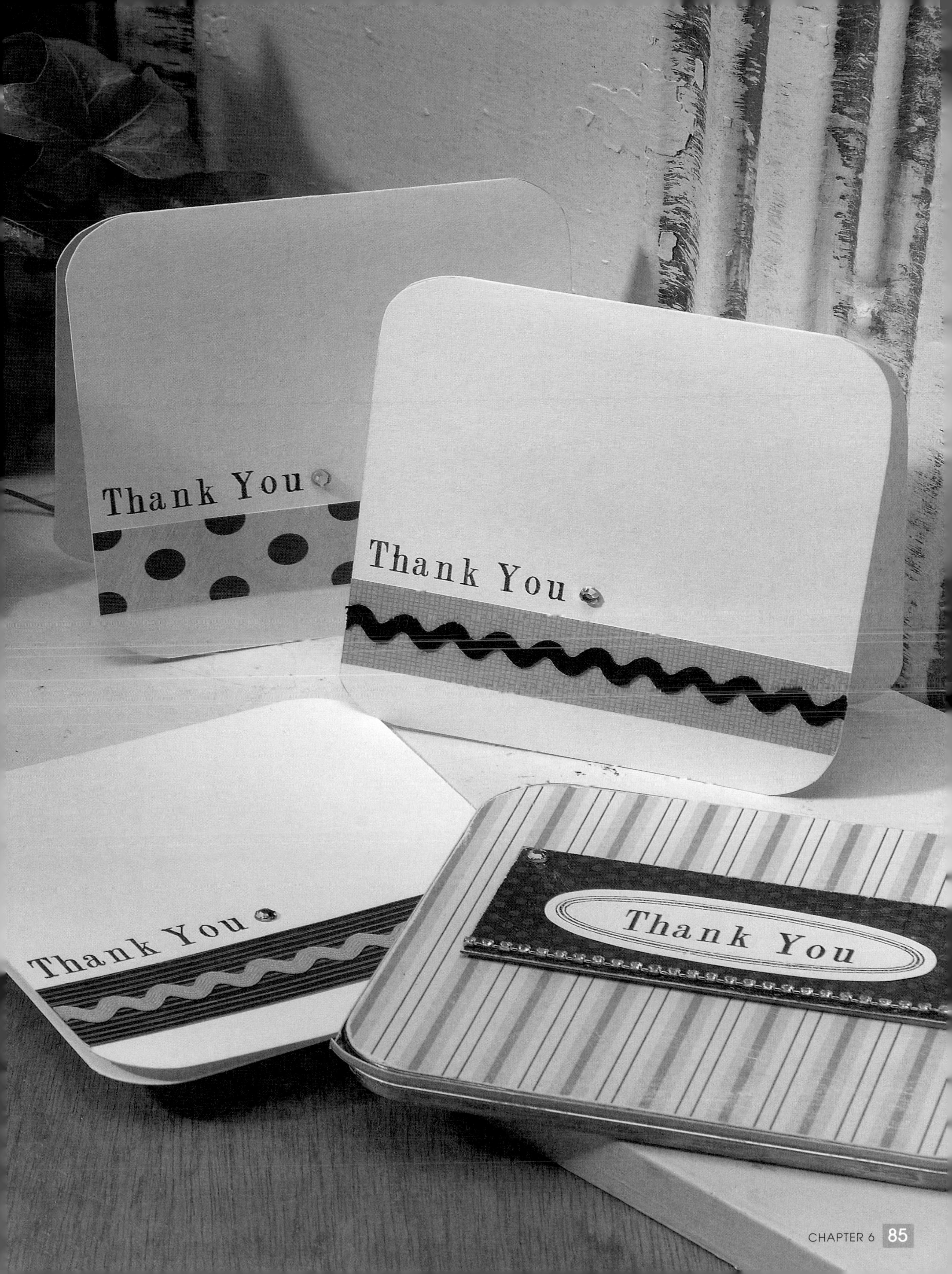
Thank You
Thank You
Thank You
Thank You

Jewelery

Vintage Broaches
Sara White

MATERIALS

Buttons: Vintage Buttons
by Benno's Buttons & Trimmings
Antique Stores, Flea Markets, Garage Sales,
Local Craft and Fabric Stores

Metal Items: Metal Pin Backs or Clasps

Fabrics: Felt

Adhesives: E-6000

Tools: Toothpicks

Other: Purchased or Junk Jewelry Pieces

Sara's Note:
For a finished look on the back, cut a small strip of felt and glue it to the back of the pin so the glue won't show. Cover the base of the pin back while still allowing it to open and close and function as a workable clasp.

Sara's Note:
Combine layered vintage buttons in any visually appealing fashion that suits you! The button is generally the base for the broach and the jewelry pieces are embellishments. Note that adding more than three items will generally appear too cluttered and too heavy to comfortably wear.

INSTRUCTIONS

1. Choose a button for the base of the broach. Larger buttons generally work best although if your intent is to create a small pin, a small button will work fine.

2. Select various smaller buttons to try on top of the base button.

3. Play with the design, trying different buttons in combination, until you find an arrangement you like. Usually two to three items work well together for an eye-catching arrangement.

4. Once you've created your arrangement, use a toothpick to apply E-6000 to adhere the pieces together. Carefully set the piece aside to dry overnight.

5. Once dry, glue the pin back to the back of the base button. The pin back should be placed towards the top of the base button, rather than at the center or bottom, so that the broach hangs properly.

Craft industry trends have recently revealed that buttons are a girl's best friend! Especially when they are transformed into stunning vintage jewelry pieces like those shown on the next few pages. Pick unusual, pretty or unique buttons and layer them to get the best results.

Be sure to check out garage sales, flea markets and antique stores for buttons. Don't forget to Google "vintage buttons" on the Internet and search eBay for rare finds as well.

TAG INSTRUCTIONS ON PAGE 88

Something 4 You Gift Tag

Amy Wellenstein

MATERIALS

Rubber Stamps: Dots and Antique Border by Stampotique Originals; La Passion No. 840938 Ornamentum by Uptown Design Company

Pigment Inkpads: Black

Dye Inkpads: Light Green; Mauve

Words, Letters or Stickers: Simply Stated Rub-on and Jigsaw Number (Philadelphia Collection) by Making Memories; Large Lower Case Alphabet in Black by Heidi Swapp

Paints: Green; Pink Acrylic

Tags: Medium Shipping Tag

Ribbons: Sheer Ribbons from Local Craft Store

Adhesives: Xyron

Other: Handcrafted Vintage Broach; Modeling Paste by Liquitex

Tools: Palette Knife

INSTRUCTIONS

1. Crumple tag and flatten back out.
2. Use a palette knife to spread modeling paste over the tag.
3. Brush the tag with diluted pink acrylic paint and let dry.
4. Rub mauve inkpad on the surface of the tag.
5. Rub black ink around the edges of the tag.
6. Stamp Antique Border along the edge using light green ink.
7. Paint a chipboard stencil using green paint.
8. Stamp Dots on the painted stencil using pink paint.
9. Stamp La Passion using black ink.
10. Use Xyron to adhere the stencil to the tag.
11. Tie ribbon through the hole at the top of the tag.
12. Pin on broach.

Happy Holidays Gift Tag with Pin

Amy Wellenstein

MATERIALS

Rubber Stamps: Antique Description by Stampotique Originals

Pigment Inkpads: Black

Tag: Medium Shipping Tag

Metal Items: Word Charm Eyelet (Happy Holidays) by Making Memories

Ribbons: Local Craft Store

Other: Hand Crafted VIntage Broach; Diluted Walnut Ink; Modeling Paste by Liquitex; Americana Stuccos "Light Heirloom Rose" by DecoArt; Leaf Border Stencil by American Traditional Designs

Tools: Palette Knife; Eyelet Setting Tools

INSTRUCTIONS

1. Crumple tag and flatten back out.
2. Use a palette knife to spread modeling paste over the tag.
3. Dip the tag in diluted walnut ink and let dry.
4. Stamp tag with Antique Description using black ink.
5. Lay stencil over tag and use palette knife to spread rose-colored stucco over a stencil.
6. Carefully lift stencil and let the tag dry.
7. Set word eyelet "Happy Holidays" at the top of the tag.
8. Attach a purchased pin or handmade broach to the tag.
9. Slip a ribbon through hole and tie a bow at the top of the tag.

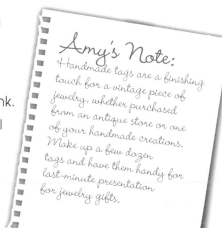

Amy's Note:

Handmade tags are a finishing touch for a vintage piece of jewelry, whether purchased from an antique store or one of your handmade creations. Make up a few dozen tags and have them handy for last-minute presentation for jewelry gifts.

Gift Tag with Flower Pin

Amy Wellenstein

MATERIALS

Rubber Stamps: Trims Cube by Stampington & Company; Flower Stamp with Text by Stampers Anonymous

Dye Inkpads: Dark Green; Walnut Stain

Tags: Medium Shipping Tag

Metal Items: Pin Back by Darice

Ribbons: Local Craft Store

Adhesives: The Ultimate! Glue by Crafter's Pick

Other: Modeling Paste by Liquitex, Silk Flower and Diluted Walnut Ink

Tools: Palette knife

INSTRUCTIONS

1. Crumple tag and flatten back out.

2. Use a palette knife to spread modeling paste over the tag.

3. Dip the tag in diluted walnut ink and let dry.

4. Stamp text from Trims Cube along the bottom of the tag using walnut stain ink.

5. Stamp flower in the upper left corner using dark green ink.

6. Glue silk flower to a pin back and secure to tag.

7. Tie ribbon through the hole at the top of the tag.

Vintage Button Bracelets
Denise Merrill

MATERIALS

Beads: 14 Small Beads (with holes large enough for the elastic to slip through)

Buttons: 28 Medium Buttons; 14 Large Buttons: Benno's Buttons & Trimmings Antique Stores, Flea Markets, Garage Sales, Local Craft and Fabric Stores

Adhesives: JudiKins Diamond Glaze

Other: 16" - 18" Fabric-Covered Elastic Cording

MATERIALS

1. Gather desired buttons. Select a color scheme and pile up one color in different shades or put piles of contrasting colors. (See photo.) Once you start your bracelet it is more fun to select buttons randomly instead of laying them all out.

2. Using 16" of elastic, start with a focal point in the middle of the cord. Pick three to four buttons as shown. (One large, two medium and one small bead).

3. Thread the smallest button onto the elastic first and center it, pulling the cord through equally on both sides. Next choose your favorite medium buttons (these are what will show most), slip cord through both buttonholes and pull tightly. If the elastic frays, just keep cutting the end a bit to give you the smoothness you need to get it through the buttons and the bead on top. Next, add the largest button ending with a medium size again. (This last button underneath can be your least favorite button as it will not be seen.) Your first grouping of threaded buttons should look

4. Push this grouping of four buttons tight and pull cord through one hole of the first button in next set again, your least favorite as it does not show at all – then through one hole of large button, and finally, one hole of the medium button; this should be one of the favorite buttons in your pile. Next, thread through one hole of a small bead and bring the cord back through the other hole on each button and pull tight. This is your second grouping.

5. Work out equally from each side of your beginning focal point, creating snug sets of fours against each other. When the bracelet is the desired size, tie the elastic in a knot twice. Paint the knot with JudiKins Diamond Glaze.

Denise's Note:

A bracelet from sweet, tiny, pearl white buttons with a pink or blue glass seed bead on the top of each set makes an unforgettable newborn baby gift.

Illustration of Button Grouping

Gifts

Distressed Heart Magnet
Amy Wellenstein

MATERIALS

Rubber Stamps: Large Cancellation by Stampington & Company

Dye Inkpads: Black

Papers: Script by Rusty Pickle

Paints: White; Black; Pink

Adhesives: Matte Mod Podge by Plaid; The Ultimate! Glue by Crafter's Pick

Other: Small Wooden Heart; Magnet; Petroleum Jelly; Photograph

Tools: Sandpaper

INSTRUCTIONS

1. Paint the edges of a wooden heart with black paint. Let dry.

2. Paint over the surface of the entire heart with white paint. Let dry.

3. Use Mod Podge to adhere a photo to the heart.

4. Seal the surface of the photo with Mod Podge. Let dry.

5. Cover the surface of the photo with petroleum jelly.

6. Paint over the entire heart with pink paint. Let dry.

7. Stamp the heart with Large Cancellation using black ink. Let dry.

8. Use a paper towel to wipe the petroleum jelly off of the photo as desired. The layer of paint and ink that was on the petroleum jelly will come off.

9. Use Mod Podge to adhere script paper to the back of the heart.

10. Sand the edges of the heart.

11. Use glue to secure a magnet to the back of the heart.

Shabby Wall Basket
Amy Wellenstein

MATERIALS

Rubber Stamps: Dingbats Foam Stamps by Making Memories

Papers: Phlirty, Aged and Confused and Phresh&Phunky by BasicGrey; Script by Rusty Pickle; Khaki Striped by Daisy D's Paper Co.

Paints: White Acrylic

Metal Items: Life's Journey Metal Art Circle by K&Company

Adhesives: Xyron; The Ultimate! Glue by Crafter's Pick

Other: Recycled Metal Basket; Rhinestone

Tools: Die Cuts (large and medium flowers) by Sizzix

INSTRUCTIONS

1. Use Xyron adhesive to adhere a piece of patterned paper to a recycled metal basket.

2. Stamp dingbat flourish image in white on the top as shown.

3. Use Sizzix machine to die cut a medium flower from script paper and a large flower from khaki striped paper.

4. Crumple the flowers, layer and glue to the front of the basket.

5. Glue a rhinestone into a round metal setting and adhere to the center of the flower.

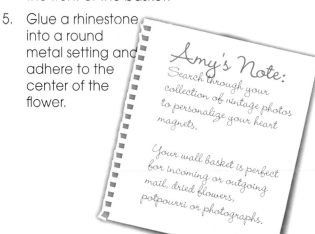

Amy's Note:
Search through your collection of vintage photos to personalize your heart magnets.

Your wall basket is perfect for incoming or outgoing mail, dried flowers, potpourri or photographs.

Every type of project in this book makes for a great gift. But this special chapter contains an assortment of fabulous ideas that refused to be categorized! We couldn't bear to leave them out and you will soon see why.

Our functional decorated wine canisters and unique heart pincushion made from an antique candlestick and stuffed wool are delightfully one-of-a-kind gifts. Adorable "pet cards" are not only fun to make but will surprise and warm the heart of the recipient to get a little special something for the critter-love their life. Think "beyond" when creating clipboards. We've included one to spark your imagination. You can theme them for a special hobby, event or holiday.

No matter the occasion, you'll enjoy digging through your stash of supplies or jaunting off to your local craft store to find fun new products for these inspiring projects.

Heart Pin Cushion

Kim Henkel

MATERIALS

Papers: Cardstock by Bazzill Basics

Rubber Stamps: Ruler by Limited Edition Rubberstamps; Tag by All Night Media; Alphabet Stamps by All Night Media/Plaid

Pigment Inkpads: White

Dye Inkpads: Light Medium and Dark Brown; Turquoise; Red

Markers: Size .05 Marking Pen

Tags: 7gypsies and DMD Industries

Metal Items: Key Charm; Straight Pins

Ribbons, Rick Rack and Twill: Local Craft Store

Fabrics: Red Wool

Other: Candlestick Base; Embroidery Floss by DMC; Piece of Tape Measure, Buttons, String; Linen Twine; Black Cording; Polyester Stuffing

Tools: Sewing Machine; Pinking Shears; Embroidery Needle

Kim's Note:
When making pin cushions add snippets of rick rack, ribbon; hang buttons and clip on saftey pins. Add stamped tags with messages, names or favorite omages for a personal touch.

Buy a glass or brass candlestick base from a local antique store, garage sale or flea market.

INSTRUCTIONS:

1. Make a pattern by drawing a heart shape on a piece of paper; cut out ³/₄" larger all the way around. Pin your pattern onto two pieces of red wool; cut out.

2. Sew ³/₄" inside the cut with right sides together all the way around heart, leaving an opening on the bottom for the candlestick. Sew once more; tracing your stitches for security.

3. Use pinking shears to cut closer to sewn heart shape.

4. Turn heart right side out and stuff firmly with polyester stuffing. Turn under raw edge of heart opening.

5. Place heart on top of candlestick base. Use embroidery needle stitch heart to candlestick. Stitch tightly around candlestick base several times for stability.

6. Use black velvet cording to tie around base of heart. Primitively stitch using embroidery floss around heart. Place your needle and thread in pincushion.

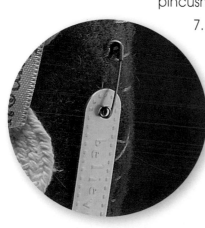

7. Thread several buttons through linen thread and tie buttons around heart. Tie rick rack around heart.

8. Use a straight pin to hold piece of measuring tape. Attach large rick rack and ribbon to heart using a straight pin.

9. Stamp tag image on cardstock and add "pinkeeper" using marking pen. Cut tag image out of cardstock into a rectangle. Attach "pinkeeper" tag to pincushion.

10. Stamp images on the other tags and attach to base of pincushion.

11. Randomly add pins for decoration and future use.

Happy Birthday Wine/Liquor Canister

Nikki Cleary

MATERIALS

Rubber Stamps: "Get Swanky" by Hampton Art; Stampendous

Inkpads: Fluid Chalk Pastel in Pink; Embossing Inkpad; Watermark Inkpad

Embossing Powders: White

Papers: Li'l Davis Designs

Paints: Various Shades of Greens

Tags: Hand-Cut

Metal Items: Chain and Fastener from Local Hardware Store

Ribbons: Local Craft Store

Adhesives: Decoupage Finish by Plaid; FABRI-TAC by Beacon Adhesives

Other: Canisters from Local Craft Store

Tools: Embossing Gun; Paper Cutter; Paintbrush; Stapler; Hole Punch

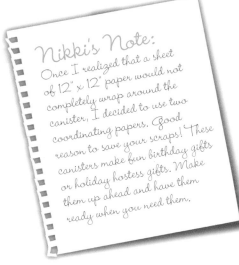

Nikki's Note:
Once I realized that a sheet of 12" x 12" paper would not completely wrap around the canister, I decided to use two coordinating papers. Good reason to save your scraps! These canisters make fun birthday gifts or holiday hostess gifts. Make them up ahead and have them ready when you need them.

INSTRUCTIONS

1. Paint canister and top of the lid and sides of lid with shades of green paint as shown.

2. Cut two coordinating papers to wrap around the canister. Ink the top and bottom edge of both papers in pink. Adhere to canister with decoupage finish.

3. Wrap ribbon around canister as shown. Adhere with FABRI-TAC.

4. Make loops with ribbon and secure with a drop of glue on each loop to make bow; trim excess ribbon.

5. Cut a wavy line in the paper on top lid and adhere to lid with decoupage finish. Dry brush light green paint over dark green paint around the sides of lid.

6. Stamp "happy birthday" and emboss with heat gun, cut the words out and adhere to bottom of canister with decoupage finish

7. Layer papers onto hand-cut tag. Stamp "get swanky" and emboss with heat gun. Staple rick rack to tag, punch hole in tag and attach to canister with chain.

Holiday Wine/Champagne Canister
Nikki Cleary

MATERIALS

Papers: Holiday Hoopla by SEI

Paints: Green; Yellow

Tags: Holiday Hoopla by SEI

Ribbons and Rick Rack: Local Craft Store

Adhesives: Decoupage Finish by Plaid; FABRI-TAC by Beacon Adhesives

Other: Buttons; Canisters from Local Craft Store

Tools: Paper Cutter; Paintbrush

INSTRUCTIONS

1. Paint canister and top of lid yellow; paint lid green.

2. Secure strips of paper on canister and lid with decoupage finish.

3. Secure rick rack and buttons on canister.

4. Adhere tag and rick rack on lid with FABRI-TAC.

5. Tie ribbon through canister and lid, tie on gift tag.

Cookie Cutter Jar

Kim Henkel

MATERIALS

Dye Inkpads: Sepia

Papers: Melissa Frances Papers; Cardstock by Bazzill Basics

Markers: Size .05 Marker

Words, Letters or Stickers: Rub-Ons by Melissa Frances

Tags: Melissa Frances

Metal Items: Mini Cookie Cutters by Melissa Frances; Clip; Safety Pin

Ribbons: Local Craft Store

Adhesives: Mod Podge by Plaid

Other: Pom Poms; Jar; Button; Gingerbread Figure by Melissa Frances

Tools: Paintbrush

INSTRUCTIONS:

1. Cut papers in different shapes to cover jar lid. Add rub-ons.

2. Brush with Mod Podge to adhere and cover papers and let dry.

3. Glue on button and gingerbread man.

4. Wrap pom poms around lid and secure in place with safety pin.

5. Write "cookie cutters" on tag.

6. Attach tag to jar using clip.

Kim's Note:
You can fill this decorated jar with anything... homemade jelly or cookies, hard candy, peanut brittle, M&Ms, Hershey's Kisses — a truly sweet treat for a hostess!

Santa's Checklist Clipboard

Karen Hamad, MD

MATERIALS

Papers: Christmas Paper Collection by Doodlebug Design

Paints: Red; Pale Yellow

Markers: Black; Red; Green; Gold

Ribbons and Fibers: Local Craft Store

Adhesives: Cheetah Tape Runner; Glue Stick; Scrappy Tape by Magic Scraps

Other: Clipboard; Jingle Bells; Jump Ring

Tools: Sponge Brush

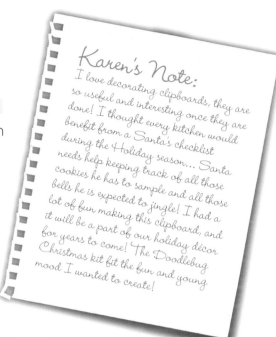

Karen's Note:
I love decorating clipboards, they are so useful and interesting once they are done! I thought every kitchen would benefit from a Santa's checklist during the Holiday season... Santa needs help keeping track of all those cookies he has to sample and all those bells he is expected to jingle! I had a lot of fun making this clipboard, and it will be a part of our holiday décor for years to come! The Doodlebug Christmas kit fit the fun and young mood I wanted to create!

INSTRUCTIONS

1. Cut several lengths of patterned paper the width of the clipboard and tear into strips. Chalk or ink torn edges. Tape or glue to clipboard.

2. Paint above and below patterned paper to finish the look of the clipboard, including the metal clip if so desired.

3. Cut white cardstock to fit into clip.

4. Print "Santa's checklist" as shown and use contrasting markers to check boxes as shown.

5. Attach jingle bells with jump ring to bottom corner of cardstock.

6. Tie green, red and white fibers and ribbons onto top of clipboard.

dec.25

Santa's Checklist

- ☑ Bb&G list
- ☑ Stuff Stockings
- ☑ Milk & Cookies
- ☑ reindeer food
- ☑ JINGLE BELLS

hohoho

Not 2 Shabby Wall Hanging

Amy Wellenstein

MATERIALS

Rubber Stamps: Philadelphia Uppercase and Lowercase and Misunderstood Uppercase Foam Stamps by Making Memories; Large "2" by Stampotique Originals; Vintage Italian Labels

Pigment Inkpads: Mauve

Paints: White and Mauve

Metal Items: Round Pewter Brads (2) by Making Memories

Ribbons: Silk Ribbon by 7gypsies; Sheer Ribbon from Local Craft Store

Adhesives: The Ultimate! Glue by Crafter's Pick

Other: Framed Screen; Rhinestone Frame by Li'l Davis Designs; Small Photo by Limited Edition Rubberstamps

INSTRUCTIONS

1. Paint frame white. Stamp frame with vintage labels using mauve ink.

2. Mix various alphabet and number stamps to stamp "Not 2 Shabby" on the screen with white acrylic paint.

3. Paint two decorative brads with white acrylic paint. Rub the paint off the surface, leaving it only in the crevices.

4. Cut a photo to fit in a plastic rhinestone frame. Glue photo in frame.

5. Glue frame to screen.

6. Use the decorative brads and glue to secure a sheer ribbon hanger to the frame.

7. Tie a piece of silk ribbon to one side.

Pet Cards

Claudine Hellmuth

MATERIALS

Papers: The Big Slab IV by Provo Craft; 140 lb. Watercolor Paper

Markers: Black

Adhesives: Matte Gel Medium by Golden

Other: Images of Pet Heads by Cre8tive Eye Studio

Tools: Paintbrushes; Pencil; Scissors

INSTRUCTIONS

1. Make a photocopy of a picture of your pet's head or use an image from Cre8tive Eye Studio.

2. Cut out head and lay on a folded piece of watercolor paper. Make sure the fold is to the left so your card will open correctly.

3. Use a pencil to trace around the pet head and then draw a pod shape body on the watercolor paper.

4. Cut out figure with scissors, making certain to not cut along the folded side.

5. Glue down pet head and scrapbook papers for clothes.

6. Outline card and add drawn elements with black marker as shown. Add a hat or a crown.

Claudine's Note:
Add a note to the inside of your card and send to a furry friend!

Clocks

Time On My Hands
Janet Klein

MATERIALS

Papers: Local Craft Store

Paints: White; Pink; Lavender; Turquoise; Green

Pencils: Fine Art Pencils by Caran d'Ache or Colored Pencils from Local Craft Store

Adhesives: Gloss Gel Medium by Golden; E-6000; Glue Stick

Other: Quartz Clock Movement; Straight Hands; White Gesso; Letter Beads

Tools: 1" Foam Brush; ½" Flat Brush; Small Paintbrush; Sanding Block; Bone Folder, Xacto Knife; Cutting Mat; Poplar Wood or Foam Core Board

Janet's Note:
The "No Place Like Home" clock on the following page is made using the same technique as for "Time On My Hands" on page 105. Cut a new shape and change out the paint and papers for an entirely different look!

INSTRUCTIONS

1. Create hand pattern and trace to desired poplar wood or foam core board. Cut out.

2. If using wood, lightly sand surface.

3. Gesso back and sides of clock face with foam brush..

4. Apply adhesive with glue stick to top of clock face. Carefully place paper over glued surface and burnish with a bone folder. Dry completely.

5. Place the paper side to the cutting mat. Use Xacto knife to trim away excess. Remove center hole for clock movement.

6. Paint hands a mix of bright colors to accent your paper choice.

7. Paint edge of clock with alternating shades of green and turquoise or desired hues with a ½" flat brush.

8. Scribble accent lines of color with Caran d'Ache or colored pencils.

9. Apply Golden gloss medium to surface. Allow to dry.

10. Use E-6000 adhesive to attach letter beads at the 12, 3, 6 and 9 hour marks.

11. Assemble quartz movement and hands following manufacturer's directions.

Janet's Note:
All my clock bases are cut from ¼" poplar wood on a scroll saw. First, I pre-drill an appropriate hole to accommodate clock movement according to manufacturer's recommendations. You can alternately use foam core for the clock base or use pre-cut and drilled clock bases available in various shapes at local craft stores.

It's time to create! Clocks are always a welcome gift, and these add color and whimsy to any space... kitchen, living room, family room, playroom, nursery, art studio, media room, music room, study, game room, foyer, even bathroom! This project looks like it should be for the ambitious crafter, but you won't believe how easy it is. You can use foam core board if you want to eliminate the scroll saw cutting time and still achieve the same effect. Once you enjoy success with one, you'll want to make more! You'll have an array of fanciful clocks in what seems like minutes... time flies when you're having fun! Choose a theme, a shape, an occasion, a time to make a special gift for someone you care about.

Coffee Time

Janet Klein

MATERIALS

Papers: Snowflake Paisley and Winter Stripe from Chatterbox; Olive Cardstock

Paints: White Acrylic; Two Shades of Blue Acrylic; White Gesso

Adhesives: Gloss Gel Medium by Golden; Glue Stick

Other: Quartz Clock Movement; Straight Hands

Tools: 1" Foam Brush; ½" Flat Brush; Small Paintbrush; Sanding Block; Bone Folder; Xacto Knife

INSTRUCTIONS

1. Create coffee cup and saucer pattern and trace to desired surface. Cut out.

2. If using wood, lightly sand surface and gesso back and sides of clock face.

3. Make a duplicate of your original pattern and cut out the cup and saucer separately. These will act as templates for your papers.

4. Choose desired papers or use the cup pattern with the paisley paper, and the saucer pattern with the contrasting stripe. Carefully cut and adjust pieces to fit clock surface.

5. Apply glue stick to back of paper. Align in position and burnish down with bone folder.

6. Once dry, turn upside-down on cutting mat and carefully trim away excess paper, close to contour of clock shape. Cut an elliptical shape from olive cardstock and glue to top of cup for "coffee".

7. Use Xacto knife to remove center hole for clock movement.

8. Paint hands using shades of blue to compliment papers. Dot patterns of white paint on the hour hand. The minute hand is striped with two shades of blue. Let dry.

9. Paint edge of clock in alternating shades of blue with a ½" flat brush. Let dry completely.

10. Assemble quartz movement and hands following manufacturer's directions.

Valentine Clock

Janet Klein

MATERIALS

Papers: DieCuts with a View; Gold Metallic; Cream Bond

Paints: White Acrylic; Brown Acrylic; White Gesso

Adhesives: Matte Gel Medium by Golden; E-6000; Glue Stick

Other: Quartz Clock Movement; Pointed Clock Hands; 1/2" Wooden Buttons; Poplar Wood or Foam Core Board

Tools: Bone Folder; Xacto Knife; Cutting Mat; Scallop Edge Scissors; 1" Foam Brush; Small Paintbrush, 1/2" Flat Brush; Sanding Block

Janet's Note:
Your choice of papers make all the difference in the "look" of the clock you make. Check out your local craft and scrapbook stores to see the wide variety available today. Pick papers that truely strike your fancy or work well for the occasion to make "creating your clock" more interesting and fun!

INSTRUCTIONS

1. Create heart pattern and trace to desired surface (wood or foam core). Cut out.

2. If using wood, lightly sand surface and gesso back and sides of clock face.

3. Apply glue to clock face surface.

4. Apply paper. Use a bone folder to burnish paper in place.

5. Once dry, turn upside-down on cutting mat and carefully trim away excess paper, close to contour of clock shape.

6. Use Xacto knife to remove center hole for clock movement.

7. Paint wooden buttons to look like chocolates: First paint buttons brown and let dry. Drizzle on white paint to look like "icing". Let dry completely.

8. Using scallop edge scissors, cut two circles 1" in diameter from gold foil and cream bond paper.

9. Glue faux chocolates to paper wrappers. Bend papers up to give appearance of candy cups.

10. Use a 1/2" flat brush with white acrylic paint to dry brush an accent line around clock edge. Allow to dry.

11. Use E-6000 to glue "chocolates" in wrappers at the 12, 3, 6 and 9 hour marks.

12. Assemble quartz movement and hands following manufacturer's directions.

Beautiful Mini Album

Kelly Lunceford

MATERIALS

Dye Inkpads: Brown

Papers: Powder Room Collection by Chatterbox

Words, Letters or Stickers: Descriptives Stickers by Chatterbox

Metal Items: Brads; Eyelets

Ribbons: Local Craft Store

Adhesives: Mono Permanent Adhesive by Tombow; Mini Glue Dots by Glue Dots International

Other: Wooden Frame by Chatterbox; Blossom and Square Button by Making Memories; Chipboard

Tools: Paper Cutter; Scissors; Bone Folder; Eyelet Hole Punch and Setter

INSTRUCTIONS

1. Cut chipboard 12" x 5 ½". Score in at 5 ½" on both ends. Crease score marks with bone folder. Cut two pieces of floral patterned paper (enough for the cover, plus some to wrap around to inside). Glue to cover and secure on inside.

2. Cut one piece of striped patterned paper 4" wide and long enough to wrap to inside. Glue to binding area. Cut another piece 4" wide and just long enough to place on the INSIDE. Glue in place.

3. Cut two pieces of floral paper, just enough to fit inside album.

4. Run the entire album through the sewing machine with a ¼" seam, keeping the album flat. With a zigzag stitch, sew along the seams where the floral and stripes meet on the front and back cover.

5. Distress edges with brown ink. Refold album using previous score marks for a crisp fold.

7. Set a row of three eyelets on the top and bottom of the binding, alternating colors if you wish.

8. Create the pages by cutting six assorted patterned papers 5 ¼" by 10 ½" and folding in half. Sandwich all papers, one inside the other, and punch holes using eyelets as guides. Thread ribbon through the holes and secure with bows on the outside of the album. Repeat the steps until you have filled your album.

9. Create the tabs by choosing meaningful words from the Descriptives stickers and securing to paper scraps. Stagger them throughout the pages, paying special attention to placement. Add ribbon and button with Mini Glue Dot.

10. Embellish cover as desired, adding blossom, frame, ribbon and stickers.

Dream Mini Album

Kelly Lunceford

MATERIALS

Rubber Stamps: Express It by Making Memories; Everyday Flexible Phrases by Stampin' Up!

Dye Inkpads: Black; Blue

Papers: Studio K by K&Company; White Cardstock

Words, Letters or Stickers: "Like it Is" by Making Memories

Metal Items: Colored Safety Pin, Book Plate and Classic Letters by Making Memories; Eyelets

Ribbons: Local Craft Store

Adhesives: Mono Permanent Adhesive by Tombow; Glue Dots

Other: Sewing Machine; Chipboard

Tools: Bone Folder; Paper Cutter; Eyelet Hole Punch and Setter

INSTRUCTIONS

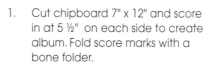

1. Cut chipboard 7" x 12" and score in at 5 ½" on each side to create album. Fold score marks with a bone folder.

2. Cut two pieces of patterned paper large enough to cover the front and back, allowing enough extra to fold onto inside. Glue in place, creating mitered corners on the inside. Cut a strip of the cracked paper large enough to cover the binding area and cover the raw seam of the other pattern paper. Glue in place.

3. Cut another piece of the cracked paper for the inside binding area and glue in place, making sure it is just slightly smaller than the inside cover. Next, cut two pieces of the patterned paper and apply to the inside, to cover the overhang.

4. Keeping your album flat, sew along the outside of the album. Use a zig-zag stitch to sew along the seam where the two patterns come together (front and back). Once it is completely sewn, you can re-fold your original score marks to keep it crisp looking.

5. Add a row of three eyelets to the top and bottom of the binding.

6. To create your pages, cut six pieces of cardstock to fit inside and fold in half like a folder. Put one inside of another. This will give you three sets of two. Use a pencil to mark where you will need to punch holes so that they will line up with your eyelets. Thread the ribbon through the pages and album and tie in a bow.

7. Add your embellishments to the front. Stamp the word "memories" on a scrap of patterned paper and add to your bookplate. Stamp the word "dream" on the metal letter "d" and let it dry. Attach to the ribbon with the safety pin.

8. Add your photos for a priceless keepsake.

PRODUCT RESOURCE GUIDE

100 Proof Press: www.100proofpress.com

3M / Scotch: www.scotchbrand.com

7gypsies: www.7gypsies.com

American Crafts: www.americancrafts.com

American Traditional Designs: www.americantraditional.com

Anna Griffin: www.annagriffin.com

Arctic Frog: www.arcticfrog.net

Around The Block: www.aroundtheblockproducts.com

Autumn Leaves: www.autumnleaves.com

BasicGrey: www.basicgrey.com

Bazzill Basics Paper: www.bazzillbasics.com

Beacon Adhesives, Inc.: www.beaconcreates.com

Beaux Regards: www.beauxregards.biz

Benno's Buttons & Trimmings: www.bennosbuttons.com

Bo-Bunny Press: www.bobunny.com

Caran d'Ache: www.carandache.ch

Carolee's Creations: www.caroleescreations.com

Catslife Press: www.catslifepress.com

Cavallini & Co.: www.cavallini.com

Chatterbox: www.chatterboxinc.com

Close to My Heart: www.closetomyheart.com

Crafter's Pick: www.crafterspick.com

Cre8tive Eye Studio: www.picturetrail.com/thecre8tivei

Hands: www.creativehands.com

Creative Imaginations: www.cigift.com

Cross-My-Heart: www.crossmyheart.com

Daisy D's Paper Co: www.daisydspaper.com

Darice: www.darice.com

DecoArt: www.decoart.com

Deja Views: www.dejaviews.com

Delta: www.deltacrafts.com

Design Originals: www.d-originals.com

DieCuts with a View: www.diecutswithaview.com

DMC: www.dmc-usa.com

DMD Industries: www.dmdind.com

Doodlebug Design: www.doodlebug.ws/

Duncan Enterprises: www.duncancrafts.com

Dymo: www.dymo.com

E-6000 Craft Adhesive/Eclectic Products: www.eclecticproducts.com

EK Success: www.eksuccess.com

Elmer's: www.elmers.com

EZ Laser Designs: www.ezlaserdesigns.com

Fibermark: www.fibermark.com

Fontwerks: www.fontwerks.com

FoofaLa: 1-800-588-6707

Glue Dots International LLC: www.gluedots.com

Golden Artist Colors, Inc.: www.goldenpaints.com

Graphic Products Corporation: www.gpcpapers.com

Hampton Art LLC: www.hamptonart.com

Heidi Swapp: www.heidiswapp.com

Hermafix: 1-888-CENTIS-6

Hero Arts: www.heroarts.com

Heidi Swapp: www.heidiswapp.com

Hermafix: 1-888-CENTIS-6

Hero Arts: www.heroarts.com

Hot Off the Press: www.paperwishes.com

Imagination Project: www.imaginationproject.com

Inkadinkado Rubber Stamps: www.inkadinkado.com

JudiKins: www.judikins.com

K&Company: www.kandcompany.com

Karen Foster Design: www.karenfosterdesign.com

KI Memories: www.kimemories.com

KMA: Local Craft Store

Krylon: www.krylon.com

Lasting Impressions for Paper, Inc.: www.lastingimpressions.com

Li'l Davis Designs: www.lildavisdesigns.com

Limited Edition Rubberstamps: www.limitededitionrubberstamps.com

Liquitex: www.liquitex.com

Magic Scraps: www.magicscraps.com

Making Memories: www.makingmemories.com

Martin/F. Weber Co.: www.weberart.com

May Arts: www.mayarts.com

Melissa Frances: www.melissafrances.com

Moda: www.modafabrics.com

My Mind's Eye: www.mymindseyeinc.com

Paperbag Studios: www.paperbagstudios.com

Paperfever: www.paperfever.com

Pebbles Inc.: www.pebblesinc.com

Plaid Enterprises, Inc.: www.plaidonline.com

Postmodern Design: 405-321-3176

Provo Craft: www.provocraft.com

Rainbow Tape: www.rainbow-tape.com

Rusty Pickle: www.rustypickle.com

Sandylion Sticker Designs: www.sandylion.com

Sanford: www.sanfordcorp.com

Scenic Route Paper Company: www.scenicroutepaper.com

Scrapworks: www.scrapworks.com

SEI: www.shopsei.com

Sissix: www.sissix.com

Stampcraft: www.eyreandbaxter.co.uk

Stampendous: www.stampendous.com

Stampers Anonymous: www.stampersanonymous.com

Stampin' Up!: www.stampinup.com

Stampington & Company: www.stampington.com

Stampotique Originals: www.stampotique.com

Sticker Studio: www.stickerstudio.com

Strano Designs: www.stranodesigns.com

Suze Weinberg: www.schmoozewithsuze.com

Tombow: www.tombowusa.com

Treehouse Memories: www.treehousememories.com

Uptown Design Company: www.uptowndesign.com

Westrim Crafts: www.westrimcrafts.com

Wordsworth: www.wordsworthstamps.com

Xyron: www.xyron.com